D0607244

VISITATIONS

YELLOW SHOE FICTION

Michael Griffith, *Series Editor*

Also by Lee Upton

Fiction
The Tao of Humiliation
The Guide to the Flying Island

Poetry
Bottle the Bottles the Bottles the Bottles
Undid in the Land of Undone
Civilian Histories
Approximate Darling
No Mercy
The Invention of Kindness

Libretto
The Masque of Edgar Allan Poe

Essays
Swallowing the Sea: On Writing & Ambition, Boredom, Purity & Secrecy

Critical Prose
Defensive Measures: The Poetry of Niedecker, Bishop, Glück, and Carson
The Muse of Abandonment: Origin, Identity, Mastery in Five American Poets
Obsession and Release: Rereading the Poetry of Louise Bogan
Jean Garrigue: A Poetics of Plenitude

VISITATIONS

stories

LEE UPTON

31652003162287

Louisiana State University Press

Baton Rouge

Published by Louisiana State University Press
Copyright © 2017 by Louisiana State University Press
All rights reserved
Manufactured in the United States of America
FIRST PRINTING

This book is a work of fiction. Names, characters, organizations, places, circumstances, and events are the product of the author's imagination, or are used fictitiously. Any resemblance to actual occurrences, institutions, or individuals, living or dead, is coincidental.

DESIGNER: *Mandy McDonald Scallan*
TYPEFACE: *Whitman*
PRINTER AND BINDER: *McNaughton & Gunn, Inc.*

Library of Congress Cataloging-in-Publication Data

Names: Upton, Lee, 1953– author.
Title: Visitations : stories / Lee Upton.
Description: Baton Rouge : Louisiana State University Press, [2017]
Identifiers: LCCN 2017008822| ISBN 978-0-8071-6812-7 (cloth : alk. paper) | ISBN 978-0-8071-6813-4 (pdf) | ISBN 978-0-8071-6814-1 (epub)
Classification: LCC PS3571.P46 A6 2017 | DDC 813/.54--dc23
LC record available at *https://lccn.loc.gov/2017008822*

The paper in this book meets the guidelines for permanence and durability of the Committee on Production Guidelines for Book Longevity of the Council on Library Resources. ∞

for Eric

CONTENTS

VISITATIONS

Visitation

Tiffany's mother is swearing at the flowers again. I am Tiffany's mother. I am swearing at the flowers again. The girlfriend of X, the ex-wife of Y, the sister of Z, the last-born daughter of A, it's me, Tiffany's mother, swearing at the flowers. Because they are pathetic flowers, and we rent a dump but someone who once lived here planted these flowers. Yesterday they were upright, sun-facing, perfume-making, soft-cheeked blabbers in the backyard, roses and daisies and peonies and flowers I have no name for—oh, and irises, too, with their caterpillar fur—and what is there now? Where are those flowers with their once-big beautiful fat-assed faces that I loved? Where? They're lawn-smashed and needle-dicked. Blipped, beheaded, slashed into bug runways, pissy misfits, just a track of bloody collapses, some of them melted into the wet grass and others scattered like filthy dirt-bagged feathers.

Tiffany's mother was going to bring them to Tiffany. I, Tiffany's mother, was going to bring them to my little girl in big bunches, big-headed big-bloomed fragrant heart-filling bunches, and the flowers would talk to Tiffany and whisper into her ear. And out of the mouths of flowers, the sweet un-fucked-up heads of those flowers, would come words, all scented, pure and private words that would say only what they could say for me: *I will regain custody. I will never let them take you from me again, Tiffany.* But no, there are no flowers for Tiffany, no bouquets so lush, none, no bouquets tumbling with petals upon petals upon petals, no way for me to gather up every green and golden stem and watch Tiffany's face when her mother lays flowers into her arms—and all week I had thought of Tiffany's eyes smile little soft hands and the flowers overflowing her arms, flowers up to her chin, and I would have stripped every thorn from every pale yellow rose and those flowers would have come to a happy rest in Tiffany's arms.

Blame the weather, says X, if you're going to blame anything. Calm down, says X. Don't get so upset. Come on, baby. Remember: You can meditate. Remember: yoga. Mindfulness. Be here now. Come on. They're just flowers. You didn't plant them yourself, even. They were here when we moved in, you know? Tiffany doesn't need flowers. She doesn't.

I can blame the weather, Tiffany's mother says. Because I am Tiffany's mother I can blame anything and anyone I want. I'm good at blame. I'm the world's greatest blamer, is that what you think? And because I am who I am I don't know the names of half the flowers. I don't know anything, do I? I'm Tiffany's mother, and Tiffany's mother doesn't do so great with names anyway, that's what some people think. Tiffany's mother gave Tiffany a stupid name, X's own father says. The name a drug addict gives a kid. Tiffany. Slap a sign on the kid that says drug addict's kid why don't you so everybody knows about Tiffany's mother.

X is backing up. The screen door slaps itself like it's having a hard time. Guilty screen door. Breathe breathe breathe. You are still Tiffany's mother. X is right. You can blame the weather—last night's storm, yes— but you can't blame only the storm. Could a storm do all this, wreck all the flowers, make corpses, lay down tracks, pluck and splinter heads?

Who would do this to flowers? Innocent stupid things all sprayed across the lawn like someone took a machine gun to them. There was some hail, yes. A few pellets. Some rain, yes. But not enough for this much damage.

And that's when the culprit gets himself noticed. Over by the back fence, the treacherous asshole. Mr. Master Blaster I name him in that instant. Because he is moving his mouth sideways, contemplatively, like he's just an innocent chump who can't stop himself and who knows every form of life belongs to him, and who secretly blasts holes in softness and eats from the inside any delicate precious thing. The way he's looking my way it's like he's about to say, "Who? Me? Little ol' me?" and he's wiggling, his neck muscles sliding back and forth as he chews like he's wearing a fur poncho, and he's almost completely round, like he's made to be hugged, like some pettable sweet stuffed animal a child would love except I know better. He can bite through anything, right? A garden hose, a steel pipe? His teeth could bite through my arm, right? And he's a burrow-loving fool—and there must be more than one burrow: at least one big hole somewhere right in the backyard so he can escape after eating through the garden, eating and eating, sampling the whole smorgasbord of flowers until his two buck teeth turn pink from teething flowers.

I'm thinking that I know everything he did: walking on his flat many-fingered feet through the soil and ripping with his black-gloved hands at any lushness the hail missed and making himself dinner, each paw like a tiny spork lifting to his puffy mouth every bloom and leaf, and here's a sip from that iris and then, liking what he tastes, he's plowing the daisies and blowing through the peonies, gorging and gorging, and that's when I clap my hands, clap them until my palms sting. And Mr. Master Blaster practically stands up to look for the commotion before he crumbles down, and his skin is loose and rolls around on him almost like some invisible hand is petting his crummy little ass. I must stop swearing. I am Tiffany's mother. And then the clumsy villain backs up and waddle-runs and he's down, invisible, ducking into his hole.

The hole—it's there by the ragged grapevines that twist around the puny-looking pine and I lie down right there by the hole. I could push rocks in—one less exit for you, you culprit, you thief, you plunderer. I could push rock after rock into that hole. But of course he has some other exit, or tons of exits. He can get out of any situation, the fur bomb, the crook. I'm dropping in some pebbles anyway.

And that's when X comes out holding a cup of tea for me. I manage to thank him. I'm calming myself. Calming myself so much that I want to be alone, and somehow X knows, putting one hand on my shoulder—lightly lightly—and backing up. I will cry later when I remember what he's done, will cry with gratitude, with guilt, but for now I want to focus. Because I'm beginning to think that this isn't the groundhog's burrow. No, what I'm looking at is a sinkhole. Pennsylvania limestone. It's like walking on a honeycomb, this state. Your house can bury you, just fold up with you in your bed, and then you're under the soil deep down and you never get a real funeral because you're already buried. It's like dirt's revenge or dirt's efficiency plan for you. Grotesque. I'm being grotesque. Tiffany's mother shouldn't be grotesque. Sometimes X says to me, Don't be grotesque. And so I get more grotesque. Like maybe I talk about shrunken heads and how whoever first thought of making shrunken heads should have been a captain of industry. Shrink shrank shrunk. I never wanted shrunken flowers—the roses, the irises, the flowers I forget the names of—but they shrank and got ripped and my head shrank with them.

For nearly a week I had walked among those flowers when they were alive and upright and they didn't ask anything of me, not even to be admired. It wasn't their fault, what happened to them, was it? Being beaten by hail and then eaten alive by a groundhog, or is the true name woodchuck? Hog. Groundhog. Grinding the flowers. A hog with all those escape plans. Easy for him to escape. He doesn't have to worry about where his next dime is coming from.

The flowers. I know they're innocent but I want to tell the shreds of those flowers: You are not worth it. You were too noisy. Your colors blared. You would never have lasted long anyway. I don't need you, you fragile creeps.

I want to be angry. I am so good at being angry. I want to be good at something.

I am trying to grow calm. I am trying to pity the flowers.

I stick my arm inside the sinkhole. Or maybe it's just a big rut, not a true sinkhole—just a trench dug by the groundhog and his groundhog friends, or maybe a deer wandered here and pawed and pawed until the earth kept opening. It would be nice to see a deer right now, clattering onto the lawn, with those big antlers like fenceposts on his head. That can't be easy, managing a head like that—with so much equipment. Maybe the deer could chase the groundhog and make the groundhog sorry for his sins.

I will be flowerless. Flowerless in front of Tiffany. My visitation. My rights. I am her mother, not simply her visitor, right? Visitation rights.

Calm down.

It must be after midnight when I hear splashing in the bathroom sink. It's X. I didn't even hear him leave the bed so I must have been asleep.

Right away he gets back in bed and, just like that, he's asleep again, breathing deep, and I'm awake. I step out onto the lawn and walk toward the fence, the grass warm-wet under my feet, like blood or entrails, like maybe something died and was dragged back here, and that's when I fall and the fall is funny. A fall that keeps falling and I'm not landing. And I think: Am I inside the sinkhole? Or maybe I'm dreaming, but I'm not dreaming because the walls of the sinkhole snag at my hair and sting and in dreams I don't feel pain. And I think when I land please let me land on something soft, but something I won't kill by falling on it, and I know that far down below is the groundhog, an orange flower petal still in his mouth, and he's so stupid or not stupid it's not his fault—animals aren't stupid—but I'm falling slowly toward him and he can't realize what's happening. He's so busy chewing. He's so selfish. He just can't get enough. You are a hog, groundhog. You'll never forgive yourself.

And I'm telling myself that I have to make time slow, stretch time because this is my life and all I have left is this falling-down-time and then light leaks into the hole and a girl is turning in the air above me and she's floating down too and I'm thinking I'll break her fall maybe with my own body. I can see her shoes right above my head, little black shoes that look almost new, hardly scuffed. And she can't help it, her legs are kicking at the air she's so afraid. And the little goof is wearing her mother's apron, and there are pockets in the apron, and I want there to be pockets for me too, like maybe pockets inside time—time when I'm not in time, when I can live without wanting anything or anyone so much that I ruin everyone and everything, time when I don't have my heart set on what's impossible. And soon the girl and I will land, and we will land on hard earth and gravel and rocks, and right then the girl drops into my arms and we float down together.

X finds me. X marks the spot. X, my good man, clean and bright in the morning light, finds me in the backyard. By then the girl has gone, running off past the hedge. It's X who pulls me out of the sinkhole.

In the kitchen I sit at the table and X dabs my legs and arms and chin with Neosporin. He makes coffee. He has washed a blouse for me in the sink so that I have something to wear. When I see Tiffany he'll have to wait in the car—he's not allowed inside—but on the drive he stops. We can't afford it, but he stops anyway. I don't want to think about what he's done to make what he's doing possible. I don't want to think. And then I am Tiffany's mother carrying in my arms so many flowers that much of me, the whole front of me, is invisible. I am all flowers.

A Shadow

Some disquieting confessions must be made in printing at last
the play of *Peter Pan;* among them this, that I have no
recollection of having written it.
—J. M. BARRIE
Dedication to *Peter Pan, or, The Boy Who Would Not Grow Up*

On the morning of J. M. Barrie's death in 1937 a maid found something
that shone on the carpet of the author's sitting room. Believing what she
spied was perhaps a lost pin-hook for a curtain, she dropped it into her
pocket. Days later, the maid's little daughter discovered that bit of metal
on the floor in the rented room where she and her mother lived. What
the child found appeared at first to be meant for a lady's dress, something
to close tiny buttons. The girl slept with her prize under her pillow, a
little star, an arrowhead, or a bayonet for the tin soldier she hid in a crack
of her bed's headboard.

Many years earlier, a boy digging in a garden with a teaspoon had
unearthed that same bit of metal. He ran with his treasure to the thin-
faced gentleman in Kensington Gardens who appeared each day with
his Saint Bernard and teased the children there. The gentleman with the
fine mustache admired the metal until the boy cried, "It's for you," and
would not take the gift back.

On that same afternoon another child was watching. To avoid being
discovered, this particular child climbed an oak. His eyeglasses were
bent at the rims and smudged, and he could hardly see without them. Off
and on, the boy wiped sweat from his lenses. He balanced on a branch
and spied while the man who accepted the little bit of metal suggested

new twists in the children's games. The boy in the tree feared that the other children knew he was listening above them, or that the man knew, or at any rate someone knew and laughed at him. The boy caught sight of his own shadow stretched far below on the ground. Panicking, he curled into a ball so that his shadow wouldn't look quite so boy-shaped and give him away.

He needn't have worried. Even the St. Bernard ignored the boy, only once sniffing in his direction.

From his perch camouflaged by leaves, the boy could not stop listening. He especially liked to listen when the man told stories. The boy's thoughts were sometimes ahead of the stories, as if he himself steered the ship of the stories into deep water.

On the day when the piece of metal slipped to the ground by the park bench, the boy saw. He waited until twilight to climb down and snatch what he had spied.

Late that very night, a shadow appeared over the boy's head. The shadow spread upon the ceiling and over the walls, and a dream came for the boy, a dream full of islands and clouds bursting with rain, and in the dream the boy washed his face in leaves. When the boy woke he was so happy that for hours he didn't grow thirsty or hungry. That day he climbed even higher in the oak while below him the men and the boys kept busy with their games and storytelling, and the St. Bernard romped in circles. Everyone on the ground laughed so often that, if he hadn't been afraid of being found out, the boy would have laughed with them.

The next night the shadow again stretched across the boy's room, and this time the boy dreamed of blood in bowls, blood that fizzed, blood that once sped within a living man through a forest. In the morning the boy stood at the window and looked out at the light and tried to forget his dream. He felt better when he saw the metal piece glitter on the window ledge.

The following night the boy slipped into the open cavern of a dream. Everywhere he looked turned green—green so green that the green was water and the green was bird wings and the green was light inside a peapod. The boy could smell cut grass. When he woke he tried to forget his dream, even the beautiful green of the dream, for in the dream a man trailed blood from his pierced side, and the blood made sticky the grass where the man's feet were dragged. That afternoon a storm broke. As the rain poured, the boy in the oak believed there were secrets everywhere, secrets hovering over the chimney tops, and secrets in the streets streaming with rain. When the boy finally returned home he was so drenched and tired he couldn't keep his eyes open any longer.

That night the shadow sped through the boy's window and demanded, "Cut off the pirate's hand."

In the dream the boy couldn't stop shrieking. No, he wouldn't! He wouldn't cut off the pirate's hand! He wouldn't! By morning, worms wriggled on the window ledge where the boy kept his eyeglasses and the piece of metal.

That afternoon the boy heard the man tell the children that a captain's hand was lopped off by a child. The boy shivered to think that someone had obeyed the shadow's command. The man told the astonished children gathered around him that a hook was then attached to the flesh where the hand was sliced. The boy listened closely, his face covered by leaves. He wondered if the same shadow that visited him at night visited the man. He shuddered and wondered who could be so cruel as to delight in cutting off a man's hand.

From then on the boy climbed to the very top of the oak and no longer needed his glasses. In the distance the treetops swayed back and forth like a school of fish in a pond. Even the faraway trees looked magnified, the bark of each tree as visible as fur on the scruff of the Saint Bernard galloping over the grass.

The boys who played in Kensington Gardens were brothers, and soon they began to call the man Uncle Jim. The oak branches turned slippery from moss that spread after many storms, and the boy who watched felt monkeylike and strange to himself as he crouched, clinging to a limb.

One afternoon the boy came crashing down from the oak. He lay on the grass for a long time, the wind knocked out of him. The laughing boys didn't apologize, although they had to be the culprits who somehow, some way, sent him crashing from the tree.

When the boy caught his breath he scrambled up to hide again among the leaves. He was too ashamed to look in the direction of the man telling stories. He stared hard into the distance as the horizon filled with a milky blue haze, and this time the boy heard the name of the child in the stories, and the boy hated the name. The child in the man's stories never grew, and he gathered around himself abandoned children, and lived where adventures never ended among glittering islands and slippery fish women and ignorant pirates. All the games played by the children were a rehearsal for the man's stories, it seemed to the boy. And the boy thought the stories were silly. He thought that his own dreams, however much they terrified him, were stronger and deeper and truer, although he wondered if the shadow in his dreams might be Peter Pan.

That night a tapping began at the boy's window and grew louder until the boy crept out of bed. A bloody hand scratched there at the glass. The boy leapt back to safety and covered his head with a blanket.

In the morning when the boy awoke he found the hand on his pillow. The hand was dissolving like sand poured into a bucket of water. The boy closed his eyes and tried to convince himself he was dreaming.

After that, the boy's ears began to prick up at the slightest sound: a mouse rolling a fragment of walnut shell, a leaf brushing against a stone, a dog's moan as she burrowed her head among her sleeping puppies. Otherwise little changed for the boy until one night the shadow appeared again at the window and made a new demand: "Cut off the pirate's other hand."

The boy cowered in a corner of the room.

The next day he put up a cloth sheet at his window to block out all light in hopes that the shadow, even in dreams, couldn't appear again when the room swam in total darkness. That night the shadow pulled down the sheet and spread across the ceiling and the walls and again made his demand, "Cut off the pirate's other hand."

From then on the boy stayed away from the man in the park and the boys, those brothers who were now orphans. He stayed away as if the stories he heard had conjured the shadow. Yet staying away made no difference, for each night the shadow swayed close to the boy's ear and demanded, "Cut off the pirate's other hand."

One night, furious with exhaustion, the boy windmilled his arms at the walls and shouted, "Who are you?"

He shouted until the shadow dwindled to the size of a man and spoke. The shadow sounded like thrashing leaves as he made his claim that he was the last shadow of the green man. The boy knew—as every boy then knew—the story of Robin Hood, whose eyes could catch the gleam of a hawk's feather seven oaks in the distance. And the boy knew that Robin Hood died from treachery, from the bloodletting that drew too much from his once happy body. And the boy knew that Robin Hood, weak as dry grass, leaning against Little John, pulled back his bowstring, and his arrow flew with a magnificent shredding sound. Afterwards, the outlaws and the poorest of the poor covered his body in oak leaves at the very spot where his arrow struck.

The bit of metal gave off light on the window's ledge.

The boy held out the metal to the shadow and said, "Take it back. It's the tip of Robin Hood's arrow. I stole it."

The shadow flew to the window and said, "You never cut off the pirate's other hand," and disappeared into the night air.

Year after year the boy remained a boy, and sometimes the shadow returned and leaned against him, and the boy felt like he was bound to a mast while the earth rocked, as if he and the shadow sailed on a ship. After a while the shadow left the boy alone, and the boy soon grew to miss the shadow.

The boy taught himself to make shadows on the wall with his hands: a claw, a duck, an old woman in a scarf, a rabbit, a bat, a wolf. And still the shadow didn't come back. The boy passed a vendor on the street one afternoon and she offered him a sample of her wares. The taste was so bitter he nearly spit out what she put in his mouth. The woman pointed to the leaf-shaped scar on his cheek, a souvenir from his many days spent in a tree top. "You're a delicate fellow, aren't you?" she said with a mean laugh. From then on, to show he wasn't frail, the boy swallowed whatever she handed him, even gnarled, pickled things. He was still a boy, but a different sort of boy after that. When he thought of the stories the gentleman in the park told, he kept getting things mixed up. Who was the pirate and who was Peter Pan? What he had heard there seemed like shadows of other stories, and he missed the shadow more than the stories, although the shadow was inside the stories, and pitiless, just like the hook poised to tear a hole through a man's body.

The boy kept his window open in case the shadow might return.

Sometimes the boy felt insubstantial and tissue-thin. Sometimes he looked at his own hands and admired his fingers, still able to clasp after all those years when he managed never more than once to fall from a limb. Sometimes he was glad that although he was still a boy he looked to others like a shrunken man. Sometimes he wondered how many of his dreams were the shadow's own dreams and never his. Yet always, no matter what, the boy was grateful that he was still a boy. Otherwise, everything everywhere around him was changing. He could feel the change on his skin. In the park a page of newsprint whirling in the wind stuck to his chest, and the black ink looked like a thousand hooks. He had never learned to read and was glad of that. Sometimes he studied the arrow tip and thought it was a tiny hook too and he believed he was unlucky. His pulse hardly beat then. He had to clap himself on his chest and crow like a rooster to get his heart started again.

In crowds he scanned faces to find another child like himself. He knew it was past time for him to leave when his loneliness became even more terrible.

One night, many years later, the boy flew to the man whose stories he listened to in what seemed like another world, that world of gardens. The boy parted the curtains at the man's open window and stood on the casement. He carried with him the bit of metal, which didn't resemble an arrow tip in the least anymore, its edges dull and ashen.

The boy dropped to the floor. He hardly knew what to say, except to explain that he was grateful for the man's stories, even the silliest ones.

The man opened his eyes, faded and dim, and blinked. "Peter?" he said. "Is that you?"

Wanting to be kind, the boy almost said yes. Instead he said nothing.

The man asked, "Didn't you used to be the green man?"

The curtains tossed in a gust of wind and floated in the night air and twisted before dropping again. "I have something that's yours," the boy said. He pressed what he'd stolen long ago into the man's hand. "No, my boy, that was always meant for you," the man said. "It belongs to Robin Hood's shadow, not to me." "No, it's always for the ones among us who won't grow old. Did you finally cut off the pirate's other hand?"

The boy swallowed and told the truth. "I couldn't kill him, sir." "But did you cut off his other hand?" "No, sir." "He would have come back anyway," the man said. Just then the shadow darted into the room, crawled up a wall, and did an awkward dance. The man went on, his voice weakening, "Their kind will always come back."

The shadow fled through the window. The boy had lost the shadow again. But by now the boy knew where he might find him.

Four years after J. M. Barrie's death, the maid's daughter who had found the arrow tip slept fitfully among rows of other children in a charity hospital in London. The ward was quiet late in the night while the girl dreamed of gardens and of children, and of children digging with teaspoons in gardens. A shadow flitted at the border of her dream and made his demand: "Cut off the pirate's other hand."

The child knew she was inside a dream. Only in a dream could she still hold tight to the arrow tip she lost when everything around her exploded in flames and smoke. With her bandaged fingers the girl lifted the arrow tip like a many-pointed star. And in her dream she cut off the other hand of the pirate, his hook, and the hands of the clock.

That night no pirate chased children, no hands, no hook, no clock. The shadow flew to the window next to the girl's bed and told her that in Never Land the pirate would grow a new hand, and another hook, but the hands of the clock for one night would always be dead, thanks to her bravery. He gave her a medal made of iron—a new arrowhead, one that wasn't meant to mark a grave.

"Will you take me with you?" the girl asked.

"This is only a dream," the shadow said. "You made the dream yourself."

"My bandages are dirty. In a dream they wouldn't be so dirty, would they?"

The shadow couldn't tell the girl how many dreams thrummed through him along with a greenness that could be imagined even when greenness ended. After all, he couldn't tell her what he was made of. He couldn't tell her what he didn't understand, and there was so much he was uncertain about. Long ago in another war the count was never exact: how many boys who once dug with teaspoons in gardens were lost in trenches.

So very much for a shadow not to know. Whatever was stolen from the poor was never determined—no one knew how much that was. Or that the greatest gift stolen from the rich was forgetfulness.

The wind from the open window blew on the sleeping girl. The shadow turned and closed the window and parted the curtains to see into the night. A boy was coming after the shadow, and the shadow had to get away before he was snatched. The shadow couldn't remember ever not playing that game. He didn't know that already the boy was on his trail, almost ready to clap hands on him.

The Odyssey

She was eleven years old and homeschooled, and one of her nonnegotiable assignments was to read the daily local newspaper. As a result, she knew a lot of things even her parents didn't. For instance, she knew there was an unidentified man going around throwing semen at women. He did it from his car window. Another fact: Two months ago the newspaper reported that someone, probably someone else, was throwing fat at people's houses. The newspaper never explained. Did someone cut the gristle off steaks, save the fat in his/her refrigerator until he/she filled an entire bucket, then throw that exact fat at people's houses? Possibly? People—the species defies logic!

Homeschooling. Maybe she wouldn't have had to be homeschooled if her parents hadn't named her Tahreen, a name that made kids step on your heels when you hurried through the halls, that caused kids to bump you into a locker, that made kids give you a nickname: Soup. Like that was funny. But maybe having a name like Tahreen wasn't all bad, given that you didn't have to go to school anymore. You could be what your mother called "a free-range kid," which also meant that for your science project you could go down to the beach and gather up a few "aquatic plants" and bring them home for "identification purposes."

That was how she found the man. The beach was a tiny strip of sand overwhelmed by giant rocks, rocks that in the morning light made Tahreen think of last week's lesson about "spatial relationships" in Monet—a lesson for high-schoolers, but what the heck, she kept skipping grades because otherwise the work was so easy. Tahreen loved that little triangle of sand where she could watch the waves ride up against those rocks and sometimes splash her face, like she was getting a warning from

Triton: This is my ocean! Dare not enter, young dark- haired wench of the land-dwellers!

The gold light—the sparkles of it—alerted her to the man, because otherwise he was pretty much the color of the sand. It was his hairs—he was hirsute! even worse than Dad—and the shining of his hairs snagged at her eyes and caused her to look down. Otherwise she was a looking-out-to-sea sort of person, always hoping to find a shore that would never emerge, for the horizon went on and on, just the way she imagined her life would go on, endlessly, as she gathered knowledge, as she swayed through the years, much like duckweed, for example.

Her first reaction didn't amount to a full thought but a cry: "Mom!" Then she saw the man's chest rise. He was alive! How embarrassing! He might have heard her call for her mother. Or not. He was breathing but otherwise not moving. She crouched a few feet away and wrapped her arms around her knees. Observation is so important! To be a diligent observer is essential for a budding scientist. But was he dying? Should she run to her parents? First, however, she must assess the situation—or is the word *access?* His big head and jaw, eyes closed, eyelids not moving, tiny whiskery hairs all along his jaw, hairs that would feel sharp. Some sort of safari shorts with big pockets. Back up to the head again. Fore-head ridge, not like Neanderthal man quite. Okay, back to the nether regions (*neither* regions?) again. Kneecaps prominent, bony and long long long legs. He was not a teenager but not all that old. His chest was bare, which was good for her ability to observe his breathing because the hairs moved. Maybe he was napping? On his left arm, what looked like a long cut, kind of open and white, not bleeding. Maybe salt water closed the slicing up?

Hypotheses:

shipwreck
kidnapping
hijacking
escaping from law
lost long-distance swimmer
regular exhausted swimmer

failed suicide

runaway from cruel or neglectful parents

merman

alien from planet without water or swimming lessons or . . .

She closed her eyes. The sun was beating down hard. She wondered if eventually she should cover the man with wet sand so that he didn't shrivel. The sun was doing things to her eyelids so that she could see even with her eyes closed. She was seeing red poppies opening. Funny how you could see the sun when you couldn't see anything else.

Sand spurted against her knee. She opened her eyes. The man was sitting up and looking at her.

He said words, but she didn't know the language. He had a man's voice but there was something pleading about him. Something boylike. He couldn't be as old as she had expected. He was a man, but he hadn't been a man for long.

He was still speaking. She wasn't good at Spanish. Knowing Spanish wouldn't help anyway. She didn't think he was speaking Spanish. What could she do? She tried translating what he said in her head. Through telepathy. Through sheer compassion. We are humans. Our neurons speak the same language. He paused, and she said what he thought he meant—in English, and she raised her voice too, because maybe being loud would help in terms of understanding.

You are saying that you are alone and have no one but me to help you. You have traveled a long way. You believe that I was put here on Earth to save you. Really, that's right. I'm here to save you. You are hungry.

She looked at him with great hope. He nodded. Of course. They could communicate through their minds! It was just like her mother always said: "I know what you're thinking." Her mother said this to Dad. Then there were fights, because Dad's thoughts were irritating, naturally.

Tahreen asked, "How's the arm?" She hoped she sounded casual. She didn't want to upset the man more than he probably already was. She pointed to the arm, casually, not letting her eyes linger. What is the meaning of the word *malinger*? Is that like bad lingering?

The man reached toward her as if to touch her face, maybe to do a pretend knock on her chin. She hated when adults did that. Like that thing they did to really little kids: "Got your nose," and then the adult's big fat stinking thumb is sticking out between his knuckles. You want to make a kid puke, go ahead and do that. The man swayed and squinted, then covered his face with his hands.

Pinpricks of tears behind the girl's eyes.

"Stay here," she said. "Don't move. Up there—right over behind where the water tower is—that's where I live. I'm going to get supplies for you!"

For the rest of her life she would remember that moment: the man looking at her gratefully, his pupils enlarging and seeming to fill her own eyes, and then she was running and aware of her strength. Homeschooling required a physical-education component, which she hated, but on that day she ran with all her force. She was flying, truly, flying so fast even though she was wearing sandals with that toe-wedgie thing that hurt. Once she was in the house she didn't bother to be quiet, didn't even say where she was headed as she filled a sack with apples and cheese and grapes and put a few olives in a baggie and then flew back to the beach—she was winged, her sandals were winged—and then she was at the exact spot and the man was gone.

Nowhere. She looked for his tracks in the sand and couldn't find them. She looked out to the horizon. She walked into the water, with each step fearing she would step on his drowned face. She looked for a glint of goldenness. She walked the beach and zigzagged around rocks and trespassed on the properties of the rich summer people and wandered all the way to Conway and could not find the man.

At least she had that: a secret. Her almost-drowned man. It was impossible not to be marked by the incident. It was like getting a tattoo visible only to herself.

⚓

Maybe you don't wind up becoming a scientist exactly, but you can be an environmentalist of course and you can work for a series of nonprofits, which is one of the more challenging routes you can take. Because, after all, unless the organization is a self-serving outright scam you can count on not making a profit, and you can almost always count on losing your position as the nonprofit flounders or is directly undercut by the industry the nonprofit opposes and exposes. So you're a floating person, in some ways, beaching up on the shores of one nonprofit after another and each time learning a new language about biodiversity and coral reefs and environmental justice and fracking fracking fracking and carbon sinks and disaster recovery. There was always more to learn and so much that was alarming and besides you were human and lonely and your social skills—never mind your social skills. The thing was: You were a worthwhile human being although you were so lonely you were finally "coming a little late to the party" (as your sometimes-friend Corinne declared). That is, you were going the online route to find a man or men. To put it bluntly. Which meant lots of coffee dates. Because you subscribed to three sites.

Of course you were a woman now, and your name, as always, was Tahreen. For dating websites you shortened it to Tahti. The name sounded friendly, even kind of Tahitian, one man informed you.

You had a little test for those men, because even if you were so lonely sometimes you kept on your television even while you slept, you could still be selective. Here was your test: At some point during those coffee dates or occasionally during dinners at a restaurant where you knew the staff and they would remember you in case your corpse had to be identified, you told the man about finding a living body on a beach. The man's response would be telling.

For instance, if the man talked over you or expressed no interest or just looked at you with a puzzled expression, you didn't have to see him again or be disappointed if he didn't want to see you again.

Sometimes a man would give a fuller response:

"Finders keepers, huh? You always wanted a man-toy right? Like a man blow-up? How old were you when this happened? I hope you were at least eighteen!"

"Tell me everything. Details, all right? You weren't hurt, were you? Is there something you're not saying? You can tell me. I want to hear everything. You were just a kid, right? A curious little devil girl."

"That was probably a dream. It's unlikely, from what you're telling me, that such a thing happened. Children's memories are often false. You probably just took too many hits off *The Little Mermaid*. I've had a terrible problem distinguishing between reality and dreams and movies and television and YouTube myself."

"So. The same thing happened to me. Exactly. Except it was a woman. Very beautiful. I like beautiful women. Sorry. You're sweet. I always want to be honest. This probably is as far as we should go. Coffee. Not to rush you. Or anything."

Did she necessarily need someone to spend her nights with, to complain about her colleagues with, to give her a ride back from Star Buick when her car died? For a while she stopped telling men about her long-ago experience on that beach. Why should she give away that part of herself? Even her parents didn't know about the incident—if it was an incident and not a dream, for lately the past seemed fuzzier. All those years ago, after the man disappeared, she kept checking the newspaper. There was never mention of anything that could have been connected to the man she found. And now, well beyond a decade later, everything was fuzzier in her life, and a low mist hung over her days. It was harder to get up in the morning and do what her latest supervisor called "God's work." The despoiling of the Earth was far gone, so how could she help turn back the horrible tide? And here she was, host to the most archaic desires, for her loneliness wasn't the sort that could be alleviated by team-building karaoke nights and elaborate gluten-free cupcakes composed partly of avocado and three-hour movies about disappearing glaciers and allegories about the digestive system/deforestation. The cupcakes almost helped, but still.

A winter night. Snow like Hollywood snow. Thick, lacy. Like chains of paper dolls. Optical-illusion snow. Sparkle-less snow. Matte snow. Like snow that had cosmetic surgery. Like end-of-the-world snow. Engineered snow.

She agreed to meet the man at a Mediterranean restaurant and set out early so she would arrive first. She always arrived first so she could find the best exit. She didn't know the neighborhood, but the chatty Uber driver said she'd like it: good rents, a decent school district (obviously the driver was a father). The restaurant, he said, was a "well-kept secret." Girded with those good opinions, she tried to think positive thoughts. Why shouldn't one date finally turn out? She knew three couples who met online. Maybe she knew even more couples who met that way but weren't advertising the fact. Two men from work who were married to each other had met online. A woman who used to tease her wickedly in grade school was promoting a matchmaking service on her blog. Good things could happen.

Oh no. No no no no no no.

He was impossibly good-looking. Better-looking than his photograph. The photo didn't capture him: the warmth in his eyes as he held out his hand to shake hers. The smooth planes of his face. The clever, quick smile. He had arrived at the restaurant first. She couldn't know immediately if the route to the restrooms led toward a rear exit.

She was glad when he handed her the menu and said, "Please. Choose now, and we can talk afterwards." She stared at the menu as if making a difficult decision. She would order the Greek salad and didn't need to study. No, she wanted to gather her thoughts with the menu as her shield. The man didn't project obvious signs of disappointment. He had, after all, seen her photograph. Therefore, he must have known, generally, what she looked like. It was just that the photograph was a lie. She hadn't doctored it, no, but she'd probably taken over a hundred selfies, using the timer, before she got the right image, and that depended on the light streaming through her balcony window and thus whiting out a portion of her face. In her profile she had spent some time describing her various positions at nonprofits. Maybe that's what appealed to him.

Which is why she decided to apply the test right away, even before they ordered drinks. The runes seemed right: Their waiter was ignoring them.

She told him about finding the man lying in the sand, about how his disappearance was something she'd never stopped thinking about, how sometimes, at odd moments, she imagined she saw him again in the street or in a store or at a restaurant. She laid it on thick, all the while thinking: I sound like a crazy woman, like an absolute freak, like someone to run from, like a wildebeest—what are they anyway, wildebeests? I'm supposed to know this crap and I still don't.

"Ah, Nausicaä," the man said. His dark lashes were all that were visible of his eyes, which were squeezed almost shut as if he was staring at the sun. "Little Nausicaä, who found a man and wanted to save him. And she did. Because of her kind heart, Odysseus returned home."

Tahreen didn't remember *The Odyssey* that well. But she could recall enough.

"But my Odysseus—the man I found—didn't return home because of anything I did."

"You don't know that. He woke up and saw an innocent little face who cared for him, who didn't threaten to call the police. You didn't make any demands. You could have turned him in or you could have ignored him, neglected him. No, you wanted to help. No, you sat there quietly watching him, and then you spoke, and then you ran off and he knew you were bringing him food."

"Why didn't he stay then—if he was hungry?"

"How could he burden a child? Or maybe he thought you were a vision?"

Why was this man so intent on her eyes? He hardly looked away from her. What could such a man want? What was he after? She couldn't bear any more. "You're looking for contacts," she said. "You're networking, right? Is that what's happening here? You're interested in working on environmental issues? This is about employment. It's not a date."

"Yes, at first. But then I didn't know I was meeting Nausicaä."

It was a pleasant evening overall. Tahreen went back to the menu and ordered grilled trout. She backtracked and chose, additionally, a salad with guava beans, and decided on mussels as an appetizer. She even had dessert and coffee and an after-dinner drink. She was sure he would reach for the bill.

"I like that you're hungry," he said. "You know, if what happened when you were a child haunts you that's a good thing and there's a way to deal with it—imaginatively."

Her scalp felt lit with embarrassment. She didn't want to know what he was proposing—and she also did want to know.

At last she said, trying to sound light-hearted, "I'm lonely, but I'm not that lonely."

He laughed. "This is what you do," he said. "You go back to that beach and you go out into the water. Not too far. Stay safe. You go out and stand in the waves for a long time and then when you're very tired—not too tired, stay safe—you stumble back to the shore—your legs will be weak—and you lie down in the sand in the exact same position as that man you found. You go to sleep. And when you open your eyes again everything will be different. You won't be locked into being the witness anymore. You'll know something about what it feels like to lie there, unprotected. And maybe, if you're lucky, a child will show up or even a dog."

"A dog?"

"Why not a dog? They're loyal. They're good luck. And whoever shows up or doesn't show up, whatever, it doesn't matter because you'll have a vision. Maybe your vision will be that you're just a stowaway on the Earth. Or maybe your vision will be that you were never alone, that there was always someone watching you the way you watched that man. And whoever was watching you is haunted by you too."

He had passed her test, she knew. But could she pass his? The thing about tests: You never know what the questions are in advance.

The man texted her a few times in the next days. She didn't text him back, and then he stopped texting. She didn't erase his number—just in case.

The next summer, on a cloudless day while her parents napped, overwhelmed by her visit, given that they were overwhelmed by any disruption to their routines, Tahreen made her way down to the beach. She'd lost her job, and a somewhat "romantic" (the quotation marks were well earned) relationship she'd tried to foster was clearly not only dead but rotting. She walked out and tried to remain standing as wave after wave pounded higher, once dragging the pebbly sand out from under her feet and sending her onto her back where she flailed, salt water plowing into her nose. She stood again and steeled herself.

By the time she walked back to the shore her legs wobbled and buckled. She stretched out and fell asleep.

It must have been at least an hour before she woke. Her cheek hurt from where she'd ground the side of her face into the sand. Her legs were burning. She turned her head, agonizingly, left to right. She was alone, except for the sun, which was brilliant, without judgment, neglecting no one.

Gods and Goddesses in Art and Legend

On the afternoon Alette moved into the house she came across the closest thing her childhood offered to a sex manual: *Gods and Goddesses in Art and Legend, with Sixty-Four Illustrations in Gravure*, by Herman J. Wechsler. When she first pored over the book as a fifth-grader, the illustrations were already muddy, the pages a darkening manila and flaking. On the cover Venus sailed on her half shell, staring impassively, one bare breast entirely visible, a handmaid rushing toward her with a robe. And the couple blowing flowers her way? The female half of that couple flaunted a fully bare breast too. No less fascinating was an illustration inside the book: Claude Lorrain's *Narcissus and Echo*. How small and naked Echo was. Like a tiny garden slug.

Alette's parents had moved to a development for seniors in Tilburne, Wisconsin, and for the last months before the rental agent took over the property Alette was staying alone in the farmhouse. To return home is frequently enacted in television dramas as life-transforming in a profound and irreversible way. In Alette's imagination the only acceptable, non-shaming reason for an adult to return home is if you were sent to investigate a murder.

North of the farm stretched the meadow where Alette used to run as a child, pretending to be a nymph and taking extreme measures to feel nymphlike. Back then she read her book of myths in that breezy meadow. Sometimes a page would turn as if moved by an invisible hand. Her father, only last year, had come back from the deep grass, his shovel drizzling with snakes. These days she didn't bother venturing into the meadow.

Instead, Alette began a routine of walking down the hill to the bridge that spanned the creek south of the farmhouse. The road to the bridge was lined with maples thrashing on windy days with a dry sound, like sandpaper, as if readying themselves for autumn by the finest increments. She walked quickly because she needed to exhaust herself, to walk off whatever in her was dangerous and world-hating. Once she had confided to Ajax about her sadness, sadness that predated the sale of the farm, sadness that included the sensation that she was always looking out from behind glass. Grinning, Ajax said, "Well, maybe it's because you're wearing your glasses today." She swatted him but felt gratitude. She was a woolly mammoth in a tar pit and there he was, a caveman with a stick, grunting to pull her out. He must have gotten tired of that.

Ajax was so unselfconscious that it was relaxing to be around him. They talked together incessantly: national politics, international politics, politics at his job—instructional technology at a university—his family (she even knew his aunts' names and dietary preferences), his onetime experience as a stunt double for a movie that went directly to Pay-Per-View. It wasn't a one-way conversation either. He knew more about her than anyone alive. In fact, their relationship was one long conversation. That he broke off.

Currently Ajax was in Nara, Japan, at a conference. She kept tabs on him through a mutual friend and his Facebook. To stop missing him she tried drawing up memories that ought to be repulsive. For instance: Ajax on a park bench, barbecue sauce twinkling on his beard like an upset ant hill. But no, she wasn't repulsed. Nothing he did, finally, could repulse her, at least not for long. If she had to put him in *Gods and Goddesses in Art and Legend* he'd be one of the portliest gods—Pan—or maybe just a mystical being: the Minotaur, if the Minotaur was free to travel. To Nara. Japan.

He had a good job even if the university where he worked was foundering. She, on the other hand, was underemployed. Except for Ajax, she didn't know anyone who wasn't.

Sizzling erupted behind her—a runner's nylon jacket. Until then she had believed she was alone on the road.

"Sorry sorry sorry," the runner said breathlessly. "I didn't mean to spook you."

"You didn't."

They exchanged names, and the runner pointed toward where he lived, just up Moss Road. She couldn't remember any houses on Moss Road for a quarter mile except for an abandoned farmhouse where, many years ago, she used to spend time playing with a boy who had been about her own age.

The man, sweating heavily, stared down at her, looking amused. Then off he went, his shorts buckling at his knees.

A week later Alette became reacquainted with someone she'd known peripherally since childhood. Kyra—direct, unsentimental, unromantic—the most transparent person Alette had ever known. Kyra liked to say, "I'm an open book." Generally if someone said that, you knew they were a closed book, but Kyra was genuine. Every indication proved it. Nothing about her was even squeamish. In junior high science she tore into owl pellets without blinking and was enthusiastic about dissecting a cat. While Alette had few friends back then and no one to share her secrets with, Kyra was a secure member of a group of girls. Practical girls whose clothes matched.

The two women were having lunch at the Wagon Wheel Inn when Kyra said, "I heard you met Paul? He was running and you met?" He was divorced, she said, and designed and built furniture. "You met him?" She didn't wait for Alette's answer but rocked forward in the booth. "The bread here—it's not really bread, is it? My sandwich—it's like eating through a foam rubber mattress a teenage boy passed out on. Sourdough is such a bad concept. Why are you so nervous?"

Alette flinched. Being nervous, wasn't that her downfall? Admittedly, the business she'd been employed by failed, but nearly everyone she worked with found new positions. They made connections, gained advocates, knew enough to distrust reassurances that the parent company was only reorganizing. The catalogs they produced were works of art, or nearly, and she'd had her hand in most landing pages and everything except the blog. What had she been doing, though, other than stimulating desires? Which sounded like pornography except she was selling sweater sets.

So what was left? Freelance work online, including designing brochures for a sports facility and an arts center, and a website upgrade. Her rates were so low it was not much better than an unpaid internship. Kyra, at least, couldn't look down on her. She worked for the county newspaper, which meant she covered everything in a twenty-five-mile radius, from school board meetings to botched break-ins, to a mysterious disease striking dairy cows. Everyone knew journalism no longer paid or hardly paid.

It was a Wednesday afternoon when Alette made her way again to the bridge. This time she took a path that led down to the creekbed. She wandered along the bank past a dam of stones, the kind built by children, and looked for mint. Long ago she'd learned what plants can't be brought home after she plucked cattails that filled the living room with a smell like urine. Any mint plant, including lemon balm, was safe.

She heard her name called at the same moment a dragonfly clicked and whirred past her eyes, bobbing on wings like transparent vanes.

Her name rang out again. From above. On the bridge.

The conjunction between the dragonfly's flight and looking up and seeing her neighbor, and then witnessing the sudden disappearance of both her neighbor and the dragonfly, afforded Alette a keen and unfamiliar sensation. She recalled her neighbor's name: Paul.

When she walked to the bridge the next afternoon she saw her neighbor again—as if he'd noted the time she walked. Or maybe she noted the time he ran. He asked if she'd like to see his work. His face was open and encouraging. She didn't know what he was talking about, and then she remembered what Kyra mentioned, that he designed and made furniture. The obvious occurred to her: She was a potential customer.

They were inside the foyer of his house. On a stand near the door lolled a blackened cluster of bananas with stickers attached. The foyer walls, surprisingly for a designer of any sort, were bare. Then again, so many people never bother to put anything on their walls. Wherever they lived looked provisional, half storage locker, half laundry bin. Ajax's apartment was like that. She felt a surge of longing for him.

As Paul led her into the front room she had to hide her surprise.

Books lined the sofa like a short boxy family, arranged by sizes. Books were ranged in towers next to a china hutch, behind the glass doors of which leaned more books. Inside an apparently unused fireplace leaned a row of behemoths, large enough to be art books. Taking up the room's center: a green leather recliner with three hard-bound atlases on its seat. A corner of the kitchen was visible, and there, on a counter, were books arranged by color, gradations of red in one tower, blue in another. Quite a few of the books looked very old, and she imagined that the spines shed. Old books, molting.

Paul's eyes met hers. The way he was looking at her! As if she could never disappoint him, as if he already trusted her completely, as if it would be impossible for her to do or say anything that would lower his estimation of her.

She stepped away from a stack that reached her waist and said, "You must be a great reader."

"People always ask if I've read them all. No one could read them all. A source of guilt and shame."

"Where did they come from?"

"Most—from library sales."

"You must go to some wonderful library sales." She went on to mention a library sale she had been to. As she spoke he was looking past her. It was like that game children play when one child pretends to see a ghost over another's shoulder. *Can I be that boring already?* she wondered.

Seconds later, light flashed through Paul's eyes and he became fully present again. She imagined she saw what he saw. Maybe he was looking at the hollows in her face, the landscape of it. She had always been a thin-faced person with eyes that were dark-circled even when she got adequate sleep. Long before she suffered from insomnia, even as a child, she looked bruised around the eyes. Elderly women in stores used to ask her what was wrong. And now, as she stood before Paul, she could feel her clothes sag, her fake velveteen pants with their elasticized waist, her old cotton shirt printed with blue roses—everything was sagging. It was "I am a safe woman" clothing, the layered cloaks of invisibility.

Just the same, as Paul examined her, she wondered if her sudden bout of self-consciousness might be a good thing. At least, in this instant, she was beginning to care about appearances. How things look does matter if you're the one who has to look at them. Because she didn't have to look at herself, she had generally stopped caring.

"You sell the books?" she asked.

"In a sense. Would you like to see?"

They left by the front door and passed around to the back of the house, stopping at a tin shed. Wind gusts rattled the metal. Once inside, Paul pulled an overhead cord.

The first thing Alette saw: a couch, made of books. An ottoman, made of books. Under a coffee table's varnished surface, pages overlapping in a repeated pattern. On a shelf: a line of whittled books, pages stiffened and clipped into shapes—a cathedral, a family farm complete with a tiny pig. The center of one book was carved out and filled with sand, atop which rested three pebbles. A Zen garden.

Books. People have odd relationships with them. In college Alette knew a girl who, if she made it past five pages, was compelled to read to the end. One friend bought books and never bothered to read them. Another friend resented returning books, assembled an illegal library, and quit school when his fines mounted.

Alette drifted her hand across a coffee table whose legs were books. Given that she did so much work on the internet, what were books to her? The words she generated online were illuminated and words no less for that. And wasn't Paul making art from art? Weren't the books likely to be destroyed otherwise? Here, at least, they'd survive, even if they'd never be opened, even if he was using a glue gun on Robert Louis Stevenson. And don't words live through whatever medium on which they appear? How did anyone expect books to be treated these days? Like a national flag in a nation that didn't burn its flag?

And didn't she dog-ear and underline books and occasionally take them into the bathtub? Hadn't she cracked their spines and written in their margins and slid them across the floor and bookmarked them with anything that came to hand, not excluding socks?

At least she didn't make them utterly unreadable. The pages that overlapped on the coffee table under her hand—she couldn't make out more than two sentences.

What power should a book have anyway—as an object? The volumes Paul used were closed crypts, dumber than bricks.

But why would anyone want any of this furniture in a home? Say the stool next to her, a simple block of what might be regarded as cheap novels, though it was hard to tell. You can't judge a book by its cover, unless you're like Paul, and then the cover is everything. Would you want to prop your feet on this block of books after a hard day? Was it a way to put words beneath you?

"You don't like it? You're sorry that I'm using books?"

"You're gifted."

"Except I'm using books."

Being attracted to someone can translate into not being honest with yourself. And then you call not being honest with yourself by another name: open-mindedness.

The wind died down by the time they left the shed. Paul asked if he could drive her home. She preferred to walk.

She was only yards past his house when she spotted, through a tangle of grapevines, a scorched foundation. Instantly she understood. This was all that remained of the abandoned house that she and a boy visited when they were children. They snuck into the house through a door strung with binder twine. The house's wallpaper had been leprous, with strafed patterns of cherries, two on a stem. Burdocks and thistles scratched at windows whitened with spiderwebs. She and the boy clambered through the rooms, knowing better than to go near the staircase, partly sawed off to feed somebody's woodstove. She loved the vines growing up the walls, the broken shelves, the piano that bedded litters of mice. Although even as a child seeing that ruined piano bothered her. Abandoning a piano—it was like abandoning a person.

The boy had lived almost a mile farther up Moss Road in the sort of house that never stays tenanted for long. Alette didn't know how many children lived there, or if they were all related. Two of the toddlers often wandered the lawn, heavy-looking diapers hanging between their pudgy bow legs. Once when Alette was walking by, three girls pressed themselves against an upstairs window—no curtains—and the girls were naked and wriggling like angleworms and laughing at her. She ran away from the sight of them.

The boy belonged to the house, but he was different, shy to the point of speechlessness. When she went to the abandoned house he was often already waiting for her. She and the boy hardly talked and frequently just huddled together, their knees touching. His black hair was thick—as thick as she imagined a bear's fur to be—and she once got up the nerve to touch it. He sat stock still, to show her he gave his permission.

That's what she remembers: a boy whose body was like a hot radiator, and how sometimes they stayed crouched until it was as if the house didn't exist and only they did. If she and the boy breathed in mouthfuls of dust as thick as smoke, if they knew a wall could collapse, or that they could fall through rotted boards or puncture their hands on nails, they nevertheless kept on visiting the house.

In late September the boy stopped showing up. When she found the courage to walk to his place it was evident a new family was living there. This family had a lot of cars—junkers on the lawn, and the air smelled like gasoline.

And now, all these years later, even overrun with grapevines and burdocks, only its foundation left, the house was somehow hanging invisible in the air. Evidence that it was once her own.

The next afternoon Alette walked down to the bridge again, choosing the time carefully. A half hour later she was ready to head back up the hill when she heard her name called.

How happy she was, waking up beside her neighbor Paul. Some part of her already knew she belonged in his house. The bedroom windows were open, and the air was fresh. On the bedside table, under layers of shellac, glimmered an old jacket cover of *A Room with a View*—a cypress on the left edge, towers of various heights in the distance, in the foreground a stone gate flocked with moss, ivy, lichen. What Alette remembered about *A Room with a View* wasn't on the cover at all. Everywhere violets were in that novel. In her memory, smoky blue violets emerged from every crevice, tinting the pages blue. The novel's two lovers kissed. But what she remembered more than the kiss was a flood of lavender and blue and bits of yellow and dark green leaves overwhelmed by the deep bluish-purple of wild violets, the ground watery with violets and softly scented. Saucers of blue were spilling with every step the lovers took. She sank back against the warmth of Paul and drifted once again into sleep.

She and Paul didn't have much to say to each other, not really. Maybe that was for the best. Look what had happened with Ajax. She and Ajax had talked and talked and talked and she'd talked him out of her life. Talk was overrated. Besides, Paul wasn't at all like Ajax. Paul's face was a forgiving mirror, or maybe an enchanted mirror. You saw in his face what you wished you could feel.

Except when, just as suddenly, you felt that you didn't exist for him, the way he could wipe a person from his consciousness. It was weirdly fascinating, that blankness that came over him. You wanted to bring him back, to make him see you again.

The great thing about being with Paul: She hardly thought about Ajax anymore. And she wasn't troubled with insomnia.

The happiness she felt—as if something wonderful buried in the landscape and undiscovered for years had sprouted. Another part of her resisted that assessment and wondered if her happiness had its source in exhaustion. She was so tired she didn't have the energy to be unhappy. And maybe the love she felt for Paul—for she loved him in an almost dizzy way, in some way instinctive and raw—was larger than happiness.

Paul offered to drive her home each morning, and each morning she refused. It was practically a ritual—his asking, her refusal. She liked to walk by herself up the road and replay the night. And she liked how at the crest of the hill the farmhouse became visible, and the old chicken coop, sagging and yellow. She liked walking by the granary, now filled with bales of wire. She liked looking past the gate to where the horse barn once stood, with its softly pounded earth broken by molehills. She liked seeing the silo at the head of the lane, and beyond the silo, the meadow with its wild clover. She tried not to think of her parents in their apartment in the development for the elderly, the hospital two blocks away, and how they must miss the farm. How contracted all their lives would be once the land was no longer in the family, once the sale went through, once renters invaded and set up their volley ball net on the lawn, their carport, their fire pit.

Upstairs in her childhood bedroom, like a broken-off piece of her past—on her bed, near her pillow during all those nights she slept away from the farmhouse: *Gods and Goddesses in Art and Legend.* She lifted the book, and the soft yellowish smell of old leaves swept up from the pages. Why had she ever left the book behind when she went away to college years ago? Those dusky illustrations: She had dreamed her way into them as a girl. And the myths. Didn't they keep happening?

Alette hadn't seen Kyra for weeks and felt guilty about it. She kept putting her friend off when she called. Finally, when Kyra asked if she'd like to take a ride out to Sinegal Lake, Alette said yes. There would still be time to meet up with Paul later.

In the years since Alette last visited, the slopes surrounding the lake had become barnacled with closely set cabins. Otherwise, it didn't look much changed. Water lapped at gravel, and the two women listened to the far-off vibration of an outboard motor. Kyra picked up a handful of pebbles, tossed them, and water churned. She was grinning. "Look down," she said. "Do you see anything?"

Inches from Alette's feet the lake water was murky. She crouched. A slew of men's belts had been dumped into the water. She jerked backward.

Kyra bent with laughter. "I probably should have warned you, but isn't the immediate unexpected impact great? It's pretty interesting, huh? You don't see this every day."

"They're what—snakes?" Alette asked. "Eels? Lampreys? "

Kyra made hard snuffing noises. She looked almost contrite before she burst into more laughter. "I know. I know. I love your face. Forgive me. I'm a terrible human being. But they're great—the eels, the infestation, once you get used to them. My brother will be in ecstasy. He travels constantly. On grants. A totally different sort of mind, that's what he has. Nothing he likes to study more than invasive species. As he'd say, 'They're so gutsy.' I emailed him about them. Fat chance I'll hear from him. He's always off to unconquered realms. Beyond email. Like any place is beyond email. He doesn't check his email hardly ever anyway. He's too busy delivering mercy to plankton. Coddling invasive species."

"I didn't know you had a brother."

"He was only a year older than we were, Alette. The school bus? He used to ask all the girls to go out on his boat? We always liked boats, our family. My father has three now. They're rotting, though. You just can't get enough of those eels, can you?"

Alette took three more steps backward. "God, it's like a great big tangled nest of them. Will they die out in winter?"

"They lasted last winter, although that was a mild winter. I bet these are hardy. Born out of industrial waste and fertilizer runoff. Maybe it's a good thing they have a place where they can thrive, maybe they're endangered otherwise. Did you notice the for-sale signs all along the lake? It's not just the economy. Nobody wants to talk about the eels because property values will plummet. Nobody wants to send little Tommy and Ahmed or whoever down here to wade either."

Alette wished she hadn't come. One minute she felt grateful to Kyra for injecting the unexpected into her life. The next minute she wanted to crawl back to the house and nap on the couch. She was so tired lately— so many nights with Paul. And she was also filled with foreboding, for something was overdue to go wrong.

Kyra coughed, bent, and a stream of vomit hit the pebbles. "It's all right," she said. "I'm getting used to it."

The knowledge must have been about to crest into Alette's consciousness. She hardly paused before asking "How far along are you?"

"Almost four months. It's going to kick soon."

"You didn't tell me."

"Isn't it obvious?"

"No."

Sunlight flickered around the edges of the lake, and the clouds' reflections stirred. "I thought you realized," Kyra said. "I keep thinking everyone must know and they're just pretending they don't."

"Does your brother know?"

"Even if he were standing here he wouldn't notice. I could grow a tusk and he wouldn't notice. I'm used to it."

You think you know a person, especially one who seems as transparent as Kyra, and you find out there are hidden panels, all of them opaque. Within minutes Alette fantasized about shopping for Kyra's baby. Already she hoped to be useful to Kyra and felt almost unbearably tender toward her.

Back in the car, Kyra said, "You're going to be different now, aren't you? I'm still myself."

Alette had wanted to open the car door for Kyra, to adjust her friend's seat belt, to buy her ice cream, to find out who the father was.

Before Kyra spoke again, Alette shivered with apprehension—because happiness is so fragile. No need to act surprised even if what's expected can be surprising when it arrives full-blown.

"It's your neighbor," Kyra said. "Paul."

Alette said, "No it's not."

"Alette, he makes furniture out of books. He's not right for you. I don't know what I was thinking either."

When her throat stopped closing Alette asked, "Does he know?"

"No."

"Will you tell him?"

Kyra lifted her hands from the wheel, dropped them back, and said, "I want to be angry and open up a dictionary and look under the letter *P* and find *Paul* there as the definition for *Prick*. But no, it's Paul. I can't get mad at him. It would be so much easier if he were, you know, the kind of guy who rides a motorcycle into your living room and ejaculates into your grandma's face. But no. It's Paul.

"You know, I should be more nervous. What will my life be like? How can I support this baby? Who will love me and the baby? Because I haven't given up on being loved. Maybe it's hormones talking. Am I the only person who feels like this? The other day I read about a woman who gave birth on a train and walked off carrying both her baby and her placenta. That could not be me. I feel tranquilized, you know, like a cow elephant. Maybe it's nature's way of protecting the baby by making me calmer. It's like nature is starting to turn me off so I don't do any more damage. Plenty of women are only nauseous. What I have: It's like an awful sleeping sickness where I keep waking up to vomit. At least I have you to complain to."

Once Alette was back at the farmhouse she pulled out a glass and turned on the tap. As she drank she thought about how water has no taste, only coldness, sensation. Everything has a taste except water—though if water has a taste it tastes like rocks and the season of spring. But no, this water had no taste. The water in the glass was very cold. She would miss even this water.

She knew she would miss Paul. She already did. All that feeling. Just feeling. They hadn't needed to talk—they were just at the beginning of things anyway. And even as a mist of pain surrounded her she knew that eventually she'd be fine. People paid too much attention to what passed for romantic love. It was sentimental, overwrought. Hyperbolic. In the end it wasn't profound. No, it was only regrettable, not tragic or even sad. Still, people shot each other in the head because of it.

The next morning she could hardly eat. A day later she could hardly stop eating. Love—it was an illusion, she told herself repeatedly. The illusory version she had thought she experienced was a product of late capitalistic individuality. Plus narcissism. She told herself she could never have held Paul's attention long enough to matter to him anyway. He brought confusion, he didn't solve confusion. He was the messenger, not the message. His presence let her know how deep her loneliness was, but that didn't mean she was lonely for him. Yes, his face was like a forgiving mirror, or maybe an enchanted mirror. She had told herself that idea about his face a number of times. You saw in his face what you wished you could feel when you looked in the mirror. That's what she told herself before she told herself other things.

One sunny but cool afternoon in late November, a day before she would have to vacate her parents' house, Alette drove up Moss Road. She had driven past Paul's the afternoon before at the same time, out of curiosity, wanting to stop but not stopping.

This time Kyra was in the driveway, wrapped in a heavy coat, undeniably pregnant.

"You look great," Kyra called over as Alette climbed out of her car. "You look so healthy."

Alette thought those were the words she should have said to Kyra.

"I wanted to catch you driving by," Kyra went on. "You're terrible about returning calls."

Alette was led inside Paul's place, or what was Kyra's place too now. The house was warm and at least visibly book-less. She was relieved that Paul wasn't there.

"You're wondering about the books?" Kyra asked. "They're all out in the shed. We need room. I can't live the way Paul was living. He's such a book fetishist. He was handling the damn things all the time. It was like I was always being displaced. At the moment I'm weaning him from a boxed set of Trollope."

Watercolors of ocean scenes lined the walls. The seascape reflections didn't match the boats or the shoreline. Everything looked off-kilter, curled on reflected surfaces.

Kyra followed her gaze. "He kept those packed away until I found them. He has so little faith in his own gifts, but I love these. At first you think they're conventional, and then you see there's something wistful about them and you can't stop staring. Oh—and I'm trying to get him interested in lumber. Books do not make good furniture. He said you hated his furniture."

"I never said that."

"You didn't need to."

"You really have changed things," Alette said, wonderingly. The house smelled like baked apples. The bowl that had held bananas was banished. "When I was here I kept thinking about the house that used to be near this lot," Alette said. "There was an abandoned house—"

"I saw what was left of the foundation," Kyra said. "But I don't remember anything standing there when we were kids."

"I'm surprised," Alette said. "You're the one with the great memory." As she spoke, she recognized the side table decorated with the paperback cover of *A Room with a View*. Either Paul or Kyra, probably Paul, had moved the table from the bedroom. Yes, it would have to be Paul. Later, Alette would check online for the full text of the novel. She would be surprised to see that the violets only appeared in a few paragraphs. She had thought they took up chapters.

Kyra asked, "Did you ever find out who lived in the house before it was abandoned?"

"No, and I don't want to know. I thought of it as our discovery, mine and a friend's. Part of me fell in love with that place."

"But not this place," Kyra said, her color deepening.

"No," Alette said quickly. "Never. Never."

They were silent until Alette went on. "There was a boy who went to that abandoned house. I still think about him sometimes. He lived about a mile from here up the road. He was, in some ways, my first love." She stopped, embarrassed.

She shouldn't have worried. Kyra, bless her, wasn't listening. "He's got to branch out," Kyra was saying. "Or else try something that doesn't involve mold—book mold. Does he listen to me? Of course not. He can't concentrate long enough to listen to anyone. I wish he'd take a few lessons and paint more. To make a boat look like a boat. I know. I know. If he wants to be taken seriously he shouldn't make a boat look like a boat. But he'd also like—eventually—to sell a few things. And people like boats that look like boats. Because they like boats. But what do I know?"

"You know boats."

"Yeah, I do."

It would be almost three years before Alette was back in the state, returning for her father's funeral. He was buried in the family plot, two miles from the farm. Alette called ahead to ask the new owner if she could stop by the farmhouse. He was between tenants and said he didn't mind.

After Alette turned into the driveway she took a long time before she got out of her car. She started toward the porch and then decided she didn't want to look through the windows. She had no plans, either, to head down to the bridge and the creek. Instead, she walked far into the meadow.

She knew that Kyra and Paul were still living on Moss Road with their child. She wouldn't visit them. Not because she was wounded anymore. And not because she had been wrong in the past to be so romantic and airy.

She thought of her mother and how lonely she would be now. And how lonely they both were, in their different ways. Yet neither of them had anything to regret.

She thought about the things she used to imagine when she was a girl, when she was, for her own purposes and by her own willful design, a nymph—how when a tractor started up over the ridge, across from the horse barn, by the fence, Pan quietly ate an apple, the chill-to-the-hand Northern Spy. Most of the other gods and goddesses were on the other side of the farm, jostling one another or playing with their reflections in the cow tank or yodeling into the silo. Artemis polished her arrows beside the corn crib. It was Venus herself who was in the meadow, floating until she stepped off her shell and into the blue ground mint that gave off its scent. Accompanying Venus was her small son, a strange little boy made from love, and the air was alive and whirring, as if somehow everyone could be enchanted—or grateful for the near possibility, grateful to be called from somewhere higher than where they once stood, even if, from where she herself stood, Alette feared she was wrecked for any life that could not become enchanted.

And now, what next? Alette told herself she was human, after all, which meant not everything could happen to her. There were simple biological matters. Rules of gravity. Rules of longevity. What is obvious is generally true, not what is wished for. Or maybe she'd just picked the wrong gods.

What new pattern was she going to make for her life? Whatever it was, her life couldn't be made only of books. Not only of books. Although partly of books, that was true.

Hello! I Am Saying Hello! Because That Is What I Do When I Say Hello!

"Hello!" I said. And then I said, "Hello! I am saying 'Hello!' because that is what I do when I say 'Hello!'"

No one ever laughed—except Anita. Because it's not funny.

I have ruined lives. My cousin William trusted my ideas, and as a consequence I ruined his restaurant. I had an idea for a Viking Christmas as the restaurant's holiday theme. Except the Vikings weren't Christians. But I had this idea: Odin's Feast.

I wanted everyone to eat with their hands. For all I know, the Vikings had cutlery. But I wanted us to serve vats of beer and big pans of chicken. But then when we had the Viking Christmas every patron was so reserved, so polite, so un-rollicking, that it was smaller than life in there despite troughs of mead and braided women and nettles in the flatbread.

So that didn't work out. Some people wanted their money back. Because of nettles in their flatbread.

For the next year William let me try again with another theme: Tiny Tim's Christmas. And some people said: So what did Tiny Tim *have* for Christmas? They had read their Dickens. Well, what did he have? Until he got taken under Scrooge's wing he had at best a skinny goose. Before then, the family was impoverished. Exploited. But I had a rejoinder: "It's Tiny Tim's *dream* of a perfect Christmas. Carriage rides. Eggnog. Hot grog. We can wear Victorian gowns with those high waists and the little ribbons tied under our breasts!" And my cousin William asked, "Who'll be Tiny Tim?" And I said, "We'll hire a short and sullen teenager. Like Tiny Tim with a tongue stud." And then I said, "I get to be Mrs. Fezziwig and wear lots of stuffing." And William said, "You mean padding." And then I knew: Oh good. William's paying attention to detail already.

But it was a disaster.

There was a problem with what William called "reservation management." And then Jamie—he's dead—no, he moved, that's all, I'm just kidding, no one ever laughs when I say somebody's dead—Jamie tried to put on a floor show, so he dressed up as Christmas Future, which made it look like we were flirting with Satanism. And then because there were so many people we had to subdivide the food and wound up giving a lot of people their money back. William wanted to give *everyone* their money back. I felt like Scrooge because I kept restraining him. But who would have thought so many people wanted to celebrate Christmas like Tiny Tim?

Restaurants close all the time. It's risky enough without me ruining your business for you. Owning any restaurant: You'd make more money offering tours of a backyard cave or knitting sweaters for kittens and selling them on Etsy. Or taking a picture of a raindrop that looks like Lincoln.

So back to *Hello*. I said, "Hello," etcetera, and there was Anita on the phone, asking me to be her maid of honor. She was returning to us. To get married. I didn't even know what had happened to her original husband until she said, "He was glad to leave me."

"Oh no!" I said, more dramatically than I meant to. "Oh no! I don't understand!"

Then she told me about the man she was going to marry. He was an artist. His name was Malcolm. But I wasn't really listening after that because I was so busy thinking: Anita is back. Am I going to ruin her life?

Because I am so good at ruining things.

I always loved Anita—maybe because I rescued her. Women need to rescue people to feel like they're superheroes. I was just ten when I met Anita, but I needed desperately to be a rescuer even though I didn't know that yet. The first time I saw her it was a June afternoon and school was out and she was wandering on our road. And because I smile too often—although kind of scarily, I admit—she confessed to me that she had run away to find her father in Milwaukee. Now she wanted to get home because of course she couldn't get all the way to Milwaukee. But she didn't remember what street she lived on. Because they had just moved to our town. From Milwaukee.

Usually when people come to me for help, as you know, I ruin things. But somehow we got lucky. We kept walking until Anita recognized her home because her mother was already in the yard, slapping her hands against her crossed forearms like a maimed duck. Anita's mother was the least forbidding-looking adult woman I had ever encountered.

If she knew her daughter had tried to run away, she wasn't going to let on.

"I'm making pancakes for supper. Can you join us, honey?" She was talking to me.

I knew I couldn't stay. I wasn't supposed to wander that far from our road. I would be sent to my room to think about my irresponsibility, because God knows there can't be more irresponsibility in this house. Although only my father would say that. My mother would beg for my release.

It was a day of surprises. My father never noticed I was gone. And I had made a friend—a friend who for years would never seem less than mysterious. Always, Anita had a way of popping up when you didn't expect it, but then suddenly she wasn't there anymore. Like an escape artist. When we were children I didn't even try to understand Anita, which maybe—I think now—ensured that she tolerated me. After she left town I always imagined she'd return. And there I'd be, her loyal and true friend, waiting to say hello again.

At twilight the development's model looked haunted, but brightly lit. Despite its imposing size, the show house reminded me of a dollhouse, like anyone could lift off the roof and the thin walls could be crushed with one swift pummeling from a frustrated child. My mother's farmhouse was located right across from the development's gates. The last remnant from an earlier world.

A card table was set up in the dining room. It meant that Uncle Rex would drive over later, and he and Aunt Louise would have a game of hearts with my mother. Aunt Louise was already in the living room, seated in the peacock-patterned chair across from my mother. Three years ago the dentist my mother used to work for gave her one of those clocks that makes the cry of a bird on the hour. We were just minutes short of the northern mockingbird.

When I was a child we were taught a song in school called "My Mother's Face." In some ways it was cruel to teach us the song. Not all of us had mothers and two who did had mothers in prison. Maybe now the school doesn't teach that song anymore because of the growing prison population of mothers. Anyway, I sang that song as if it had to be about my own mother's face, her beautiful face. Even now it's not like my mother and I talk all that much. I just like to feel the radiance of her presence, and admittedly sometimes it's like being irradiated, but most of the time I don't feel genetically modified or anything. Actually it's kind of the reverse.

"I remember her very well," Aunt Louise said. "A bright, pretty girl. Very quiet but you always felt she was up to something. And then she just left everybody without a word."

All three of us were silent, conjuring Anita.

"Why'd she leave her husband in the first place?" Aunt Louise went on, turning to me.

I told my aunt I couldn't even begin to understand. "Will you go to the wedding?" I asked her and my mother.

"I'm going to send a gift," my aunt said. "And I want to see you in your maid of honor dress. But no, I don't think I'll go. I think that before eating anyone's food and drinking their wine, you should know the person. I haven't seen Anita in at least nine years. And she was unknowable to begin with."

"Aren't you curious?" I asked.

"It's nice of her to ask, but I wouldn't feel right about attending. I always had a feeling about her. And then when she disappeared I thought: That's the kind of person who won't get straightened out for a long time. I know full well that people like her cause havoc for any decent person involved with them—and that worried me. As a mother."

"So there we have it," my mother said. "You're worried that William could be preyed on."

"William, never." My aunt hesitated. Her features softened. "Actually I'd like to see someone try to prey on him."

My mother and I exchanged a look. In the emotional economy of my aunt's household, Uncle Rex was besotted by Aunt Louise, and Aunt Louise was besotted by William. Which left William free to enjoy his parents in the least demanding way, while regularly avoiding them. My aunt never spoke critically of William even when he was a boy, although criticism of children, a sly, fawning sort of criticism, was practically a sport among women in our town. My aunt always spoke of William as if no one anywhere was remotely like him. She believed herself lucky to have a son with such an "uncompromising temperament." She had to be the only person in the world who thought he had an uncompromising temperament. There was a while when I could get him to do anything. Like, say, let me accidentally ruin his business.

"There was never any calculation in Anita's behavior," my mother said. "She acted without thinking."

"I'm not so sure about that," my aunt said.

What was I doing in that living room? Supposedly, a grown person shouldn't visit her immediate family too often because they have this weird power—it's like brine. You feel pickled in the past. There you are, a person who pays her water bill on time and her cable bill only three weeks late, and you go home and you're pickled in brine. You're listening to your mother and her sister as if their low expectations make sense. Although I don't mean to implicate my mother. I've always held "Daddy's girls" and "Mama's boys" in contempt. But there's no negative term for a girl who loves her mother. That's just natural. And the thing is: I kept finding myself with my family, what there was of it, now that my father was no longer alive. But then again I was always with my mother and Aunt Louise and Uncle Rex even when my father was alive.

It was two days before the wedding, and given that William's restaurant had been turned into a low-budget craft store, Anita must have wanted to show her fiancé the one restaurant in the immediate area with any reputation at all. Then too, she must have wanted him to meet a few of us locals.

The Cuckoo Inn was known for Bavarian decor and chicken: chicken that was more breading than chicken, chicken that was encastled with turrets of breading.

As soon as I arrived, my eyes snagged on a man's upper lip. It was a thin lip but an expressive one. You expected those lips to speak a Romance language. And then the man spoke with the flat Midwestern voice of any of us. "You must be Natalie," he said.

A woman stood and leaned over the table toward me. I gasped in recognition and spoke her name. All the while I thought, What happened to Anita? The vividness had drained from her face.

"I've heard from nearly everyone we used to know," Anita said. The warmth in her voice couldn't be mistaken. Her voice was still her own.

Looking around wearily with his thin lips, Malcolm said, "And too many of them are actually coming." I noticed then that Malcolm's nose was unusually thin, his eyes heavily lidded. He looked like a rare dog breed. I am sorry, but he did. And I was very tempted to begin talking about rare dog breeds, how there must be some that are as inbred as royal families but are maybe less aggressive?

A chair was pulled out for me, and Anita introduced me to the others. "You remember my mother—Agnes," she said, and honestly I wouldn't have without prompting. Agnes was now a solid-looking woman in an aqua-colored dress with inflated shoulder pads. The weight was good for her; it made her seem less easy to abuse. And then there were other names: Grace, Joyce, women I remembered as girls from a class behind Anita's and mine. They were to be the bridesmaids. I hadn't realized they'd been close friends with Anita, or that she had kept in touch with them. The best man's flight was late, so I wouldn't be meeting him that night. There were two older women—friends of Agnes's, and then, and this struck me as insanely peculiar, my cousin William.

"I've never seen so much food in my life," Malcolm said.

"It's called family style," William said enthusiastically, though enthusiasm had never, to my knowledge, been an emotion he entertained, and I felt immediately embarrassed on his behalf.

How can I explain the irritation I felt toward William? It can really make you irritated when you see somebody whose life you ruined. Especially when they never get mad at you about it. It was so patronizing. William. He was eight years older, and when we were growing up, in child years, that was like he was forty. And now there he was, trying to look comfortable and at ease when I knew better. We're cousins, after all. Similar blood eddies through our veins. His face was the color of oatmeal, like the blood ran down to his feet and just pooled there. When he was a boy William liked his adventure books but not adventure, his airplane models but not flying. He never even learned to gut a fish.

The whole situation was vaguely embarrassing in another way—all those waiters in lederhosen hefting platters enormous enough for the appetites of farm animals. This was the sort of place I knew enough to avoid working in. And not just because of the lederhosen, but because of the chicken. I don't know why anyone bothers with the lederhosen. Or the cuckoo clocks. Or the billboard-sized menus. People came to the Cuckoo Inn as if it were a duty to gorge themselves, a discipline, which is the problem with all-you-can-eat restaurants. It's not restful. It's manual labor.

Anita was stroking Malcolm's forearm, her hand breezing across his sleeve. She kept it up, not descending to a pat of any sort. Like he needed petting or he might bolt.

When she stopped she asked, "Would you like to see Malcolm's work?" She passed me her cellphone. The image was upside down. From across the table William was angling for a look.

"Malcolm wraps things?" I said.

"Yes. He uses common materials."

"This is very interesting. Is this a mannequin that he's wrapped?"

"Never ask him about what's under the wrapping."

Malcolm turned toward us and glared in self-parody, I think, and said, "Those sensitive artist types."

I said something about how I was drawn to the images, and I wasn't lying. I'm too proud to lie or I'd lie a lot. I was actually drawn to what Malcolm made. I was drawn to want to unwrap them. To unbandage all the little forms. I wanted to free every tiny hostage, every shrink-wrapped mummy.

I looked up at my cousin, wondering if he felt the same way. But

William had turned toward the plate glass window and was looking out at the parking lot.

Before the desserts were wheeled in, I pulled up an empty chair at the far end of the table and sat next to Agnes. She wasn't in that perpetual state of alertness from years ago, a state that told you she was so self-protective she couldn't possibly mount an offensive against anyone else.

She began talking quietly.

"Her ex-husband: Now that was sad. They adored each other. Really. But you know Anita." She looked toward the center of the table where Anita, oblivious to us, prodded at her plate with a fork. "You know how she is. Running away. Ten months old and I turned my back and couldn't find her. She'd crawled under the living room couch. Hiding."

"Wasn't he good to her?"

"You know Anita. Goodness doesn't matter. He must have thought she'd give him another heart attack. She would have, too. You can't help but love her. No one can. But then you know Anita. She's here and then she's gone."

Later Anita changed seats, and while Malcolm was talking to her mother and out of earshot she told me her history with him. They met at "a retreat for musical singles," she said. "I know. I don't have a musical bone in my body. I attended on the advice of a friend—and there was Malcolm, another imposter."

"How long have you known him?"

"I hate to admit it. You'll think I'm crazy. We began planning for the wedding after two nights together. He wanted that. I had no good reason to leave him." It took me a moment to understand that she wasn't referring to Malcolm but to her former husband.

"I made Andrew's head hurt. Me or his head. One of us had to go. You make me sick, he said. He meant it."

"You couldn't make anyone sick. Wasn't Andrew sick to begin with?"

"He recovered enough to find another woman before he asked me to leave."

I didn't believe her. My guess was that Anita herself had undone the marriage deliberately but carefully, the way a good tailor might rip out a seam without harming delicate fabric.

When Anita returned to her spot, Joyce was pulling photographs out of her purse as if Anita had opened the gates for that sort of thing with her cellphone.

"Have you seen what Anita looked like in high school?" Joyce asked Malcolm.

"Oh no you don't," Anita said, thrusting her hand across the table for the photographs.

Joyce feinted sideways and passed the photos to Malcolm. He laughed, a very nice laugh, I had to admit. He looked closely at the photographs, frowning, and said to Anita, "You looked like this?"

I only caught a glimpse of the snapshots. It was the old Anita, blindingly so. That's when it occurred to me that Malcolm might feel cheated, assuming he'd gotten the lesser version of Anita.

And that's also when I noticed Malcolm's mole. He had one of those moles that didn't look real, like in those old *Gunsmoke* reruns where the elderly saloon boss Kitty wears one above her lip and it seems too dark and hairless to be real. Like that. Like a facial punctuation mark that says, "Pause here." Like the mole is this tiny entryway into another dimension on the other side of the face. Like a fantasy mole.

When Malcolm left the photographs on the table, William picked them up and handed the packet to Joyce.

That's when something peculiar happened. Malcolm lifted Anita's arm and dropped it back on the table, wiped his hands on a napkin, and drew his chair back. Anita was wearing a white blouse with bell sleeves, the kind popular decades ago, and the lower sleeve must have been resting in the bowl of cranberries because a red stain had crept up to her elbow. Malcolm didn't look at her much after that—as if because of that stain she wasn't the woman he wanted to marry.

When William called the next afternoon and invited me to his place I was so surprised that I asked him, "Why?"

He answered the door, his hair still wet from the shower, looking thinner than the night before—maybe because I'd seen him in a heavy jacket. He had probably come to the dinner straight from work and wore the jacket to cover whatever shirt he'd greased up. Ever since he lost the restaurant he had been managing rental properties for absentee land-lords. He was good at it. He could fix anything and he was trusted. He showed up to fix things when people were out of their apartments. It was a decent job for someone so shy.

Then I saw the two of us in the foyer mirror: We had more of the same sorts of features than I was comfortable acknowledging. But then I told myself I really should stop obsessing about helping to ruin his restaurant. We looked so much alike you'd think he ruined his restaurant himself.

A pitcher of lemonade stood on the coffee table. Next to the pitcher: a fresh bowl of ice, two glasses, and a pint of gin. I felt myself cheering up.

"So," he said.

"Well."

"So is it good to have Anita back?" he asked.

"It's wonderful. Not that she's back for long, but it's wonderful none-theless."

He took a deep breath before plunging into the question he had ap-parently been wanting to ask. "Don't you think it's odd that she's back?"

"Yes."

"Why do you think it's odd?"

"Why do you think it's odd?"

We waited one another out. Which wasn't hard for me because right then I had a memory of running through the room we were in. William's place used to be my aunt and uncle's "starter home." I remembered dark-ness and another room deep in the house. We'd played hide and seek in that room, under his parents' bed. There were fringes in front of my face. William had found me. I must have been not much older than a toddler. It was deliciously thrilling to be found.

William spoke first. "I know next to nothing about Malcolm. Can you tell me anything about him? Would you say—he's not what you would have expected?"

"Why would I say that?"

"I'm just trying to imagine your response," William said. "I never can imagine what you're thinking."

"I'll tell you if you stop trying to imagine it. All right?"

"I only want to know if there's something we should be worried about."

"I probably don't know any more than you do. What do you know? And why do I hate you."

I felt the world fall out from under me. I didn't mean to say I hated William. William is un-hateable. I must have been talking to myself. "I'm sorry," I said. "I don't know why I said that. I don't understand why I could ever say that."

"All right, Natalie, all right. You always say things you feel but don't mean. And then you cry." He was smiling a genuine smile, and stupidly I started to cry with gratitude, which led William to feel so comfortable with me that he began a rant.

"He's preposterous," William said—meaning Malcolm. "I can't tell if he's such a copy that he's an original. And he's too young. Is he reliving another decade or . . ."

"He lifted Anita's arm like it was just some kind of thing," I said.

I told William everything as if he hadn't witnessed it for himself: Anita's sleeve dipping in the cranberry sauce, Malcolm's way of dropping her arm with distaste.

The muscles of William's face composed themselves. "Maybe he doesn't like cranberries," he said.

"You're acting like you don't understand the implications of what I've said so that I'll tell you more about my reactions." I felt wild irritation. No wonder we so seldom talked. I was right to tell William I hated him. He could be counted on to grow ever more cryptic, and I could be counted on to cry. I felt like ruining his restaurant all over again, and I also felt: Why should I always feel so guilty? What's wrong with me?

Then I knew exactly what to say to drive William momentarily insane so that I wouldn't be the only insane one. I said, "He probably adores her, for all we know."

William practically levitated. "Tell me the truth," he said. "Do women like that sort of thing—that arty crap?"

"Anita must. She keeps those photos of his art on her phone."

"They're mummies. They belong in a natural history museum."

"I don't know if we should extrapolate from his art to his likely tendencies as her husband . . . but why not?"

William sat forward. "Mummies," he said. "Do women like mummies?"

I couldn't help myself. "Oh yes. Some."

"He looks like a high-school sophomore's vision of Byron."

"There's something to be said for that. Many women do like that. Except high-school sophomores don't read Byron anymore. What world are you from, William? I wouldn't think you would have paid much attention to her anyway."

Then I was in for it: one of William's fugue-like recall sessions. "She came up the road all the time when she was a kid," he began. "It used to bother me—a kid alone. This little skinny girl with sad eyes. I felt better when she was with you. There used to be a stump across the road and she'd sit there. It would drive my mother nuts. 'Come on, sweetie,' she'd say. 'Come in and have cookies.' Anita completely disarmed her. She acted like she didn't need anything. She wouldn't come in. She liked sitting there and staring at the house. Not talking. She still hardly talks— except to you. I always wanted to send her back up to your house—to give her some company. She was like a stray cat. A pitiful little kid."

"But she wasn't pitiful," I protested. "Everybody loved her. The mothers all wanted her as a friend for their daughters. By the time we were teenagers she had more dates than any other girl in the school. Everybody adored her."

"Because they couldn't get to know her. There's safety in that for people. Why'd she come back? Anita never had much use for anyone but you."

I felt a blast of warmth and repeated my cousin's words in my head: *Anita never had much use for anyone but you.* I thought I shouldn't admit it, but I never had much use for anyone but her either—except for my family, including William, even though he could be so reliably frustrating.

"Probably Anita's happy and just wants us to know it?" I said. "Maybe that's why she's back—so we know how happy she is?"

Immediately, I realized that I shouldn't have said that. William's face let me know. All I could say was: "Oh, William, I'm sorry."

The ceremony passed quickly despite my participatory role as maid of honor. The best man was an old friend of Malcolm's—a guy with the beginnings of muttonchop sideburns like you see in photographs of

Civil War soldiers. He was an artist like Malcolm, except he didn't wrap things. Instead he videotaped himself smoking cigarettes that were filled with famous people's hair. His tuxedo was torn up in spots, as if he'd climbed over a barbed-wire fence before arriving at the hall.

During the reception Anita's mother looked more peaceful than she had at the Cuckoo Inn. Nothing disastrous had happened on her daughter's wedding day. No one had bolted. All was going according to plan, and the room was filling with more guests than anyone, including Anita, had expected. It was likely that a good many of those assembled hadn't even been invited.

But there were no children at the wedding and I missed that. Children at weddings are like really old people. Children at weddings let you relax your guard, especially little girls, because they come all fluffed out in starchy dresses like enhanced cupcake liners. Within an hour they're missing a sock, and their hair bow drips down the side of their head like an egg sliding on a wave of grease. And they rock their little patent leather shoes back and forth violently, and even if they don't whine you know the whine is there, pressing up behind their sometimes partially toothless gums.

Given that there weren't children to watch, I watched Malcolm. I tried to be objective, and I had to admit it was possible to see why Anita was attracted to him. He really was a beautiful human being, and William was right—he had that Byronic thing going for him, the one bang that fell in a curl over his forehead, glittering eyes, and a bit of a sneer that some people probably can't resist. It's kind of sad. Some people are like cats—they go right to the person in the room who doesn't like them.

But why had Malcolm married Anita? Had he already begun mummifying her, wrapping her up? And had she acquiesced? But why should I insult her by worrying about her? Could my worrying simply be a way to deny jealousy, of both her and Malcolm? Wherever my thoughts veered, I couldn't escape a sensation of dread. Anita's wedding marked a change I had hardly prepared for. I tried to think thoughts that would help me, and nothing worked.

So I just kept watching. Who was Malcolm, beautiful Malcolm? Who treated Anita's arm as if it wasn't attached to a woman who should be cherished? And where were his eyes alighting while Anita was laughing with a gaggle of her guests, her giant gown floating around her—that surprising dress, so filmy, like ectoplasm, like she'd been plunged in a bucket of highly concentrated ghosts? Oh, Malcolm, he was looking not at Anita but at Joyce, the woman who brought photos of Anita to the Cuckoo Inn. It wasn't normal, his way of looking at Joyce, maybe because she was looking at him too. They'd just met at the dinner at the Cuckoo Inn, hadn't they? But his look was enough for me to know. He was wrapping her with his eyes, turning her around and around, and she was letting him. I must not have been the only one who saw and understood. Although, to be honest, I think people should admit that it's not only peace that passeth understanding, it's understanding that passeth understanding.

I looked toward where Anita had been. She had stepped away from her guests and was at the edge of the dance floor. Our eyes met, briefly, in a shuddering way.

And then, while I was sunk in horrible understanding, William wobbled up to me. He was so drunk he looked blurry.

"Drink yourself into oblivion," I told him. "But not regularly. That's my best advice. Do I sound like your mother or what?"

He wobbled away. And that was the last I saw of him or Anita that night.

The next afternoon I got a call from my mother. I didn't even get a chance to say "Hello! Hello! I am saying 'Hello!' because that is what I do when I say 'Hello.'"

Immediately my mother said, "She's staying at William's."

I didn't understand.

"He pried her away from that psychopath."

"A psychopath?"

"Yes, he's a psychopath."

"Malcolm? You mean Malcolm? A psychopath? How do you know?"

"I heard from that girl—what's her name, in the wedding party? She told me he believes he's a pharaoh. He mummifies things. He does all this late-night reading about Egyptian preservation of the dead."

"I mean: How do you know Anita's with William?"

The details followed. Anita had moved in with William the very night of the wedding.

"She'll destroy him," I said, awestruck.

"Good."

"Good?"

"It's about time," my mother said. "Eventually Louise and Rex will even agree. After the first fainting attacks. I think Rex will particularly like the idea that he stole her."

"But what about Malcolm, the injured party?"

A moment of silence for Malcolm.

I imagined it—Malcolm weeping in Anita's arms. His anger and, beneath it, his relief. Or maybe Anita ditched Malcolm without even bothering to make excuses. Because even if he was attracted to Joyce and maybe already had slept with her—if you want to call it that—when your wife leaves you on your wedding night you don't appreciate it, at least not in public.

"We don't know if she's staying for good or not," my mother continued. "But she's there. She's hiding out. William could have brought her here, but no."

It was hard to picture Anita at William's. How had William managed it? Why had Anita allowed it? I tried out scenarios: Maybe Anita had loved William since she was a child. Or when Anita saw William again she realized for the first time that she loved him. Or maybe Anita had realized what Malcolm wanted from her, and William was the appropriate pair of scissors to cut her free? Or was it the form of William's desire that changed everything—because she could feel his need for her, and it was as palpable as, as, I don't know, as lard—and she wanted to be covered in that lard. That sounds wrong, but it's maybe precise. Lard—if I made that connection out loud people would stop listening because it's too close to the truth, and part of the truth always seems trivial and wrong, like laughing at a funeral, when that's a natural thing to do given the horror of it all. In fact, I knew a woman who laughed at her own father's funeral even though she loved him deeply, but she laughed because the minister mixed him up with another man and began talking about what a good grandfather her father was, as if the woman—an only child—had children, which she didn't. And then this poor woman at her father's funeral started thinking about her own fallopian tubes and how *fallopian tubes* sounds like a comedy act in an old variety show. And here they are—a big hand for The Fallopian Tubes.

William and Anita didn't invite anyone over. They barricaded themselves. I told myself I never understood Anita anyway. It was all a projection. She just listened a lot or pretended to listen and didn't tell you much about herself. It was like trying to have a friendship with thistledown. Though maybe that was right for William.

And then, three months later, William and Anita moved away. To Milwaukee. Of course Uncle Rex and Aunt Louise were told first, and we all had a stiff little dinner together before William and Anita left, but nothing much was explained. Not even the awful tilapia that Aunt Louise made. Which was unexplainable, I told myself.

Eventually I got a job at a new restaurant, The TimBuck2. As a hostess. Standing behind a counter near the door and marinating in the smells from the kitchen.

"We were all born for different things," my mother said.

"I suppose it's a good way to meet men," my aunt said. "Do you meet men?"

"Oh, I meet and greet men," I said. "I lead them to tables. I establish an atmosphere of trust. And they immediately forget me. It's like being their mother or something."

"Oh no," my mother said.

"Or worse. They can't differentiate between me and the menu. No, they notice the menu more. Which they should. Because they came to eat."

At least I had a job. Long ago Freud talked about how important love and work are, but nobody listens to Freud anymore. Instead they staple metal into pigeons' brains because that is so much more reliable than the talking cure. And they are right.

On every table in the restaurant small lamps with red shades were hung with finely beaded gold fringe. The owners, Buck and Tim, were fond of those lamps, and I liked them too, though I couldn't help but think of them as fire hazards. I trimmed those lamps' ratty rims every other day, but the threads cascaded relentlessly. Sometimes I meditated on those lamps and tried to convince myself that they wouldn't eventually burst into flame. On at least three occasions I talked to Buck about the safety of the lamps but he wouldn't listen. I tried Tim on the topic too. When I applied for the job, Buck's first question was: What's your cup size? The place was so new that I didn't know that on weekends after 10 p.m. there were strippers. The pole in the middle of the restaurant on weekdays was just a pole. But on weekends two women were up there— imports from Sheboygan, twin sisters I tried to pity but who resented me. Meanwhile I worried about the lamps.

And then, on June 2, a couple came in and of course—at last, I had dreaded it—it was William and Anita. It had been five years since I'd seen them in the flesh. I knew they would be coming into town—we'd got a warning from Aunt Louise, but I didn't know they'd show up where I worked.

They had always been too thin, and now they were a little past plump. They looked comfortable with each other, like people who have large couches in their living room so they can snuggle. It was a Saturday night and after ten, and I knew that behind me would be one of the Zipper Twins doing this thing she called "Deep Fried Ice Cream."

I pretended not to recognize William and Anita.

"Hello. Hello. That's what I say when I say 'Hello' because that's what I do. I say Hello."

It was Anita who said that, holding out her arms, and so I had to act as if I just realized at that second who she was. It was a slow night, but I behaved like it wasn't and led them to a table as if I didn't have time to talk.

"This is going to catch on fire," William said, passing his hand over a lamp tassel even before he sat down—which broke me, and then I was crying, as I tended to do with William. William and Anita had abandoned us, left us, left me in town with nothing, left me so that I was working at an awful restaurant that deserved to burst into flames. William and Anita had ruined me by leaving, and I didn't know until then that I was ruined—but of course even as I was crying I felt better, as if we were even, William and I. We were both ruin-ers.

A group of too-rowdy men came in, already drunk, but Tim—bless his heart—was on to it and took one look at me sitting with William and Anita and trotted over and whispered into my ear, "You're fired." I'd been trying to get fired for weeks—kind of passively, and so for once he must have felt like helping me out. The problem was always how much I was crying. And now I was crying again.

It turned out that William and Anita were co-managing three steak-house franchises, but pretty soon I was telling myself I was wasting my life—staying in town, tied to my mother and my uncle and aunt. Two years ago I had had to move back in with my mother. You might as well attach a sticker to your driver's license that says "I'm Not an Organ Donor Because I Am Gutless." The fact was, I was thirty-seven years old and read obituaries with Uncle Rex and pretended I wasn't relieved that my tiny blurry picture wasn't featured the way Uncle Rex was relieved—that should be shameful, according to everybody.

And why had William and Anita come back for me—for they had hunted me down, I was sure of it. What for? They talked about how they just got back from a cruise, how everyone got sick except for them, even though Anita accidentally touched vomit on a railing. And then just as suddenly after downing crab cakes and beers William and Anita were gone again. It was like in an old movie where there's a cruise ship and people are waving goodbye because it's possible they'll never see each other again and sometimes they don't. But William and Anita weren't in a cruise ship, they were in an SUV, the kind where you have to pull your-self up to get inside, the kind where people, when they get out, do a little jiggly jump and then half-limp into the nearest Cracker Barrel. William and Anita had become happy, satisfied people whose lives weren't at all ruined. It was like they were both bullet-proof couch cushions. And I was this skinless human being who had not changed at all over the last five years but was just hanging there, like the shad the fishermen around here catch in the spring and dry out on boards in the sun. And William had the right to be self-satisfied. It was like he had rescued Anita from mummification, like she'd followed him out of hell and neither of them ever looked back.

And it occurred to me that there was something cruel about Anita but maybe something I could use a shot of, like maybe I should be sprayed with BBs—BBs of her ability to get away without explanation. I mean, what was keeping me from leaving town? That's what people asked. That's what even the Zipper Twins asked.

The next day my mother called and said that William and Anita had left me a check for one thousand dollars and a request that I take a bus trip to a casino in the Lehigh Valley. They supplied tickets not only for me but for my mother and Aunt Louise and Uncle Rex. Malcolm had an exhibit in a gallery connected to the casino that they wanted me to see. They were his patrons. They'd bought him out so they didn't have to feel guilty about ruining his wedding.

The gallery turned out to be this tucked-out-of-the-way room in the community center adjacent to the casino, and there I saw Malcolm's mummies. They were his, certainly. These were participatory mummies; you were supposed to unravel them. According to a plaque the "sculptures" were re-rolled at night, but in the daytime, gallery visitors were encouraged to see what was under the wrapping. I spent fifteen minutes or so unwrapping my mummy and the mummy was just wrapping. There was nothing there. Well, that was predictable.

And then there he was: Malcolm. He didn't recognize me but I recognized him—the same Byronic looks, supplemented by ruffles on his shirt, ruffles that seemed foppish and pretentious, but now he was getting a little bit bald, as was I, from what turned out to be a vitamin deficiency. Or maybe because I had been convinced that I lived very much like certain fish in underground caves, miles below the surface of the earth.

"What do you think?" he asked.

What did I think? What did I think about what? I stared at him, my arms covered with loops of ace bandages.

"What was the experience like for you?"

Then I understood. He was asking what I thought of his art.

"I like unwrapping things," I said. "For a while I wanted to be a dental hygienist because of the way they pack and unpack cotton around a tooth."

It is a puzzling thing to see recognition "dawn." Because dawn it does, like the sun of understanding rises behind the other person's eyelids, like the sun is hurting them, and there you are, hurting them with the realization that they know who you are. You don't even directly have to hurt some people and you wind up hurting them. You just have to see that they're hurt and you've hurt them. I once knew a guy who said that his head could explode at any time and this turns out to be a true phenomenon—heads can explode—and so without meaning to when that man told me about his head potentially exploding I stepped back. I felt guilty about that. But now, given that the memory came to mind, I was thinking that maybe guys with the head problems would do better if they were wrapped the way Malcolm wrapped things, and then I chastised myself for being insensitive, because you know how it is: Lately you can't think a thought without subjecting the thought to a tribunal.

"I know what you told Anita about me," Malcolm said.

What did I tell Anita? "I don't understand," I said.

"You say that because you do understand."

"I don't understand. I don't know what you mean. What did I say?" Just then a shadow passed over my eyes because I realized that maybe I did ruin his marriage, because maybe I spoke with my eyes. After I saw Malcolm unwrapping with his own eyes that woman—Joyce—I turned to Anita and my eyes must have given everything away. But that would be a stupid thing to be guilty about, and arrogant too. As if one look from me sealed Malcolm's fate. When his fate was already sealed: He did not love my friend Anita.

I heard clacking, the sound of my mother and Aunt Louise and Uncle Rex above us on this sort of transparent sky bridge. Malcolm looked up too, and then looked back at me and said, "You're always with those old people. You're like someone from another century—you're like an ugly little spinster." The word *spinster* sounded strange, archaic, like he had never used the word before and never would again and had been saving it up for me.

And though he meant to harm me, though the way he looked at me told me I had harmed him first, that I knew too much about him and Anita (I didn't—not really), that my response to his art was inadequate (and it was), the thing was: I took what he said seriously. A spinster? Living in a cottage covered with roses and cuddling a gray tabby and eventually dying from old age or a bad oyster? And Malcolm was also right about old people. I was always with old people, and why was that? Yes, I like people at least two decades older than I am. Anyway, everybody's old. I'm ancient to people younger than I am. I can remember when I was in fourth grade and thought eighth-graders were old. I bet there are babies who think toddlers are old. Everybody's old. And yes, I like these old people in my family.

And now they were coming for me—my mother's and aunt's heels clacking and my uncle's stomach that always reminded me of one of those old schoolroom globes and could easily have latitude and longitude tattooed on it—there was room—and they knew me and loved me. What did people of my generation understand? William, Anita, Malcolm—they were all busy wrapping one another up, but my family, my mother, my uncle, and my aunt—they were coming unwrapped already, and Uncle Rex loved Aunt Louise even though you just knew some things were pretty much over. Like he couldn't even mount a flight of stairs. Yet he laughed and laughed, and sometimes like a braying mule, or a sump pump, or very wheezily like he had to laugh through a bird's nest. And someday they would all move away, I mean die, or I would die but not move away, and as I was thinking this Malcolm left through a back exit, his hair floating behind him like a cloud frayed by a stiff wind. And I still had ace bandages in my hands, and I let them drop to the floor where they made a loop of sorts, like a tapeworm which, by the way, reminded me of what a great-grandfather of mine once reportedly said: that he knew a man who "passed" a tapeworm so long it stretched all the way from his barn to the milk house.

"Was that Malcolm?" my mother asked. I knew she wanted to race after him and pull him back into the gallery.

So I said nothing, as if I didn't hear my mother.

It bothered me, though, that I didn't have a chance to say good-bye to Malcolm, because that is what I do when I say good-bye: I say good-bye.

A Meadow

The wife isn't supposed to know, but Lucy knew. She knew about her husband and the woman who had been her best friend, Maria. Had known for nearly two years. And now Maria's brother—a stranger—was coming to visit. Had he known about Maria and Owen? Did he think he was visiting to reveal the affair, to confess on Maria's behalf even now? Lucy hoped not. She would resent that.

Lucy got the news from Owen before he left for work. He turned at the front door and told her—as if he almost forgot something so important. He didn't want to be late, and so there wasn't time to talk. She followed him outside.

"He's coming when?"

Owen looked innocent and blank-faced, freshly shaved and showered, and nevertheless a little sleepy. "I'm not sure of the time," he said, standing next to the car and jiggling his legs. "When he called he only said he'd be here around dinner time. He's in town."

"So he invited himself over."

The crease in Owen's forehead deepened. He looked fully awake now. "Practically. I suppose so."

"I guess he really must be Maria's brother. That's what she would have done. I'm assuming then we're okay until at least five."

Less than two weeks before Maria's death her family had transported her to a hospital in Austin, in one last burst of hope that amounted, Lucy imagined, to horror for Maria. Independent-minded Maria. She had been worse about taking care of herself than Lucy was—wearing that light salt-and-pepper coat through the worst weather, never buttoning the collar, skipping meals. Stubborn Maria with her slouchy way of walking. And with that brave thatch of black hair. Maria's hostility to greed and intolerance was right on the surface, ready to spark at any moment. Listening to her talk was such an experience. She could be indignant, so committed to justice that she pounded the table. Maria chose to avoid marriage or having a child. She had been free. The freest person Lucy had ever known.

When Maria's brother arrived he thrust his hand out to Lucy with a self-consciousness that was like his sister's. He had Maria's eyes: alert, assessing, expectant. The room was turning, and Lucy had to steady herself against the arm of a chair.

While Maria's brother talked with Owen in the living room, Lucy went to retrieve a bottle of wine. The bottle was cool in her hand. She allowed the sensation of coolness to quiet her mind. There it was: the strongest sense of having experienced this moment before, exactly this moment.

She took a good swallow of wine. May all non-drinkers writhe in hell, she told herself. I don't drink enough. I really ought to drink more often.

There's a lot you should do more often: That would have been Maria's likely answer.

The men were still talking quietly when she reentered the living room. They hadn't wanted her to be with them. Something about the way they wouldn't look at her told her so.

Lucy returned to the kitchen. What had happened outside the window, in that meadow that was dark now? Lucy let herself imagine a young person coming to the meadow, like in that James Joyce story, except it wouldn't be a boy but a woman, someone full of longing, a woman standing there to watch the lights of the house every night, a woman who came for years until she became the place, unaware that she was dead, unfeeling toward her own death. Unsympathetic to her own death.

Or another possibility: A man and a woman killed the man's wife and buried her in the meadow. Something out of a murder mystery. It was not easy, killing the wife—a bloody, running-through-the-house murder, and it struck the husband, the woman he loved, and even the wife in her terror as being like a children's game. A wild children's game. Except with so much blood.

Or something else happened: a fire that couldn't be stopped. Or someone was visited by God and the whole meadow lit up with the visitation. Lucy knew what Maria would say: "It's just an empty field—it's overrun with dead weeds. Don't get all mystical on me."

After dinner Owen was telling a story about one of their neighbors, a city councilman notorious for letting developers have their way. There was to be a hearing. Owen lamented the poor planning that went on as farmland was bought up in the county. He said they couldn't be sure what would happen behind their house. They didn't own the meadow.

No matter how she tried, Lucy couldn't quite get a feel for Maria's brother. He was standoffish, tight-lipped. His appearance—deceiving. He looked so much like a male version of his sister it was unnerving. Except with Maria there would be laughter, teasing, easy conversation. Maria, for instance, would be making fun of the polka-dotted blouse Lucy was wearing.

Owen pushed his chair back as if everyone should be finished eating when he was.

Maria's brother pushed back too and asked, "Could we—what do you think?—would it be all right if we went out for a walk?"

"It's dark," Owen said.

"Will you be warm enough?" Lucy asked. "Owen has some extra coats. Heavier ones than yours is." Maria's brother would be more relaxed after the walk, she thought. He'll talk more about Maria then.

"I'll be fine."

There was a clenched sensation in the air. Maybe a snowstorm was headed their way. Lucy felt as if she were breaking through a chilled honeycomb. The grass was sharpened from frost. She could hardly make out the skeletal outlines of birches. The sound of water came from the east.

They made their way along the meadow's periphery. Bundled up, booted, Lucy forged ahead. She swung her flashlight. Neither Owen nor Maria's brother had wanted a flashlight.

Within minutes the men's voices were growing quieter. Why weren't they keeping up?

When she turned and swung her flashlight in an arc she couldn't see either of the men. She called out Owen's name and swung her light again.

The men must have taken another path. She headed back toward the house. In spring the magnolia on the lawn would be bursting with thick, creamy cups of froth. Among the branches, and flashing as the wind stirred the darkness against the kitchen window's light, were the small prisms Lucy strung last year. Light from the window caught at the magnolia in swirling splashes, as if the November branches were strung with wind-rippled water.

She was nearing the driveway when she saw a figure on the edge of the lawn. She held her breath—it was her friend. Yet it couldn't be Maria, Maria who looked starkly beautiful, light from the window illuminating her face. It couldn't ever again be Maria. What Lucy saw must be a shadow, branches moving.

The men were crossing the lawn. Owen called out, "Let's go in. I could use another drink. How about it?"

"Sorry we lost you back there," Maria's brother said. "I don't know—I was thinking about Maria, how she loved you two. I just lost it. We had to stop. And then we lost sight of you, and then I don't know where we ended up."

They were almost at the door when Lucy turned and saw she hadn't been entirely wrong. Someone was there. A boy. A little boy. By the magnolia. His face looked strange, twisted. She hurried to him. He didn't run from her. "Are you lost?" she asked. He nodded. "Come with me. No one will hurt you."

She recognized him. She'd seen him in his yard several houses down the road when she drove by. She questioned the boy. He didn't know his phone number. She told her husband, "You'll need to go to his house. Let them know where he is. "

Maria's brother left with Owen. Meanwhile, Lucy made hot chocolate. The boy sat in the kitchen while she worked. He kept his head down. He couldn't be more than nine years old. She let herself imagine he was her child, that it was just the two of them always in the house.

"Did anyone hurt you?" she said.

"I got mad," he answered. He drank the hot chocolate. There was still some pie from dinner. He ate everything she put in front of him.

The boy's parents didn't come inside. Instead, they stayed in their car and waited. When the boy ran outside he didn't look back at Lucy, who watched from the window.

Owen said the parents weren't friendly, never thanked him or Maria's brother. About the little boy he said, "He'll keep coming back if you feed him."

"He's not a stray dog."

Maria's brother was swaying from side to side. He wanted to leave. That was obvious. "I miss your sister so much," Lucy said. She couldn't help herself now.

"I can tell."

"Don't go yet," she said. "I loved Maria. No matter what. Stay, all right?"

The foyer filled with the air of hurried emergency. Maria's brother had his coat on and was looking for a glove he'd dropped.

Owen opened the door, and with a draft of air—the wind had picked up—Maria's brother was gone.

"She wasn't any kind of threat to us," Owen said later that night. He was standing in their bedroom near the full-length mirror when he confessed. "Didn't you think so? You probably could have guessed four years ago. You could have figured it out."

"Is it my responsibility to know who's lying to me?"

"I don't know."

"Why are you telling me this? You don't think I knew?" But she hadn't known as much as she thought. Four years. Not two years. Surprise surprise. It must have been so hard for Maria.

She imagined throwing her whole weight at her husband and watching him topple backward against the mirror. She was crying by then, ready to howl. Maria—it was like losing an arm, like losing the skin off her face. What did she care about what Maria and Owen did? Everything had been better when Maria was alive.

The next morning Lucy sat up from the sewing room couch where she had been sleeping. She went into the kitchen. When she looked out the window she saw that the meadow's soil had shrunk overnight, turned hardened and gouged-looking. Owen was there.

Lucy dressed hurriedly to confront him. It was time to tell him. There was no reason to stay with him anymore now that Maria was gone. On the horizon a rolling mist was cut through by pale morning sunlight.

Flakes swirled in the air. The first snow of the season was always like that, so pure. So fine, almost invisible.

She turned around. Looking toward the kitchen window . . . How much that window left out when anyone stood on the opposite side. From the meadow it looked like a child's miniature. Irresistible to a child.

When she turned back she saw the boy. Head bent, he was walking toward her across the open ground. He wasn't wearing a coat. She ran to him and asked, "Are you hungry? You didn't run away again, did you?" He shook his head. She asked again, "Are you hungry?"

When he nodded she led him toward the house. The boy clutched her hand. They were alike, she thought, she and the boy. "I hope you're hungry," she said.

When Owen came inside he said, "See. I told you you'd never get rid of him. You keep feeding him and you'll never get rid of him."

She looked up at her husband, unblinking, for what did it matter now, and asked, "Is that how it's done?"

Portrait of the Artist's Son

Artists and their mothers. Whatever information might be gleaned by tireless, avid biographers, the evidence lay nearer at hand, stroked into being in each portrait. The portrait of any artist's mother—what temerity, what an act of love, or betrayal, or trespass. Take the brush and make a presence that gives off heat and a pulse. And fail. Always fail.

What does it mean to make something that represents one's own mother? To show respect, to wait up for yourself? A mother as a tunnel, a long hallway, and you're running backwards?

Or was a portrait a way to shake off a living ghost or to make a cage, a border, a wire henhouse for a mother? Your first home: That is a thought to pull back from. Any artist comes into the world with predecessors but probably wishes otherwise. The first predecessor: the mother.

Somewhere in every work of art: a road, so you can find your way out.

Nick was thinking these thoughts as he looked through *The Artist's Mother*. Introduction by Judith Thurman. Published by Overlook Duckworth, Peter Mayer, Inc. A coworker had given it to him as a present. She said she wanted to lure him out of himself. He kept the book in his locker at work. Occasionally, during lunch, he looked through the book. He was an artist and had a mother. Why shouldn't he be interested?

He didn't bring the book to his studio. His studio was his citadel. His studio was also his apartment. He felt elevated when he was there, elevated and removed from the ordinariness of his life. In his studio he wasn't working in the mineral plant as a custodian. He wasn't disentangling used tampons from the waste disposal unit or running a floor buffer that burbled like a hookah. No, his studio was consecrated space. Everything there was devoted to his own art—unlike his friend Birder's apartment, stuffed with his former wife's piñata collection and dozens of guitars he didn't play.

Nick's apartment was a mess, but it was a mess for art. A pure mess for art.

He was running up the walkway toward his apartment, ducking raindrops, when a woman stepped in front of him. He nearly stumbled into her, instinctively reached out, caught himself, apologized. The droopy hood of her sweatshirt hid much of the woman's face. When he recognized her his stomach sank. The story he heard about Nance when she left the plant: He'd only been a temporary stand-in for another custodian who had a wife. She hadn't tried to kill herself over him. It was about the other guy.

"Are you all right?" he asked. He couldn't tell if Nance was fighting back laughter or tears.

"No. I'm not all right. I've missed you." Her hands dragged down the pockets of her sweatshirt. He wondered if she ever again wore the beret he'd returned to the mineral plant for her.

She walked ahead of him into his apartment. The bottom of a white tunic peeked from below her sweatshirt and skimmed her rear.

"I'm sorry," she said, scuffing her feet, spreading rain from her hood onto the floor.

"Don't worry," he said. "You can't hurt anything in here. Not with rain anyway. Damage could probably help a few things."

Her sweatshirt—even sopping wet it looked like it cost something. He wondered if doing custodial work was connected to a course she took in college, a course taught by a neo-Leninist with a wine cellar who thought every young person should spend a few months with members of the working class. The beret she wore when she worked: Last month he thought that maybe she'd come late to the French existentialists. More recently he wondered if she'd come late to Che Guevara.

"You live like a vampire," she said, pulling her hood back. "Is your whole family like that?"

He had a disconcerting sensation, like when he first met her, as if she was looking for something in his face that would never be there. The last time she'd been at his place she showed up in her black beret and striped stockings like a French version of the Wicked Witch of the East. Later that night—at the worst moment for it—she stared up at him like someone taking a multiple choice test when two answers look identical. He wished he'd never let her in then and now. He picked up a roll of masking tape from a chair so she could sit down. She didn't sit.

"When I said that about vampires—I just meant the light," she said. "It's dark in here. It's like it's raining inside. You heard what happened?"

"You're all right now?" He allowed himself to hope. Maybe she only arrived at his apartment to have a heart-to-heart about the married man he heard she was seeing.

"You hadn't meant to send me over," she said.

"I thought—I thought it wasn't about me." He could hardly concentrate because of the pressure in his ears. How could she have been hurt because of him? He meant nothing to her.

"It's like being in a movie," she said, "being with you. You're very detached, you know that? It must be a family trait. Thank you, by the way, for returning my beret. They sent it to me. You're always so polite. I love that about you. Your mother must have raised you well."

Why wasn't she drying off? Even her nose looked wet. Her damp hair was the color of an almond. Every fiber in his being wanted her out of his apartment. And felt guilty for wanting her out. She said something. What?

"Who can help me?"

He caught sight of the wiggle of suffering in her chin. A blast of pity roared through him.

"Is there anyone you know who can help me?" she asked. "Now? Immediately?"

The look in her eyes—hurt, longing, disappointment. He was reading his own feelings as much as hers. She had become real to him: this sad, wet-faced young woman, shifting to stand squarely in front of him and demanding his help.

The knocking made both of them jump. Nick sprang for the door.

Birder lunged into the apartment, letting in a wet wool smell, and came to a standstill, blinking.

Before Nick could introduce his friend, Nance announced, "Nick is going to take me to see his mother. Now."

"Why?" Birder asked. He raised his hands in front of his face, like someone blocking an attack.

Nick, baffled, turned to Nance. Could Nance know his mother from somewhere? How could she? The insight shot through him. A client, yes. He had slept with one of his mother's clients.

"I'll come along," Birder said. "We can take your car, Nick."

As Nance got into the car, Birder whispered to Nick, "Nothing's wrong with her." Birder: afflicted with wishful thinking. Birder: generous to everybody. Optimistic. Too optimistic. Helping everyone he knew was one way Birder kept his mind off his ex-wife. Having Birder as a friend—it was like having Jay Gatsby as a friend. Sometimes Birder, who had reread *The Great Gatsby* at least five times, actually threw parties, hoping his ex-wife would show up again. Like Gatsby, Birder didn't have genuine friends except for Nick.

Nick didn't imagine his mother's office—the inner sanctum beyond the waiting room—had changed much since the last time he managed to visit. Her old straight-backed chair would be there opposite a soft couch. Beside the chair, a plaid basket for her dog. A lost-and-found box pushed in the corner. Symptomatically, his mother's clients were always forgetting things: sweaters, scarves, mittens, sunglasses. If only they could forget what they ought to, she liked to say: their entire families.

No doubt her new dog would be battened down inside the plaid basket. Her dogs had all been versions of one another. They looked up through fluffy fringes of hair with the flirty expression teenagers assume on Facebook. They compensated for their minuscule size and alarmingly short life cycles by their high-pitched vocal range and easily startled nervous systems. Each dog went with his mother to her office, defended her from her clients, apparently read her mind.

The receptionist pursed her lips and made a shushing noise. No one was talking, so who was she shushing? Other than herself. Was his mother already making this woman's life miserable? Then he realized. The receptionist wasn't shushing anyone. She was peeling the lid and blowing on a microwaved cup of soup. She reminded Nick of a large animal that looks harmless but isn't. Maybe a somewhat deflated hippo. Nick whispered the basics of the situation and the receptionist asked him to have a seat "with your friends."

She opened the inner-office door and entered sideways, her chunky amber pendant clanging against the doorknob. Before the door closed, a pug ventured into the waiting room on wide-set stubby legs.

It surprised Nick that his mother's new dog was a pug. Constance's dogs tended to be delicate-looking and high-strung, like the Platonic form of a neurotic. The dog turned, its tail curled up to avoid its own ass. In her chair Nance was drying off like a sidewalk after a rain—in spots. Her sweatshirt was proving to be the bright green of a child's crayon. The hair around her face looked like an exploded pillow. Her profile was taut, the muscles around her jaw drawn up.

When Nance entered his mother's office, the dog trotting behind her, Nick could allow himself to panic—and to think. One night in his apartment should not have been enough to throw Nance into depression. One night should not wreck anyone. But then, of course, he was wrong. A night was enough. An instant. And now Nance was talking it all out with his mother, Constance.

Nick couldn't remember ever not calling his parents Constance and Scott, as if he had outgrown the role of being their son by the time he could speak. His brother, Nelson, refused to use their parents' first names, and by the time he was twenty-three weaponized himself with a wife. Then a son. Then another son. Nelson might as well enter family gatherings in a tank.

Would his mother imitate Nance? Constance mimicked her clients—which disturbed Nick when he was a kid even as it sent him into fits of laughter. "You are what you are"—the words his mother claimed she would like to tell most clients. "You are what you are—get over it." In Nick's memory of when they were kids, Nelson was always prissily telling their mother that she ought to treat people who came to her for help like human beings. Whereupon Constance said: "You're thirteen. It's a judgmental age. Okay, buddy. Think about how much more judgmental I have the right to be at my age." She swiveled around to include Nick. "Do either of you boys want me to lose my mind? I work with nuts, and I'm not even counting your father. Get a life, guys, before you insult mine."

He'd loved that speech, Nick had.

He hadn't loved all her speeches. "You're like your father," she once told him. He was twelve at the time and endured a hot wave of revulsion. He remembered his own answer: "I'm not that bored." By then it was obvious to Nick that his father fit the definition of an easy word in his seventh-grade vocabulary test: *philanderer*.

Birder bent forward, his elbows digging into his thighs, and threw his tie over his shoulder. He broke into a one-incisor grin. "I told you: Nothing is wrong with her. I've seen her dance. Salsa. Colombo's."

"She nearly killed herself a few weeks ago. She had to quit work."

"She must have said that to get off work. And to make quitting easier."

"She's under treatment—obviously—with my mother. You and I— we're not exactly professionals. We don't know what's wrong with her." He hoped his mother didn't make Nance's condition worse. Constance saved lives, his father liked to say. Why was that so hard to believe?

"She's lonely," Birder said. "That's her problem."

Nick could imagine the scene: Constance would be in that straight-backed chair of hers, with its gnawed-on arms. How many years had his mother sat in that chair, listening or pretending to listen? Dispensing hard, ugly advice. It's a wonder people didn't kill themselves. She opened up other people's lives while her own stayed secret. Sometimes she complained that her clients expected too much. "Boys," she'd say to her sons, "some days I just want to die."

When Nance returned to the waiting room, her hood up, she kept her head low like a lightweight boxer who just stepped out of the ring, withdrawing from a fight.

Outside, the air smelled like car exhaust and baking bread. Puddles on the pavement reflected sky. Nance sat in the backseat with Birder. As if Nick was their chauffeur.

A mother as an interior. A room that cannot be reentered. You were made of the room. Embarrassing, queasy making, a reversal, so you want to take care of her.

That beautiful blackness in Mary Cassatt's portrait of her mother, "Mrs. Robert S. Cassatt, the Artist's Mother." At first glance the mother looked like a priest: the black robe, the white blot of paint at the throat, the hair tight to the head and the expression, pensive, watchful. Or the mother of Jacques-Émile Blanche, again in black, the depth of blackness, in contrast to her white umbrella, her white bonnet, the extravagant blossoming white and pink roses, the hand holding the umbrella, the fingers over the lips, the soft, almost furred face . . .

So often the mother in the portrait was seated.

"Why are you such an idiot?"—his mother's first words when Nick picked up his cell. "Weeks ago I sent her to Germaine Mallick. She's Germaine's client."

"She said she needed help. It seemed like an emergency. I thought you could help her."

His mother breathed heavily into the phone. "She used you as a battering ram to get to me. She thought she could embarrass me in front of you. As if that were possible. I do have ethics. Listen. She's cute as a button but not batty as a loon. She was using you."

"Are you encouraged—in your profession—to call clients 'batty as a loon'?"

"Get a life, sourpuss. Listen. I don't want to see that girl again. I've seen enough. She's a maggot. A very cute aggressive maggot who refuses to grow up into the best she can hope for: a housefly. You didn't even call before you brought her over to frighten my receptionist. You just drove her over. And dumped her out on the waiting room rug. God. To think I raised you."

"We must both be idiots, huh?" Nick hoped she'd miss a beat.

"Good," Constance said. "At last. You've almost restored my hope. I would love it if—once in a while—you'd fight back."

Like you? he wanted to say. You never win a match with Scott. She was weak when it came to her own husband. And she didn't know her own son if she thought he didn't have to fight—fight every treacherous self-doubt, fight to resist whatever drained him of the will to make an art that no one wanted.

She was still talking. "If I didn't have such a dimwit for a receptionist—she's new—that kid would never have made it past the waiting room."

"New dog. New breed. New receptionist. It's all new for you, I guess. Everything."

"At least the dog wasn't a mistake," Constance said. "I know all about your history with Nance. If you can call one wretched night history. She sought you out. I guess reality has to impinge on us all."

"So now she's reality."

"Not exactly, buddy. More like one of reality's ambassadors. You have your own life. I wish you'd figure that out. Someday your life is going to speed up and you're going to be sorry you didn't take the right risks when you could have. You're going to have to learn to listen better. People are trying to tell you something."

"That's what your life is—listening," Nick said. "Sitting there and taking it."

"There are worse lives," she said. "You'd be surprised."

The note of hurt in her voice. Something he never expected. For once, he couldn't help but feel superior, at least for an instant. The odd thing was that he suspected she'd be glad he felt superior. But then, soon after he hung up, Nick felt punched in the throat. It was pity for his mother—pity for her life, pity that she was married to his father. Pity for her and anger that he was powerless to help her. If she called, Nick would come. If she insulted him the way she'd really like to insult his father, he'd take it. How could Nick abandon her even if she dragged him down with her, weighted in the antigravity boots of being her son?

At lunch he opened *The Artist's Mother.*

Whistler's Mother: windblown hush. A study in shades of gray and black, not an erasure but a fierceness there, a mother who was once useful but was now a source of nostalgia for the painter.

Georges Seurat's mother: all black and white dots, every molecule of her swarming.

Vincent van Gogh's mother: looking so much like her son it had to be anxiety-producing. The eyes bright, the mouth curved. As if the artist dressed himself in his mother's clothing.

Archibald Motley's mother in "Portrait of a Woman in a Wicker Settee": her beautiful, calm face, her dress just reaching to her knees, her flesh visible below the hem, a mother adorned and adored.

"She never suffered," his father said over the phone.

Scott had been out late, arriving home after two to find his wife in their bedroom, no longer breathing, "not suffering." He felt compelled to repeat those words to Nick. *Not suffering.* The note in his father's voice—Nick hadn't heard it before. Until that moment he thought he had heard everything he ever would from his father.

Nick was numb from the feet up, like a dying tree. His father stood beside a thick-shouldered woman, her hair shaved close to her head. "She was strong," Scott was saying. "She had to be strong to listen to all that stuff she heard. It took strength. She just never burdened any of us with it. People needed what she gave them. Some people. There are people who need that. She saved them."

Appreciative murmurs erupted.

It was easy to spot Nick's brother, Nelson. Like Nick, he towered over everyone else. And there was Nelson's wife, Marcie. And with her were their two sons in suits that made them look like miniatures of their grandfather. Nick stumbled toward a chair and caught the impression at the room's far end of the blue satin lining of the coffin's raised lid.

Soon Marcie was standing in front of him, holding out a tissue above her swelling stomach. Her face was fuller than in her last pregnancy, her eyes glossy. She had liked Constance, possibly even loved her. It occurred to Nick that the new baby would be insurance against Nelson becoming useful in the hard days to come.

Marcie pointed at her own forehead. Nick managed to focus his eyes. When he touched his forehead his hand came back bloody.

"What happened to you?" Marcie asked. "Are you all right?"

He had to think. "I fell on the steps—coming in." Until now, his fall hadn't registered.

His sister-in-law drew another tissue from her purse. He mumbled thanks and pressed the tissue against his forehead. He was matching his breathing to Marcie's. Even though he had gotten hold of himself because of her kindness, he wished she would disappear. A few years ago he had speculated that Marcie might understand things about his parents that he and Nelson never figured out. That speculation subsided after he witnessed Marcie playing charades. Nelson practically spelled words for her. Small chance she could comprehend the czarist manipulations of her in-laws.

When the last tissue came back unbloodied Marcie kissed his cheek and walked away like the figurehead on a ship's prow, her abdomen leading, and headed back toward ever-fortunate Nelson.

Over the phone his father had told Nick the improbable facts about Constance's gift to a church she never, to any of their knowledge, attended. She had recently changed her will and, bizarrely, submitted to St. Joseph's a descriptive plan for her own funeral rites. Because of her new allegiance to the Roman Catholic Church it was assumed she wanted a traditional viewing. Despite her plans for the funeral itself, Nick couldn't imagine Constance had considered even the remote possibility of a viewing.

He recognized Constance's secretary standing over the coffin. After she left, a brunette in a too-tight purple suit replaced her, blocking Nick's view. Wrong. Wrong for anyone to be able to gawk, to take advantage of Constance. Why was this barbaric ritual even called a "viewing"? Why should a person, an inestimable, singular being, be displayed like evidence? When the woman at the coffin drifted away, Nick advanced and studied his mother. She was wearing the sort of clothes she would have chosen if she dressed herself that morning: a beige suit. Her lips looked as if they could part to speak but were being prevented by some sort of device.

He counted three gold bracelets thin as wires on her wrist. He touched her folded hands. Cold. Refrigerated.

By the time Nick got back to his chair word must have gotten around about who he was. One after another came the hand-shakers, most of them women dressed like his mother had dressed, in subdued suits. They looked like women who could survive easily at committee meetings, bureaucrats capable of displaying appropriate levels of interest while they sat at conference tables for hours, suppressing their instincts. His mother had only pretended to be like them.

For the service at St. Joseph's, Nelson and his family rode in a separate car and Nick rode with his father. They passed the river, swollen from spring rains and brimming to street level, the dark wash stealing upon the pavement. At the church Nick and Nelson sat on either side of their father. Marcie and their two sons occupied the rest of the row. The casket, now closed, was draped with an ivory cloth.

Nick smelled mingling perfumes from the women in the pew to his left: lemons and dried blossoms and dead mums. Some of the women couldn't resist looking over at him, rubbernecking, not even trying to disguise their curiosity. Why so many women, parked in a row, holding themselves tensely, as if about to race one another toward an invisible finishing line? He hadn't seen a single one of them an hour earlier at the funeral home viewing. Tiny pink fruits were embroidered on one woman's dark blouse. Something girlish about her and the other women. Something overexcited and juvenile. The sort of women his father never stopped wanting. Scott could be anywhere, in a hardware store, at a sports bar, at a drugstore, it didn't matter. It didn't matter because, too often, women turned up, standing close to Nick's father. When Nick was twelve—too old not to notice—his father brought him along to lunch with a woman very much like some of those to Nick's left. Even at that age Nick knew he was serving a purpose, someone for a woman to fawn over, someone to humanize his father, to augment his supposed charm.

Nick tried not to think of his mother inside the closed coffin. She had suffered from claustrophobia. Not full panic attacks, she used to assure him, but unpredictable onsets of breathlessness. "Don't tell Scott," she said. "This is our secret." Had he ever looked at her as fully as in those moments when she needed him? She was so fierce that usually your gaze ricocheted back. "I just need someone I can trust, someone to understand this thing I go through." She had said that to him, her son: She trusted him. He was a sophomore in college that year, and when he admitted that he failed a 200-level course in Shakespeare's comedies she railed at him for a half hour. He hadn't done any of the reading.

What could Nick remember about his mother that would help now? What memory could hold her? A rainy afternoon when he had the flu. He must have been in second grade. Constance bent over him with a washcloth that wasn't properly wrung out. Cold water dripped into his eyes. He had loved that. And loved her, and even then, for a moment, pitied her. She was trying so hard to be the kind of mother she must have thought he wanted, and she just couldn't be.

Knocking rang from inside the coffin. Loud, angry, the knocking echoed throughout the church. She wants out, Nick thought. Get her out. It's a mistake. Idiots. Maggots. Get her out.

A little kid in a pew, slamming down the kneeler—that was all. Nick was shuddering and could not stop when his father put an arm around his shoulder.

When Nick recovered he felt heat on the side of his face. The women in the opposite pew were staring again. He was overtaken by a vision: his father pulling up the sweater of the woman at the end of the row, nuzzling his head between her breasts. Hot acid burned in Nick's throat. So this was the same acid that turned his mother into the dry little cynic she was.

When he was able to look up again, the women to his left were jostling one another. In a line they marched toward the coffin, toward his mother, straightening their shoulders and stretching their necks as if an invisible string pulled each head up.

The St. Joseph's Women's Chorus began their hymn:

> Hail to Mary, mother of God,
> all glorious tidings
> to the mother of the suffering Son,
> Son risen in God's name.
> Mary, glorious mother of light.

Nick's father doubled over in the pew, a croak escaping him. But Nick wasn't thinking of his father's suffering but of his mother's sorrow and her cunning. He wondered if she had chosen the hymn. He was sure she had chosen the chorus.

Forms to fill out, finances to sort through. Constance always was the one to do that sort of thing. Practically all the income she and Scott earned came from her practice. Nelson's willingness to use the excuse of Marcie's pregnancy made Nick the likely person to do the paperwork. Their father's energies were called for elsewhere. He was moving out of the house he'd lived in with Constance for thirty-three years.

Boxes were stacked throughout the first floor. The house had been turned inside out, all its once-hidden clutter revealed, pulled from beige drawers and eggshell white cupboards. The silver framed photographs, the mounted Audubon prints, the deep forest green of the dining room's walls offset by ivory-colored crown molding: The house was such a display of his mother's taste that Nick felt vertigo.

While Nick worked on files on the dining room table, Tracey— that was the name of his father's friend—passed in and out, smelling like cotton candy, her face glittery with iridescent makeup. She had a habit of blowing her bangs away and whispering to herself. Nick could imagine his mother's irritation at seeing this woman puffing around her house. It helped to imagine her irritation—made Constance seem momentarily alive, as if her irritation had been so powerful it lingered after her death.

When Tracey tossed back her hair again Nick knew where he'd seen her before. The chorus at the funeral. He remembered her high forehead, unusually domelike for a woman's, the rest of her face diminishing, ending with a near-elfin chin, much like his mother's. Had his father chosen Tracey, or had she chosen him? She was probably in her late forties. Divorced. Anxious to be of use. Passive. Easily hurt. Child of an alcoholic. Her eyes froze when she caught him staring. Nick was tempted to say the wrong thing. But why should she suffer because of his presence? She would suffer enough because of his father.

Shamefully, Nick felt his anger recede, replaced by pricklings of relief. His father would be taken care of. Scott had found a tiny blond savior in Tracey.

Near the stairwell, Scott called out to his son, "Anything you want, it's yours." Nick imagined picking up one of the boxes Tracey was working through and shoving it at his father, whose chest would cave in like so much paper.

There was one thing he would like to keep, he told his father: the framed photograph on the side table in the dining room. The photograph must have been taken when Constance was probably younger than Nick was now. Hard to tell. Her deep stare never aged. Even when she was a young woman there must have been something preposterous about her, something incisive and vivid and yet unworldly. Protecting her— hadn't that always been Nick's wish? Although she wouldn't stand for it. No, she wanted everyone to be like her: irreverent and restless and impatient. She pulled people down to earth and kept them there. She ridiculed you, jolting you out of yourself, or tried to. People took themselves too seriously, she liked to say. Her clients must have struggled to create more severe problems for themselves, to impress her. The thought struck him—had she wanted a daughter? Someone like her?

Vinegar. That was the smell seeping into the dining room. Tracey was making "an indoor picnic." She set before him a plate of cucumbers bumpy with salt crystals and left the room just as Scott came back in. His voice was a half-whisper. "It's not what you think," he said.

Nick couldn't resist saying, "What do I think?"

"You think it's the memories. That all those years of my life with your mother are haunting me and that I can't stay in the house because of them. That's not even close. Your mother would understand. I want a smaller place. And less of a lawn. Your mother loved a big lawn. Believe me, a lawn doesn't love you back. It just takes and takes and you're left used."

Nick had hoped for an admission, some awareness, some guilt on Scott's part. For betraying Constance. For being vain and shallow and egotistical and disloyal. But no. Scott was worried about lawn care.

"Sure," Nick said. "You know, you could hire people to help you pack up the rest of the house. I can call around and help make arrangements with the movers."

"I bet you can. You know where I'm headed—there's a tenants' association?" Scott paused dramatically, and Nick was swamped by a sense of familiarity. What did Scott want? There had to be an agenda. His father exhaled, shook his head. "They don't take dogs. Any tenants' association is run by fascists. That's the nature of a place with a tenants' association. Everything goes tits up in a place like that. I may need some help getting settled." Scott studied his hands. "And then there's your mother's dog."

Nick realized: Despite Tracey, he would have to keep helping his father in the ways his mother had helped his father. And now Nick would be the caretaker of his mother's dog.

"Bonnie's in the bedroom," Scott said. With his foot he nudged a cardboard box away from the leg of the table. "She's waiting for your mother in there. Your mother only had her for a few weeks but that doesn't matter. They bonded. Bonnie was her idea of a joke—an ugly pug like that. Vicious to anyone but her. But you know your mother. Never without a joke. You won't believe how much she willed to that church. She punished me more often for what I wouldn't do than for what I did. I suppose she could have been even more extravagant when it came to the goddamn church. That's how I know it was only her *idea* of a joke. She left more for you than for anyone. I guess she thought of herself as a patron of the arts."

"Maybe in her own way she was," Nick said.

Scott sighed so heavily that Nick endured another wave of annoyance. "You were the right sort of son for her. Whether I was the right sort of father for you and Nelson I won't say. I'll say this: No one ever died under her care. Given her profession, that might be a record."

Was that the standard under which his mother had judged herself? Nick had no idea if it was a high or a low standard.

Scott's next pronouncement was delivered while he was packing a set of Bavarian beer steins. "Listen, she loved you and Nelson. If she hadn't—you particularly—would be more messed up than you are."

It was eerie how much his father sounded, suddenly, like Constance. "Why couldn't you have given her what she wanted?" Nick said. It was a question he had never before asked.

"Who?"

"Constance. My mother."

"I did," Scott said. "I tried."

To Nick the answer sounded self-pitying. As if his father actually believed he had tried. "That woman who's here," Nick began, his voice lowering. He fought to remember her name. "That woman—Tracey—I guess she'll take over now. There were so many women, weren't there?"

"Who do you think they were for?"

The question hung in the air.

Scott continued, "Did you think they were for me? They made your mother happy. I guess we could have let you get to know us better. I guess we owed you that."

"I think—." Nick stopped. "There are things I don't need to know. That aren't my business."

"That's what we thought, too. That's something you'll have to outgrow eventually: being a prig. Listen. I'm going to be fine."

Nick thought of Nance and the time she left her black beret on his bed. A symbol he hadn't read correctly. Probably even Birder recognized what was going on.

"Don't worry," Scott said. "I might need a little help getting settled. That's all. I'm glad Bonnie will have a home."

"Are you sure you're all right?" Nick asked.

"Oh no. Of course not. This isn't something to recover from. You can't prepare for it either. There's no preparation. Your mother and I—we were each other's lives."

Birder's ex-wife had collected piñatas but grew tired of them by the time she left him. And so piñatas had hung from the ceiling in nearly every room of Birder's place, swinging sullenly: clusters of donkeys, bunnies, a horned creature like a minor-league devil. Then, too, there was a green and gray turtle, its shell topped off with a small, grimy head and an expression of absolute bafflement.

Nick unclipped Bonnie's leash. The pug wriggled from her ears to her rolled-up tail as if shaking off from a lake swim. She settled on her haunches and looked up at Nick's friend. Birder searched for a compliment. "She's a—"

"Small hog?" Nick squatted next to the pug. "Nah. She's a gem. Aren't you—a gem." Bonnie nudged her head against his knees.

"You know, you disappeared on me."

"Sorry," Nick said. "Just—"

"That's okay. We're good." Birder's open smile made it clear he didn't know about Constance's death. It wasn't like Birder spent time reading obituaries.

"Her name's Bonnie. I'm taking care of her for a while."

"Great," Birder said, clapping. "I remember her—your mom's dog. Aren't you going to ask where the piñatas went? I dumped most of them outside with a big 'Free' sign. I don't know why they don't disappear. I tried donating them to a school. Easier to smuggle in a handgun. How's the art coming?"

"It's not."

A shuffling sound erupted from behind a closed door.

Nick raised his shoulders, mouthed, "You're not alone?'

Before Birder could answer, the bedroom door swung open. For a bare moment Nick thought he was staring at a small boy. The apparition opened its mouth: a woman's voice. Nick's eyes adjusted, took in the teardrop tattoos under each small glittering eye. The woman was extraordinarily pale. Nick thought of a bird blown out of a nest, a yellow custardy thing, blue veined.

Birder introduced her as Doree. "You're the artist," she said to Nick. "I've heard so much about you."

Nick almost said, "Already?" He felt like one of his legs suddenly shrank.

"Oh!" she said, "your dog!" Bonnie waddled toward her, butting against the young woman's calves. Nick noticed then: Doree was wearing a faded yellow sweatshirt he'd seen on Birder. The inscription was mercifully so faded as to be almost illegible: *Save the Beaver.*

Birder scrambled into the kitchen while Nick watched Doree fondling Bonnie. When Birder returned he was waving beers.

"Let's celebrate," he said. Doree laughed as if Birder had said something wonderful. Nick felt dizzy with envy. He didn't ask what they were celebrating.

"I was going to tell him about the guitars—you don't mind?" Birder said. Doree laughed and shook her head. "Be right back," she said. Bonnie, sniffling, galloped behind Doree. The pug's back legs slid on the hardwood floor. Doree disappeared behind the door, taking her beer and Bonnie with her.

Birder sighed and said, "I thought she stole two of my guitars."

"What? You don't mean it."

"She doesn't have any permanent home right now. She's staying with friends. I didn't even notice the guitars were missing, and then the day after the party she shows up with the guitars. Saying I can press charges. You'll think that was cynical. As if I'd ever press charges."

"She could murder you and you wouldn't press charges."

"Exactly. You have art. I have charity. Who says charity's not an art?"

"I can tell you right now that art isn't charity."

Birder went on, "The thing about her having nowhere to live. That's temporary. For her. And for her nephew. He's only three years younger than she is, but he's her nephew. He was the one who took the guitars."

"You'll help them both out."

"An honor, believe me."

When Doree emerged from the bedroom the tattoos were gone. What Nick saw must have been smudged mascara. Had she and Birder been in bed before he arrived, smearing her makeup? Had Birder, the *Gatsby* fan, found his Daisy? Doree's voice didn't sound like money—it sounded more like poverty. And Birder would fix that.

Bonnie circled Doree, demanding more attention. "She's an amazing dog," Birder said. "You could pack a sandwich under those head wrinkles. And those eyes. Do you have to pop them back in every night?"

"You forgot to critique her tail."

"It's like a fur doughnut—that's alive."

"There you go."

Indignant, Bonnie sat with her back to Birder.

By then Doree was hanging on Birder's arm. Nick missed much of what Doree was saying until he realized she was addressing him. He caught up with her when she said, "I didn't even know Birder's name. I mean, I kept noticing him at the co-op, and then when Amos came back with the guitars I knew it was a prank. It's not like Amos to steal anything valuable. It was just—a joke. He wouldn't have kept anything. But you know it was so so so wrong. Thank God he remembered the address and then when I opened the door and it was Birder—."

"If I saw you at the co-op I would have made sure to get to know you. In a heartbeat. Half a heartbeat. A quarter of a heartbeat."

"Amos—he's just—impulsive."

"I don't even remember him at the party," Birder said. "There were so many people. A good party. He can have the guitars. What do I need so many guitars for now?" Birder leaned down to Doree, his jaw grazing the top of her head.

Nick was so depressed he could hardly lift his beer bottle to his mouth.

"Take a piñata, okay?" Birder said when Nick edged toward the door.

"Sure." Nick hesitated. "Is the turtle piñata out there on the curb? My favorite. My totem animal."

Crepe paper runneled across the sidewalk. Some of the piñatas were inside out, elephant colored. Nick imagined kids jumping into the piñatas, cracking them open. The rain was finishing off the whole sopping mess. He couldn't make out the turtle piñata from the others. Its shell must have been flattened, its bewildered face crushed. Then he spotted it—almost whole.

He was nearly at his apartment, the partially crushed turtle piñata under his arm, Bonnie trotting on ahead, when the possibility came to Nick and quickened his breathing. He could reassemble the piñatas, remake them into art. And then fill them with—what?

Stupid idea.

The stupid ideas were the only ones that eventually became something that could work. If he woke up tomorrow and the idea was still there, he wouldn't need to dismiss it.

It took three trips. He stashed the drenched piñatas on the back porch of his apartment under the awning and stood on the steps listening to the rain.

Behind him, scrabbling and a hollow thump: Bonnie's head against the window. She was balancing on the back of the sofa to keep him in her sights. When he first brought her to his apartment she had been at loose ends until he remembered her plaid basket, still locked in his car's trunk along with extra pet supplies from his father's house. Once he brought the basket, Bonnie wedged herself inside, comforted at last. Otherwise she liked to slither around on her slippery claws, nosing at remnants of his art or drinking from her bowl in the kitchen and carrying mouthfuls back to spray across his studio floor. And here she was, her thin tongue curled, peering at him through the window with her worried-looking pop-out eyes. She would make, in bulk and shape, a remarkable piñata.

In the dark Nick looked across the back lawn. A gust of wind blew raindrops from the maple. The mist reached his forehead.

Birder. So Birder moped for years, wallowed and no doubt sobbed through dozens of nights. Then a woman shows up with his stolen guitars and the past is over. Out go the piñatas. Doree: home delivery. Except Birder hadn't even ordered her. She simply showed up. Maybe all Birder's charitable deeds had flown back to him in the form of Doree, or maybe Doree was a tiny demon come for his soul. Whatever the case, it was an improvement.

By the time he turned around Bonnie had vacated the window. He could hear her claws on the kitchen linoleum. Then, instantly, she slingshotted herself back to the window, for him.

Nick used to think he had to keep his life clear to serve his art. He should have mentioned that to his mother. He could have benefited from corrective laughter.

Those artists who painted their mothers—who made a likeness that was considered recognizable—for at least some of them, most, almost all, did the brush rebel? The one he liked best in the book Nance had given him: Henri de Toulouse-Lautrec's portrait of his mother. She was coming off the canvas, like a vine curling, the flowerpots behind her, the bench a green blue, and there she was, like a being who was part of the world and growing from it, yet beyond the world at the same time. She was looking down. Not seeing her son or even imagining what he was making of her.

Nick took Bonnie out for regular walks. One afternoon Bonnie's leash tangled with another dog's. It would have been romantic except that the dog's owner had to be at least eighty-five. She was a lovely woman, though, and running up behind her came her very pretty granddaughter. His mother had been right: Time started speeding up. He couldn't otherwise pretend to have understood his mother, or how other artists portrayed their mothers.

Nick dated the young woman for five months. After they broke up he began seeing a friend of her sister's—and that was the woman he eventually married. Selena was an artist herself. He often sat for her. She painted him in his boxers or in his pajama pants patterned with antlers. By the time they were married Nick didn't paint anymore. He made art only with things he found, ruined things, what others discarded.

Eventually he and Selena and two other friends exhibited together in a group show. He created an installation: a chair in an empty room. It was the chair from his mother's office. The arms were scarred, and one leg, worn down, was shorter than the others. For the first time he felt he was a successful artist. He took off work so that during the hours the gallery was open he could sit on the exhibited chair as people filed by. Those who saw the installation referred to its power, for the installation suggested the horrors of interrogation, surveillance, authorized brutality. It was incredible, he told Selena—the things he heard, just sitting there as part of his own installation. It made him feel safe somehow, though that's something he couldn't confess to her. A sign behind him was printed with a line from Shakespeare's *Twelfth Night:* "I was adored once too."

The installation was titled by a number: 148. Only Nick's wife knew it was a portrait of the artist's mother.

After *The Turn of the Screw*

When Douglas finishing reading the governess's account we were silent for a long time, depleted, exhausted. It was, after all, a very long account. One of us argued that the entire story was a ruse—that Douglas had been fooled by the pretty older woman who wanted to make herself intriguing. Another said the account was obviously composed by a madwoman. Another called the governess a perverse and evil woman, and insisted that the entire tale should be destroyed. Another—there were too many of us gathered in the drawing room, where the fire had gone out long ago and all the servants were settled into bed—argued for pity, that the governess was a victim of her own fantasies and guilt, that she meant no harm. One of us alleged that the governess should never have found another position in any household and should have been imprisoned. "She killed the child herself and made up the story later," he proposed.

Yet another quietly claimed that the governess was so isolated, so young, and endured such a claustrophobic and unnatural situation that her mind could hardly have done other than create fantasies. Two of us were silent, believing the governess's story and not questioning a word of it. Another of us—Trebells—the one this particular account will focus upon—was silent and enraged, for he believed that Douglas had made up the whole farrago or, if not, that certain details were intentionally and maliciously amplified. Surely the narrative was meant to implicate Trebells who, like the diabolical Peter Quint, was red haired and possessed a rather foxlike face, and had a history concerning his own wife and a young governess that was known by more than one of the assembled party.

After the complete tale was read—an endeavor that occupied three nights—Trebells didn't join the others on the road but set off on foot across the fields. Already daybreak was coming on. A light rain had fallen in the night, though the path along the field's verge wasn't muddy. Eventually, the path widened and met up with the main road. There, pockets of mud sucked at Trebells's feet and made him curse with annoyance. By then, he didn't have to wonder if he'd meet any of the other guests. They would have been safely well ahead, at home in their beds after such a late night. He felt wings beat above him just as a starling whisked near enough to pluck at the crown of his head.

When he was a boy he hated shooting birds. Other boys teased him about his squeamishness. After a while, at first grudgingly, he came to enjoy what a slingshot could do.

Fog crept across the road, obscuring the wintery landscape. Trebells had been walking for less than a mile when he came upon a figure moving yards ahead of him. The conclusion of the night's ghost story had put Trebells in an eerie mood, and for some time he slowed, not wanting to pass whoever walked the road. At last, irritated by his own nervousness, he quickened his pace. The fog was thickening, and it seemed that the person might have disappeared into a gully or turned off into a lane. And then, a few feet ahead, the form came into visibility.

As he stepped closer the woman turned, and he saw that she was young and lovely. He kept stride with her. When she didn't register alarm about his presence he put an arm around her waist. She didn't flinch, nor did her breathing change—as if she was hardly aware of his presence, or as if she accepted, even welcomed it. His hand shifted, and it was then he realized and dropped his arm. A woman expecting a child and alone on the road—how defenseless she was. "I'll see you home," he said. "No need to fear anything. I'll see that you make your way safely."

The feeling of satisfaction that came over him, how seldom he'd felt such a sensation. His wife had been dead for nearly twenty years, and the governess he'd dallied with—she, too, was no longer alive, taken by disease he'd heard, which was no wonder given the eagerness she displayed with him, the desperation. There had to have been other men after him, and not the best sort. Of course it was clear that she hadn't been fit to guide his children or anyone else's. Governesses—he knew them to be willful. The problem of servants, particularly governesses: They seethed, and some were all too willing to be tipped out of their small lives in hopes of some gain, some advancement. Governesses so often borrowed or retrieved things that belonged to their mistresses. Each was a spy in the house, and a witness. Yet they were necessary, as lonely and bored as they were in their stations. He could, in his way, sympathize. Why shouldn't they be resentful and make up stories? Lacking love, they became wrapped up, some of them, in the children in their care, giving themselves over to their young charges. His wife—the abscess on the left side of her face he remembered too well: anger eating its way out of her. And her trip to her mother's home and the accident there, the terrible accident, although arrangements were made and difficulties overcome so that a churchyard burial was accomplished. Eventually, given the declining health of his wife's mother, his two children were put under the care of another governess, another pretty young governess, and he made her vow not to trouble him over trifles. Weren't children's problems, almost inevitably, trifles?

Even Douglas should understand as much. The first governess, the one who caused all the trouble in Trebell's life, was of course not in the least like the governess in Douglas's account. The last time Trebells saw that particular governess she was playing pick-up sticks with his children. The long sticks of the game were spread like hay across the parlor rug. The more Trebells considered the account that Douglas read, the more certain he became that Douglas had meant to create havoc, and that details had been forged to conform to Trebells's past miseries. His children were adults now. Agnes was married with twin sons, and Vernon Thomas was a staff officer and would work his way up the ranks in good time. Neither child had been marred by Trebell's decisions in any way that was apparent.

The fog was lifting in swirling curtains. The woman turned her face toward Trebells, and he saw gratitude in her eyes. He vowed again to walk with her as far as she needed him. Within minutes she was moving off the main road. Ahead: a house Trebells had never seen before, set off at the end of a long path and almost lost in vines. He shuddered to think of the woman, clearly soon to give birth, being forced to live in such a hovel. When he came closer he saw he had been mistaken. The house stretched through the vines, stretched luxuriously ahead so far that there was something preposterous about it, as if the structure and its ostentatious turret had been erected by a whimsical and half-mad architect. This impression was reinforced once Trebells stepped inside, for staircases appeared to both his left and right. Rooms were at odd angles with corridors that receded. At one juncture a wall of mirrors made the whole all the more confusing. A spindle-legged table stood covered with letters, so many that when Trebells passed they fluttered up to touch his fingers. The handwriting on the envelopes looked like a child's. He felt unnerved and was about to back away when a fresh beam of light struck through a window, and he saw that he had once again been mistaken. As the woman doffed her heavy cloak it became clear that her waist was remarkably slim. She looked into his eyes and let down her hair, shining black as a crow. He followed her past room after room and allowed himself a fantasy that she was luring him toward a haven deep in the house where a bed laid with a soft coverlet awaited them both. The memory of ivory-colored bedding floated before him, a memory that seemed snatched from nowhere, the memory so insubstantial and cobwebbed that he wondered if he was remembering a dream.

In the next corridor he had to be careful to keep his arms close to his sides to avoid the walls, which were made of some material that scratched his arms. He passed a room full of feather beds plumped high, nearly to the ceiling.

When they reached a wall of windows the light turned brilliant, and a scene outside the glass grew clearly illuminated. What he saw froze his blood, for in the near distance was a pond, and at its center in a rowboat stood a small child, alone and tottering. Surely the child would drop into the pond and drown. The sense of panicked responsibility, as fresh and taunting as a wound, made him dash away and hurtle down the stairs. He didn't even wonder if the child was the woman's. He only knew he must save the child, boy or girl, he couldn't be sure—the little body staggering as the boat revolved slowly in the water, turning while the child on wrenlike legs teetered dangerously.

The first plunge into the water—he wished to be a good man, he must be a good man, he wished again for goodness—was a blade at his throat. The iciness sliced him. As he pushed himself forward, the violence of his frantic motions sent the rowboat veering. The child dropped into the boat, then stood again. Trebells was almost sure now that the child was a girl, a fragile thing who did not know what danger she was in and that in instants she could disappear under the blue-black water. The more he struggled the more the boat rocked away from his grasping hands. He fought until he could hardly stay afloat. Too soon, his lungs gasping, arms weakening, he felt himself sinking. When his body, of its own accord, spun toward shore, he saw the child there among reeds, laughing. How had she flown there? How had she saved herself? When he turned back, the boat was empty.

The woman who had led him to her house stood on the bank. Beside her, and resting his arm on her waist, was a scowling man, tall and lean faced. He picked up the child from the reeds and held her. Then the woman and the man, the girl tucked against the man's chest, turned their backs on Trebells as he dragged himself from the water. Trebells's coat hung heavily, sopping, and he was half-delirious with exhaustion. He didn't see the house ahead of him, nor did he have the energy to crane his neck to make out any signs of its inhabitants. After he gained his breath he struggled to find his way back to the lane that first led him to the house. When at last he staggered onto the main road he saw that he hadn't traveled as far as he thought. His own home was still a great distance away. It would be best to return to Douglas's estate.

Up ahead a familiar form emerged in the winter light. It was Douglas himself. Above Trebells's friend swirled a scarf of birds. So many and so high in the air were they, that the birds looked like flecks, like the print from newspapers or fragments from an explosion from a war happening somewhere far away.

Douglas cried out in a hearty voice. "What? Wanting breakfast, is that it?" Laughter, all good cheer. The birds above him swung higher, the flock outlined in the white winter light. As Trebells looked up, the birds swarmed as if inside his own eyes, wheeling and dizzying him.

Rage filled Trebells. Douglas had led him to this, had fogged his mind with his lying story, his ghost story of governesses, one living and another dead. Douglas, who had droned on, three nights in all, reading an account meant to embarrass Trebells. An account that would embarrass any man with a conscience.

Trebells could hardly stand, so depleted was he, his rage as heavy as the drenched coat on his shoulders.

Douglas rushed forward and took Trebells's arm and exclaimed, "What on earth?"

"So she loved you," Trebells said.

Douglas tried holding Trebells by the shoulders, as if his friend would dissolve any instant. "Who are you talking about?" he nearly shouted.

"Your governess in your horror story," Trebells managed to say.

"Didn't you listen to what I read?" Douglas asked. His knees were ready to buckle with the weight of his friend—ridiculous Trebells, whom he presumed drunk. Douglas went on, his voice tight. "She didn't love a grown man ever. She wasn't capable. She loved a child. The boy. That was the horror of it."

Two nights later, after recovering before the fire at Douglas's estate, Trebells was back in his own bed, tended by a servant. "Did I forget something?" he asked the man holding a cup to his mouth. "I missed something. There was something I forgot." He was filled with panic. The sound of a thud made him almost remember. "A bird, sir," the servant said. "A bird has hit the window." It was then that Trebells remembered his strange adventure and thought how odd it was that he could no longer feel superior to the governess in Douglas's account: her panic, her sense of responsibility, the fear she had of herself, of her charges, her fear for children. Like her, he too knew guilt, his heart in his chest like stagnant water.

He'd relinquish that feeling eventually, although as spring began to arrive Trebells often could be found listening for the sound of one particular bird's cry at dawn. It was a bird whose song he remembered from childhood, a bird he'd encountered often as a child, little anticipating that within years, not long after the first of the world wars, that particular species would be extinct.

Escape from the Dark Forest

Dhara's car lurched, shuddered, died, and started again, grindingly, only to sputter and die entirely after she steered to the road's shoulder. She wasn't as alarmed as she might have been, for far ahead beamed a pole light, and the light must belong to a house. She retrieved her purse and set off, full stride, almost enjoying the night air.

Soon, on both sides of the road, gullies roared with snowmelt. If a car came barreling she would have nowhere to escape but into a howling channel. Her brother, if he could see her, would be proud of how her heart wasn't in her throat. When she was a child she would wake to find her brother asleep on the floor of her room. He used to be afraid of the dark. When they were children he terrified her in broad daylight, like a reverse vampire. She could never be as daring as he was now—the way he went with hardly anything more than a camera to Malaysia, the Philippines, Indonesia.

The clouds drew away from the moon. A farmhouse, its windows lit, rose into view. Dhara was on the driveway when a dog began howling. She realized her mistake. It wasn't a dog's howl but a human's. The howl was horrible, like someone being burned to death.

She waited for the clouds to pass from the moon so she could get her bearings. She put her face in her hands. Her skin felt cold and smooth and artificial. When she took her hands away, a woman was next to her.

Dhara explained what had happened with her car. The woman, taking Dhara's elbow, said, "You're trespassing." The woman didn't let go even when Dhara tried again to explain her situation.

The moon cast stripes on the farmhouse lawn. Zebra night, zebra life,

Dhara was thinking, repeating the phrase in her mind the way people will when they're terrorized.

The kitchen was bright under a fluorescent light, and a boy in a chair at the table looked up when Dhara entered. As if time had altered in some magical way, Dhara realized it was her brother, who had been missing for nearly a year, almost a full year to the day. The boy was her brother—but something was wrong. Her fear stunned her into silence. Next to her brother the chair was empty. Dhara sat there, unable to catch her breath. If it was her brother, shouldn't he recognize her and apologize for disappearing on his adventure and destroying their family?

Something could be heard snapping and shriveling on the stove burners. Dhara made herself look at her brother. His chest was thin, concave. The boy in the chair was younger by at least five years than she was. How could he possibly be her older brother?

Her brother: People were still talking about him. Dhara had met one of them only two weeks ago at a reception, a woman with hair as orange as a Cheeto. "He doesn't love any of you," the woman told Dhara. "He isn't capable of love." Uh oh. One of the fallen. Her brother had a terrible track record with women. But why would the woman think he didn't love his family? Only a week before her brother disappeared he sent Dhara—from Seattle—a digital image of orchids suspended like shadowy, unreal faces, heart-stoppingly beautiful.

Underneath the spitting sound—Dhara realized it was eggs frying—she detected a scrabbling, like cockroaches in a drawer lined with loose paper.

"She doesn't look like a crackhead," the boy said.

"They don't all look like what they are," the woman said.

"My car broke down," Dhara said again, wondering if the woman couldn't hear well. "I was trying to find somewhere where I could call. I left my cellphone at home."

"You all say that. You want the syringes. You think you can find anything you want here."

The boy laughed. It was the oddest laugh Dhara had ever heard, odder than her brother's but almost an amplification of her brother's. A laugh with grit in it, like kernels of grain rattling in a throat.

A cat jumped on her lap and instantly jumped off. For the first time she noticed that there were several cats in the kitchen. Three were as entwined as baby snakes inside a cardboard box. On a stool across the room a gray cat hunched, its ears swiveling.

"My car," Dhara said. She explained yet again that her car had broken down. She didn't mean to cause trouble for them, she just needed to make a call. That was all, then she could leave.

"Do you remember that baby doll I bought you?" the boy said. He was her brother again. Because, yes, her brother had bought her a doll. The doll's eyes blinked and clicked. The head was as large as her own, or nearly. In the spring the doll turned up in the weeping cherry tree, lodged between branches, its legs dangling.

"You're Bluey Cluff's daughter," the boy said. "Mom, that's Bluey's daughter. I gave her a doll years ago. She remembered. I saw it in her eyes."

"No. No." Dhara took out her driver's license to show proof.

"Those can be faked," the boy said.

"Plenty have faked them," the woman said. She and the boy stared at Dhara, their eyes glazing with what must have been memories.

Near a box of newspapers a calico cat stretched its legs, drawing its tail up like a question mark. "She can't get enough cats," the boy said. He jerked his head toward the woman. "She hates cats. But they come here anyway." The boy smiled, a smile so much like her brother's that Dhara's head swam.

She had wanted a signal for months. Possibly this boy was a sign that her brother was still alive. Otherwise what could she think—that an entire life, her brother's life, could be a fleck of ash, and there would be no mark in the universe, no message, no clue left about what happened to him?

Amnesia—that was what her mother had said. Dhara and her father couldn't help but groan at the word. Or he was ill. Or kidnapped. Or he didn't want to be found. Her mother and father couldn't believe their son was dead, only that he was temporarily unwilling to appear. Dhara thought of the depth of her love for her brother, how it kept deepening, as if inside her a canyon opened because of his beautiful strange wildness, and there at the base of a canyon ran the river of her love for her brother.

There was no way to control what happened with her love and there was always the possibility that eventually she would grow numb. That would be natural, a means of self-preservation. How could she keep reaching to make sure all her love for him stayed alive? It was like trying to reach between her ribs to touch her own heart.

The woman was swaying at the stove on her thick shoes—a nurse's shoes, cracked, yellowed. She turned the pan over onto a plate and carried the plate to the table. For a bewildered moment, until the woman sat down and slid eggs into her mouth, Dhara thought the woman wanted her to eat. A cat leapt on the table. With her forearm the woman knocked the cat off.

"I'll just be heading out now," Dhara said. Her feet weren't on the linoleum but sliding over a cushion of air.

"It's cold," the woman said, "but do what you like. I'll tell you what. You wait on the porch a minute if you feel more comfortable out there, and I'll make a call for you to the service station."

"I can make the call."

"Now you just let me handle this."

Paint cans, a stepladder, a barrel filled with what might be axle grease—she could see all this surrounding her on the porch, visible in the pole lamp's blue light. When the boy stepped out, Dhara told him, "You look like my brother." Something about the boy's eyes, too, made her think of what happened years ago when she and her brother were in the backseat of a rental car their father was driving. Above the passenger seat rose the back of their mother's head, newly permanented. Her head appeared inflated, like Ronald McDonald's. Dhara and her brother were looking for bears, each peering out one side of the car and into the forest. "Oooh, dark forest," her brother chanted. It was broad daylight, but the deeper in they looked, the darker the forest grew. "I see one!" her brother cried. The next afternoon they drove to a bear park. The man who took their money warned them: "Keep your windows up. Don't let the bears get ahold of you." They had driven only yards into the park when a bear bumbled past their car and sat down on the side of the roadway. Outside the car's back window another bear yawned. In the reflected image Dhara's brother looked like he was inside the bear's mouth. As they drove past, her brother rolled down the window and stuck his hand out and stroked the tail end of the bear. Their parents hadn't seen what he did. Dhara would never forget it. The way he took a swipe at that bear's fur, cuffed it. The way he turned to her afterwards, eyes wide, making fun of her fear.

"Come on back in," the boy said. "My mom said to get you out of the cold."

At the doorway Dhara stepped over what at first looked like a wad of rags. "How many cats do you have?" she asked.

"We don't count. She—" the boy nodded toward his mother who was scraping out a pan over the sink, "hates them, but they come anyway. There are too many cats in the world."

The house was growing warmer. The boy bent next to his mother over the sink. They whispered, and Dhara heard "Cluff, Cluff."

"The doctor told you that you can have another baby someday," the woman said. Who was she talking to? "But you have to be careful. You're not repaired. You should thank those people. Maybe it was good you weren't allowed to hold the baby. They didn't want you to look at it. It was a girl. You should know that. Although I suspect you know that. They didn't blindfold you."

"I'm not the person you think I am," Dhara said. "That girl. She must look like me, that's all."

"She doesn't look like anybody but you because that's who you are," the boy said.

Dhara knew it then: The man named Bluey Cluff would arrive, not someone from a service station. The woman had phoned Cluff, believing Dhara was his daughter.

Dhara watched her own hand reach out and push at the screen door. As she was running across the yard she heard shrieks. Then she was on the road, running next to the gullies where water churned and roared. She wasn't sure if the boy was chasing her or if it was her own heart she heard. When she couldn't run any longer she stopped, vomiting into the road.

A silvery streak illuminated the edges of a block of darkness. After she unlocked the car door her hands slipped. She dropped her keys on the mat. She felt around and found the keys, and then, as if nothing had been wrong, as if the car only needed to cool down and had sufficiently recovered, as if it only required rest—like something made of flesh—the engine started. She managed to turn around on the narrow road without a wheel dropping into the ditch.

When she pulled into the lot of her apartment building Dhara was so relieved she rested her head on the steering wheel. She told herself her escape was a real sign, an unmistakable near-miracle. Why else would the motor have turned over unless she was receiving a message that everything would be fine, not only for herself but for her brother?

As she drew out the car key, she saw the animal.

In the light from the dashboard the fur looked almost like a raccoon's markings. She opened the car door before she was struck with the realization that the cat might starve or be run over in traffic. She reached out and, with an intake of breath, picked up the cat. Like something wounded, the animal rested its full weight in her arms.

After she turned the light on inside her apartment the cat sprang away, its paws meeting the floor with a thud. The cat followed her to the coat closet, and into the kitchen. It stared up at her knowingly until she found a can of tuna and a bowl of water.

When she let the cat outside it disappeared. She waited for a rustling in the bushes. If the cat came back, that would be another sign that her brother was alive.

She had overreacted earlier, she told herself. The boy and his mother meant to do what was right. They only confused her with someone else, someone missing. The problem would have been cleared up. Or maybe— and this was the oddest thought of all—maybe they had been playing a trick. Maybe it was a game they played together? Maybe they liked scaring her?

When the cat didn't reappear, Dhara made meowing noises. After what seemed like a very long time she felt a wash of dampness against her ankle. The cat's fur sparkled in the beam from the streetlight.

She was tired but had a hard time falling asleep. The cat kept bumping its head against her cheek. Finally the animal settled on her chest, curling its front paws, another sign of the new peace that Dhara was demanding from life. Only in the full morning light did she see that under the cat's fluffy mane ran a ring of pus where someone had tried to hang it.

Even then she couldn't believe it was a sign that her brother was never coming home, despite every indication that the actual world offered. His silence foremost among those signs. As she searched online sites for a veterinarian, she thought of Bluey Cluff's daughter and that girl's baby. Would that girl and the baby she wasn't allowed to hold ever find one another? What must it have been like for that girl to lose her baby like that? At least, Dhara told herself, her own awful adventure meant she had rescued a creature, even if the cat's chances of surviving appeared slight.

The cat uttered a cry—mechanical-sounding, like a tiny door opening, a tiny door on the other side of the earth. The poor thing's neck was oozing.

Dhara returned from the vet with the cat's neck shaved and two ointments as well as an antibiotic she was supposed to shoot into the cat's mouth. The cat didn't mind having the top of its head petted.

She kept her new happiness close and secret. Why was she now flooded—flooded!—with the conviction that her brother was alive and would make his way back? He must be teasing them. She was sure of it. It was a conviction as real to her as the cat was real. The river of love in her heart—she couldn't touch it. But it was real. Her brother was real and would come back to her and her mother and father—who were dying from the loss of him.

When he returned she was going to make sure he knew they were all lost without him. And she was going to touch his heart. They all were.

A Stalker

"You think you know what you're capable of but you don't," I told the man I was accused of harassing.

"Sheilah, you're talking about yourself," he said, and I agreed.

Not that I meant to stalk a coworker. I just couldn't stop myself from driving by his house. Phoning his cell. Pausing long minutes by his desk at work. Another person might have waited for everything to blow over. I wasn't dangerous, was I? Only deluded and lonely. Besides, it's true for most people—isn't it?—that half the time you're walking yourself around the block not knowing your leash is broken.

After I got fired, Arethna called and asked me to housesit. I knew she was doing me a favor, that I really wasn't needed. She owned the tavern across the lot from her house at the New Jersey shore, and her bartender, an old friend, always watched her place for her when she left every winter. Arethna was my stepfather's cousin, and when my mother was married to my stepfather we visited her often, but I had only visited Selden Point during summer. Arethna informed me that despite the spill from Merckler Pharmaceuticals streets bristled with rows of new mansions with white-pebbled lawns and three-tiered decks. After the first cold rains of autumn, those mansions' owners evacuated Selden Point, every hotel closed down, and most shop windows darkened. Only hardcore locals remained. The town was reduced to a bakery, a sandwich shop, three antique stores, and Arethna's tavern. "It's pretty desolate," Arethna warned. Which sounded perfect for me.

I had hardly settled in when I was startled by a whipping sound. A flap of tarp had worked loose from Arethna's swimming pool. The wind sent the tarp's edge rustling before snapping against the concrete. The pool was deep—deep enough that years ago my brother Max and a gang of boys dove from the concrete edge in daily competitions. During our phone conversation Arethna had said that two years ago in winter the man who looked after the place discovered a deer at the bottom of the pool, its legs broken.

I drew on my coat and checked the darkness under the tarp. When I discovered nothing I secured the tarp to its peg and felt almost proud of myself: Yes, I am trustworthy. Yes, I am responsible.

The tavern was closed so I used my key and opened the back room. Mud tracks mottled the area where liquor boxes were piled, and the floor gave slightly under my feet. Inside the barroom a soft whirring echoed from the refrigeration unit. I was thinking about calling Arethna and thanking her again for giving me a place to hide from my shame when a voice wormed into my ear. The voice seemed to be coming from inside and close by. A trick of acoustics? Maybe from a television or a radio? The neighbors had technology that something in the tavern picked up and transmitted?

And then—a clear voice. Unmistakable. Not coming from inside the tavern or my own head. Clearly from outside.

I pushed open the door. Snow dashed through the air in almost invisible streaks. At first I saw no one, and then, under the streetlights, a leather jacket gleamed and a man looked up, his face almost silvery. Something in the way he gazed toward me made me think he expected to see me. I lifted my hand to wave. The man turned away. The last I saw of him: the pale flash of something at his neck. I wanted to run after him, ask who he was. The impulse frightened me. Could I trust myself? I was afraid that I would do something that was self-defeating. Evidently I could, because I had.

The memory of that voice lingered. I wanted the voice to tell me: You are safe; everything you loved—almost everything—will return, in some form, somehow, without your having to beg. Besides, you won't stalk that man you just saw tonight. You're not an obsessive person anymore. You're cured of whatever drove you. You never have to be fascinated by anyone ever again, not in that way.

Arethna called in the morning. The bartender who worked for her had come down with pneumonia. "His wife let me know. I'll email the phone numbers of some people in town who could do his job. If you could just call a few numbers and see if anyone's available?" She apologized, evidently thinking she was causing me immense trouble. I was happy to be useful. After she sent the list I tried every name. No one could help out except the last person I called, who said he'd recommend a friend.

Glen Gardner appeared an hour later. How to describe him? Beautiful. Beautiful. Beautiful. Small, dark, mischievous eyes. He was the opposite of Eddie, the man I'd stalked. Eddie was a bit chubby, with a round, boyish face and small arms often buried by the long sleeves of his jackets. The man in front of me seemed Eddie's opposite, his features snapped perfectly into place to serve as a reminder that there were other sorts of men besides Eddie.

"I've never hired anyone for anything," I confessed.

"Or fired anyone, then. Good. I have plenty of experience. In mixology."

We were in Arethna's living room. On the wall above Glen Gardner's head hung a wonderfully hideous painting. I tried not to stare at it, for the same reason I don't stare at myself in the mirror as I'm changing clothes. The woman's naked cloudlike fleshiness blended into the fainting couch on which she was stretched eternally. She waited there, in all her stupidity. Arethna's house had been redecorated multiple times, but one thing hadn't changed: that gorgeous monstrosity. Even when I was a child I knew it wasn't a good painting. The woman's elbow looked like a knee.

Glen Gardner's eyes darted around the room before focusing on my own. "By hiring me you'll be doing Arethna a favor," he said. "And frankly, you're doing my family a favor. My mother and father—I help support them. We could use the money." He didn't plan on staying in Selden Point indefinitely. But if he had to leave before the regular bartender recovered he'd give notice and help me find a replacement. He shifted in his chair. The woman's breast in the painting came to rest on his left ear.

"I saw you the other night," I said. "That was you walking by." I remembered the way he passed under the streetlight.

"No, I don't think so," he said, sounding puzzled. He swiveled. "What are you staring at? This?" He pointed at the painting.

"It's so ugly," I said. "But I almost like it."

"Then I love it, Sheilah. That's your name, right? Sheilah?"

Of course I hired him.

Through the foyer window I first saw a woman's coat, purple and yellow squiggles strobed on black, like a cape stolen from a sorcerer's apprentice. I opened the door and the woman rushed in, pivoted, and shouted behind her: "Come on, boys! Play!" She closed the door and introduced herself as Melanie Trowbridge. She wore red rubber boots. "You have to beg kids to play. They're mine, by the way—not just some random kids I'm hanging out with. George and Jeff. Arethna used to allow them to run across the property. Is that all right with you too? We're instituting some races. They need the exercise. I tell Jack—that's my husband—that it's like raising turtles. Here's your paper, by the way."

I took the newspaper, it was cold and stiff, and asked if the woman needed anything. "No, if that's an offer for alcohol. We're alcohol-free. I've never set foot in Arethna's tavern—sad to say, I suppose. Just wanted your permission for the twins. I don't want to put you out."

"You're not—"

"No, no. Thoroughly no. The boys are homeschooled. Which means I have to observe their play or it doesn't count as phys ed."

"Good luck," I said, realizing I sounded sarcastic though I didn't mean to.

She leaned into the window, and I endured a momentary vision of the glass cracking and Melanie Trowbridge falling through the pane, her red boots going last. "Oh God, they're like syrup out there, aren't they?" she said. "I guess they've got each other. They don't need other goals. By the way, how're you liking Selden Point? It's a pit, isn't it? Oh God, I'm sorry I said that. It's just too true."

"Have you lived here a long time?"

She moved away from the window. "I was raised less than a mile away. We bought the house three years ago. Room for the boys to roam.

Not that they roam. My garden snail offspring." She swiveled and looked out the window again. "That's cute. They're picking up speed. I call that trudging. Look at that."

The boys were dragging as they passed the tarp-covered pool. It looked like a parody of a desert film before the mirage is discovered. Moments later, Melanie Trowbridge stomped off, her sons leaning against her, possibly exhausted by her vitality. She turned to wave at me, one boy at each side of her. It was then that I had the strangest vision, so forgive me: Melanie was an upright penis and her short little boys were a couple of balls.

Maybe it was self-defense, what my mind was doing.

Two days later Melanie Trowbridge invited me to her place, three houses over. Her living room was so dark my eyes had trouble adjusting. I sank into what was less of a couch than a giant absorbent sponge. On the coffee table close to my knees a terrarium held one cactus bearing a tiny yellow bloom surrounded by fierce needles that would glint if a speck of sunlight ever invaded the room.

"Go ahead," Melanie said. "Take off your shoes. Get comfy, girl." She was wearing beaded moccasins and fuzzy purple socks. "You look so cold. You've been ice fishing or something?"

Noises—like boxes being hurled—erupted from beneath my feet.

"That's Jack in the basement with the ferret," she explained. "He's giving it exercise." She shouted into the floorboards. "Jack, leave the ferret! Start a fire, good God." She turned back to me. "We're eco-friendly about heat, you probably can tell. The ferret's kind of our one concession to vice. They're addictive, let me tell you. Fern died—the brother. Terry—that's the remaining ferret—Terry is lonely. So Jack is just so guilt-tripped. I mean it, Terry guilt-trips him."

"Can he bring the ferret up? Or can I go down and see the ferret?"

"You don't mean that. He'll be up in your panties in no time. We try to spare our guests. I have a history with animals, so I can take it. We used to have raccoons when I was a kid. My brother had a boa, too. It's not like a ferret is news to me. It's more like a hybrid from my childhood."

"Those sounds—it's only Jack and the ferret? It sounds like a crowd."

"Terry gets behind the washer. He gets stuck behind every damn appliance in the house. That's just normal behavior for him. That and being fed. He's always hungry."

Jack came up the stairs and into the room. He was wearing a bathrobe, which made him look monkish. He was at least a foot shorter than his wife. At first I didn't notice the ferret tucked under his arm.

The ferret noticed me, however, and dropped to the floor, pulled itself onto the couch like an unraveling slinky, sat halfway up, and gawked. It was an awful-looking thing. Like an overactive, hypervigilant tube.

"He's never done that before," Jack said, winking. "He likes you."

A funny thought: If I owned a ferret or a dog it wouldn't necessarily have looked like I was stalking Eddie in his neighborhood. I could have said, "What? I'm just giving my pet some exercise. Lay off!"

"Oh—you're probably wondering about the twins?" Melanie said. "They're in Frenchtown with Jack's mom. We're going to pick them up and spend some time at Jack's auntie's place. We kept postponing the trip, but we're making it after all, and I was wondering: Could you water our plants?" She bounced in her moccasins. "The plants have their own room. They need heat."

"Do you need someone to look after your ferret?"

"Oh no. They're inseparable, Jack and Terry. Jack would sooner leave me behind."

On the way to the plant room we passed two tables piled with games and a collection of Sudoku booklets. Melanie opened a door, and the air turned foggy. Above an electric heater sprawled spider plants, tendrils quivering in the breeze from a second heater.

Melanie tapped me on the shoulder. "They're something, aren't they? You know, I think I like you. A lot. You seem like someone instinctively aware of your least savory inclinations. I mean that."

"How can you know such a thing?" I said.

"I just know things."

I walked back to Arethna's with the plants, one under each arm, the tendrils waving, and set the pots near the foyer radiator and felt like a responsible person—the sort everyone trusts to watch a home or water plants.

A message was on my cellphone. From Arethna: "I should have warned you about the Trowbridges, by the way. I hope you're not having trouble with those twins. If any children ever deserved to be called assholes those two do. Whatever you do, don't let Glen Gardner con you into giving him a job."

I called Arethna and confessed.

"What's wrong with Glen Gardner?" I asked. "Does he have a criminal record?"

"No, but obviously he's dangerous for someone like you."

"Arethna, I don't think I've ever been so insulted."

"Of course you have."

Freezing rain fell on Selden Point like syrup, clinging to powerlines and roofs. No one was foolish enough to be on the road. Two days later the Trowbridges' van was once again in their driveway. Brilliant of them to miss the ice storm. In midafternoon I carried over their spider plants. At the door I was met by one of the twins. His brother plowed in from behind and kicked him. The twin at the door looked up at me angrily, as if I kicked him myself.

About an hour after I returned the spider plants, there was a knock. Melanie, I assumed. But no.

Doneta, my sister-in-law, was hardly inside before she began apologizing. "I'm sorry. It's not a fight with Max or anything. Nothing like that. You know how Max is. Worrying about you."

She collapsed onto the couch and pulled an afghan up to her shoulders. The thing about Doneta: At first you don't notice her body, small and softly rounded, an appendage to her puff of yellowish hair. Nevertheless, there is something distinctly attractive about her. Maybe it's because she's so addled and pudding-like, seemingly ready to take the imprint of anyone who bothers to exert the slightest pressure. Like certain wobbly desserts that tempt you to stick a spoon in them.

"Why didn't Max come too?"

"Because he has a job, unlike some of us. I hope it's not a bother, my coming. Max kept telling me you wouldn't mind the surprise."

"You're welcome to stay. Of course. But I know you don't really want to be here. Max forced you to come."

Doneta's eyes brightened with what I hoped weren't tears. "He never forces me. He would do no such thing."

"He forced you. I'm familiar with his ways. He gave you the silent treatment. Until you agreed. He probably hasn't taken you out to a restaurant in months, but he doesn't mind paying your flight to put you on a spying mission."

It was clear that I was enduring an intervention. Doneta's arrival was probably planned at least a week ago. Housesitting for Arethna was part of the intervention too. Everyone meant well, I supposed. I forced myself to simmer down and said, "Doneta, I think you need a vacation. And you're welcome here."

My sister-in-law curled her legs under her bottom. "You're not glad. You're just saying that. A minute ago you looked like you would rip my head off. I don't understand you."

"I can't be any more mystifying than Max."

"Well." Doneta would speak no evil of her husband.

"Don't you ever get tired of being controlled?"

"I don't understand what you mean. You've never understood him and he's your brother."

"What were Max's instructions?"

"I'm to check up on you. To see if you're—absolutely okay. Really, Sheilah, honey. If you don't mind, I could use a drink."

In the morning: grilled cheese sandwiches with tomatoes, for breakfast. Made by Doneta.

"Sheilah, sorry—there were little boys on the porch this morning. They looked exactly alike. I've never been so freaked out in my life. They were reading your newspaper, and they looked at me with hatred in their eyes."

"Oh. The Trowbridge twins. I've never noticed their eyes."

"I'd watch it around them. Two bad seeds."

"Their mother's exceptionally nice."

"It's the nice mothers who give birth to demons. Have you ever seen *Rosemary's Baby?* Max and I are trying for a baby—without luck. I don't mean . . . You know what I mean. Since your mom died. You know how anxious Max gets. If he lost you—I don't know. So he wants kids. Not that a child would replace a sister. Or the reverse. You know what I mean. He's been pretty beat up about you."

I set down my napkin. "Tell Max I'm fine. And tell him I hope you'll have kids. Really."

Doneta was taking on color. Maybe she was like the desert: After a while you learn to detect a variety of hues. "Oh—speaking of sex," she said. "Arethna was concerned about a new bartender you hired? Arethna says he's fatal to women? One of those kinds of guys?"

"You want to meet him, don't you? Admit it."

"And you want to introduce me so you can use me as an excuse to talk to him, huh?"

I asked myself a question I never thought I would pose: Why have I underestimated Max's wife?

Doneta took my car into town—her idea—to pick up "some things," so she was gone when Melanie Trowbridge, her face a knot of worry, arrived at the door that afternoon. I was hoping to tell her about Doneta and wanted the two of them to meet when my sister-in-law returned.

"You haven't seen Terry?" Melanie asked. Her twin sons stood behind her.

When I said I hadn't, Melanie and her boys turned away, calling the ferret's name into the gray afternoon.

I pulled on my coat and began my own search. I tried the swimming pool first, drawing back the tarp. Only leaves scurried on the concrete bottom. Next I tried around the perimeter of the house, and then around the tavern.

Once I got to the rear of the building the sensation of remembered time swept through me. Years ago I spread a blanket on the patch of dirt behind the back exit, under the maple—diseased-looking, bare-limbed now. This was where I read my books, looking up from time to time, catching sight of the tavern's back porch, with its screened windows that weren't boarded up then. Maybe there hadn't been an overflowing dumpster either. And maybe the walls of the tavern didn't look half-scraped, like someone gave up after prepping for a paint job. Was Arethna having money problems?

I shuffled around in piles of frost-stiffened leaves. Hummocky, saturated dirt and ice-blasted grass were visible everywhere the concrete left off. I stepped onto a soft patch and gasped. A discarded sweater, half-buried in slush.

I was working back toward the house when another possibility occurred to me: the patch of soil under the tavern's back porch. The ferret could burrow and from there wriggle up and inside where the wood was decayed.

I fetched the tavern key and was crossing the parking lot when Glen Gardner's truck pulled in. I told him about the ferret situation.

"I can get the rake," he said. "To pull back old leaves or anything. You won't want to use your hands. Wait. I've got plenty of time before we open. You realize it's a pretty good bet that that ferret is frozen."

The back door of the tavern opened hard. Tiny mud tracks splayed everywhere I stepped. I pushed boxes away from the wall. Light shot up from flickering bubbles next to a box of O'Doul's. The ferret shoved free, slinking against my ankle.

Glen scooped up Terry, juggling the squirmy body from hand to hand. I took over, and the animal buried its head under my arm. We were laughing, Glen Gardner and I, and just like that, without preamble, I kissed him. I pulled away almost instantly, my face aching with embarrassment, and apologized. "I didn't mean to do that," I said. "I'm not myself."

"Well, good," he said. "I'm glad you're not yourself. If that's what it takes."

Just then Melanie jogged into the tavern with the boys right behind her, all three anxious to reclaim the ferret. She tugged the animal out from under my arm and gazed into its face—a face that was all furry neck—and admonished the poor hapless thing. "You don't know how to leave anyone alone, do you?"

One of the twins' voices was aimed at me and sounded weirdly low, almost like a man's. He asked, "Did you steal Terry?"

"Of course she didn't," Melanie said. "Terry's the one who steals things. He's taken the channel changer, my tights, lots of the kids' balled up socks. He probably was out looking for more things to steal. Leave it to Terry to try to steal from a tavern."

An hour later the Trowbridge twins popped over with a thank-you card and a package. By the time I turned around from putting the package on the table, the twins had disappeared. I found them in the living room. As soon as they caught sight of me they scooted away. I tried to imagine what the twins saw. The woman in the painting seemed to have enlarged, a trick of the light. Her navel winked. She looked like a tuber dug up from a garden.

I opened the package the boys left. Chocolates. Three of the brown paper skirts were empty and two of the caramels were poked into. A nougat bore teeth marks.

I didn't want to go to the tavern the next night, but Doneta kept insisting. The truth is: I was afraid that Glen Gardner would think I followed him. I didn't know if I could take the humiliation. I resolved to ignore him. I lent Doneta my own coat, given that her jacket was too light for the weather. She protested and kept saying "I'm fine. I'm fine."

"We both should bundle up. See. I'm wearing layers. Plus this hat." I pushed my crocheted cap down until it covered most of my forehead.

"What a great hat," Doneta said. "It's kind of quiche."

"Quiche?"

"That's not the right word, is it? Damn my high-school French."

As we passed the pool I thought I heard something and checked under the tarp. I told Doneta about the deer that had fallen in—to make sure she didn't think I was anxious about nothing.

"Poor little deer," she said. "That must have been such a surprise. You're walking around and whoops. The moral: Keep out of people's yards. Do you suppose the deer was drunk? I hope so."

On the other side of the bar Glen Gardner was drawing a beer. Doneta didn't wait to be introduced. "So you're Glen!" she exclaimed, angling a shoulder at him over the bar railing. Glen grinned, hunching his shoulders, copying Doneta's posture.

I claimed a table for the two of us. It took Doneta a few minutes of chatting up Glen Gardner before she swung over, clutching beers for both of us. She whispered into my ear. "My God. No wonder Arethna worried you'd rush to get involved with him. I feel pretty helpless around him too."

From behind the bar, Glen gave me a quick nod, his eyes communicating sympathy.

After a few minutes I said to Doneta, "Maybe I shouldn't ask, but do you always drink like this?" Around us, men's eyes were glowing moistly in the near dark. I was reminded of a cartoon I once saw of a cave filled with bears.

"It's been months since I've had even a glass of wine," Doneta said. "This is just—fun. A blowout. Soon I'll have to go back to the evil land of sobriety. Don't worry. It's not like every day is *Carnevale*. What is it we're doing tomorrow?" Before I could answer, she said, "Let's walk the beach, visit any store that's open, and then drink ourselves into oblivion."

"You've needed a vacation, haven't you?"

"All right. I give up. Your brother is hell. Absolute hell. I'm tempted to shoot myself in front of him. At least I'm not tempted to shoot him. And you know exactly what I mean. And you're not even married to him. I'm hungry, by the way."

Several men sat near us, listening to Doneta, watching her throw her head back. She kept crossing and uncrossing her legs. I had visions again—visions of her as a caramel pudding with a spoon stuck in her middle. I worried that a stranger in the bar would follow us home.

I didn't say goodbye to Glen Gardner, and later I worried that by not saying goodbye I was proving I was overly interested in him. Like I was engaged in reverse stalking.

"Do you always wake up like this?" Doneta asked the next morning in an infuriatingly chipper voice.

"Like what?"

"Like you've been crushed. You were just as bad yesterday. You're worse than Max. Are you sure you're not clinically depressed?"

"I'm too tired to know what I am. It's called lack of coffee."

The coffee Doneta made was so strong I could taste grains on my tongue. We took our cups into the living room. I imagined that Doneta would want to go everywhere in town, given her stated preferences last night. Instead she said, "I just need a quiet day. Feet up. I want to hear everything. Don't look agog. I won't be here long at all. I have to return to Max with concrete reassurances. Quotes from you. The works."

"Max should have come himself."

"Are you kidding? You're kidding. Like he can communicate. Come on. He leaves that up to me. Think of this—you have power too. It just depends on what sort of man will resent it."

I was desperate to change the subject and asked her to turn around. "What do you think of this painting?"

"Max never mentioned it."

"Therefore it doesn't exist."

"No, I just meant he told me about this place in detail. He loved those vacations. I heard about every room and about the adults passing out in the parking lot by the tavern. Maybe this painting wasn't here back then?"

"Oh, it was here."

"Well, we're both better looking than that hag, and that should give us hope. I like how she's just lying there like a big old lazy ass."

"Something to aspire to," I said.

"Does the painting have a name?"

I examined the plaque, tarnished a soft brown. "It's called 'After the Dance.'"

"I'm sure that's a euphemism. Listen. There are lots of men in the sea."

"You mean fish."

"No, I mean men. You should take a cruise. And remember—you're not alone. You've got Arethna, Max, me. Glen Gardner—all he could talk about was you. Those men in the bar. Who do you think they were looking at?"

"You."

"Well, that's true. But it's because I gave them something to look at. There's someone already out there—for you. Waiting for the signal."

"The hand signal?"

"I'm sure that's another euphemism."

The next day Doneta asked for a lift to the airport. "I've abused your hospitality for too long," she said.

I hadn't known she was leaving so soon. "I was just getting to know you—at last," I told her.

A sensation of sickness overcame me in the airport, with its white shadowless light, and the insecticide-like smell, and the feeling that we're all in a kill box and scrambling around.

A purse, sunflower patterned, was tucked under Doneta's armpit. She had straightened her normally puffy hair, and her eyeliner was thicker on her lower lids. It was hard not to hug her. Then I did.

"No Fear," Doneta said. "Not that I'm nervous about flying or anything. I just remembered that I've always wanted mud flaps that say that. No Fear. Like the truckers."

"Reassure Max," I said, and then—with a leap that made me more sick to my stomach, I added, "Tell him I'm fine and that I miss him. And reassure him. Repeatedly."

"That's kind of my full-time job. Reassuring him. I should confess. I'm not going directly back home. I have a couple of old friends in Coral Gables. So I rebooked. Don't tell Max. Let him think I'm still here."

Now I understood the summer handbag peeking from under Doneta's arm.

She went on, "Yeah. I've jumped at the chance for recuperation. And a little fun. Honey, listen. Don't be ashamed anymore. You were a little overly enthusiastic about a coworker, but I'll tell Max you're fine now."

"I was just—I thought differently then."

"You were kind of acting like you were, you know, a man. I guess there are still some things we can't get away with."

I was tempted to defend myself, to say I hadn't stalked Eddie without provocation, hadn't done anything much, except be mistaken. I was also tempted to ask, "Who are you really seeing in Florida?"

Then again, who was I to interrogate her? And what does it mean when you see your neighbor and her two sons as male genitalia and your sister-in-law as a pudding? I thought then, too, that maybe you have to be ashamed of yourself and humbled before people reveal the hidden parts of themselves, or before you're capable of seeing those parts. Just at that moment Doneta changed form. She wasn't a pudding but a sandwich—she'd eaten enough of them in the past days. I had a vision of her as one of those stacked sandwiches. A club sandwich. When in reality she was a brilliant tactician on the order of Marcus Aurelius.

I never did get a chance to introduce Doneta to Melanie Trowbridge. I would have liked to see them side by side. They were beginning to represent something to me besides genitalia, puddings, and sandwiches. You could be like Melanie Trowbridge, and you're the beleaguered star in a situation comedy about your family—and everything's funny and you can complain about your children because tragedy hasn't hit them. Or you could be sneaky, like Doneta, and only pretend to be what everyone thought you were, and then, even if you blew your cover, if you blew it with the right person—say, your sister-in-law—you knew you were safe. The person you trusted would never tell because she knew too much about shame.

It was the same with Eddie. He had loved me—for almost two months, before he accused me of stalking him. That was the part of the story that was always left out. I hadn't said anything, nor had he, about what happened earlier between us. He was married. He knew I wouldn't betray him.

Eddie used to spend some nights at my place, used to contact me every day, and then stopped cold. That's when I began following him and doing stupid embarrassing things. The truth is: It was like being taken over when I stalked Eddie, like someone was steering me. Or like I was the host to a parasite, a terrible gross worm. Being wanted—it was like a worm that delivers a drug right into your bloodstream. Then you're unwanted, but the worm wants more.

At least I had wanted something. And now I didn't want what I had wanted. I could start over, knowing more about what I was capable of. How far I could trust myself, at least. I suppose that was my revelation—up until then.

In the middle of that night—hours after Doneta left—I woke, startled. Someone was in the house. In the foyer. The door of my bedroom pounded. A spattering of sounds like rainfall on cement. I opened the door to the furry, stocking-like length of the Trowbridges' ferret. I studied the animal, trying not to think it was ugly. No, but sleek and restless, and persistent. The animal, in turn, was studying me.

I called Melanie. She appeared at my door without the twins. Jack was still in bed, she said. The twins were sleeping too. She picked up the ferret, snuggling her face against its fur as the valiant thing struggled to break free.

She murmured, half asleep: "You're just a wild one, aren't you? You just need your adventures, don't you? You criminal, don't you know you're loved?"

Experimental Theater

You slept in until noon, when Rebecca popped over and announced you were going with her to a matinee—The Community Playas. "We can deride this together. It's an original play—don't weaken—by Edgar Winebatten. He's a cousin of my editor, so I have to pretend to be interested."

"You have to write a review?"

"No. They're closing after today. We don't really do reviews. It's more a puff piece, a feature about The Community Playas. Why does that name bother me so much? It sounds like they're a bunch of fat-assed adulterers. What have we got here? A bunch of community playas. I'll have to find something nice to say. That's why you need to come with me."

"Me?" You were more baffled than flattered. You suspected Rebecca wanted you to accompany her because you were accustomed to failure. You worked in Customer Service, or Customers Raging as you called it. You listened to people complain and exhausted them with sympathy and then redirected their calls.

The ushers were out of programs by the time you and Rebecca arrived. As soon as you sat down, the curtains opened and two men squatted on the edge of the stage and then dangled their legs near the front row. The men pivoted their wrists and made circles with their right hands.

"They're fishing," Rebecca whispered, awe in her voice.

"Lookee there," said the bigger man, in suspenders.

"Lookee there," said the smaller man, in suspenders.

This went on for a full five minutes. You checked your watch. It was 2:12. Rebecca squirmed. Her arm rest trembled. She sideways-glanced at you apologetically while you smiled to give the impression you were enjoying two of the most boring activities possible to witness: fishing and mime.

A woman in the front row flopped forward. She was *flopping* because her legs were bound with sequined shiny material. It took a while for you to realize she was supposed to be a mermaid, a mermaid sitting right in the audience. When you came into the theater you had noticed her cotton candy blonde spun hair, but you hadn't seen below her neck.

"Lookee there," the smaller man said, swinging his legs off the side of the stage wildly, like a kid. Was he supposed to be the young son or grandson of the other man? He looked about forty-five.

"Lookee there," said the presumably older man, pointing to the mermaid.

You leaned forward to watch the mermaid slumping in the center aisle. In a film, terrible things would have happened by now: a helicopter's blade slicing one of the fishermen in half or a squid pulling both men off the dock or seagulls pecking out their eyes.

Next an enormous man with an ax and suspenders took giant steps across the stage. Paul Bunyan? His overalls were cut off above the knee, and his thighs were oiled. His eyebrows looked mortified, meeting in an inverted V in a futile attempt to crawl off his head. His hands resembled enlarged ping-pong paddles. And then you saw that his hands actually were encased in ping-pong paddles.

"Lookee here," Paul Bunyan said. He pulled out a hand puppet of a weasel.

Beside you, Rebecca whispered, "No."

"I see what you want," said Paul Bunyan as he attempted to move the weasel's mouth with his paddle hand. "You want a period costume. A love song. A concubine."

During times like this, when you can't concentrate and can't leave, where there's nothing to occupy your mind, almost anybody starts hating their surroundings. Then you have to ask yourself: What specifically is so wrong about what you are experiencing? After all, you've seen plenty of odd or offbeat moments in other plays: an actor's pants falling off, the nurse in *Romeo and Juliet* forgetting every other line, actors who dissolved in helpless tears, the blonde in *Noises Off* who at curtain call shouted *Shit asses!*

You have nothing against experimental theater, so why should you be having such a bad time, like you were strapped in your seat by the air pressure of pity for the actors? Like what transpired on stage was worse than that other excruciating category: bad musical theater starring children who sing. It wasn't that you were closed-minded, was it? Several of the plays you bought tickets for in the last five years could be classified as experimental. In one performance, a man in the bottom half of a horse costume sipped milk through a seven-foot straw, and you enjoyed that.

When bored, you often engage in erotic fantasies. Frustratingly, Paul Bunyan was the only candidate for your fantasies. And he wore a beard and sideburns that wouldn't have met the approval of a third grader portraying Lincoln. Please let my mind fantasize about him, you told yourself. Dear life, please grant such riches to your unworthy daughter.

Your former husband—small boned, with his stretchy, mobile face— you were developing an allergy to those attributes in any man. And yet the enormous man on stage, wide of shoulder, wide of forehead—you couldn't imagine your way into fantasies about him, despite his spectacular un-resemblance to your former husband. Your one and only fantasy at that moment: clutching Paul Bunyan's giant paddle hand and dragging him off the stage.

Clapping. A bearded bald man in a turtleneck strode across stage and continued clapping: vigorous, shoulder-shaking clapping.

"No. All wrong! Terrible. Hopeless. Victor, pull your pants up."

Sounds of hammering, sawing offstage.

"Can you keep it down?" the clapping man shouted.

You understood then. You were in agreed-upon reality after all. Or in partially agreed-upon reality. An experimental theater company's director was interrupting a particularly bad rehearsal. You had been watching a play within a play. Within minutes a romance ensued, as well as two monologues on the attractions of atheism.

That was when Rebecca stiffened beside you—which turned out to be a good thing, her stiffening. Otherwise you would believe she set you up, because there on the stage, after a blistering eternity of boredom, arrived a woman whose life you almost ruined. You can say "almost" because she married Jason after all. And who was coming up behind

Abigail on the stage but Jason himself? By then your right leg was doing this galloping thing, and you had to use all your willpower to stop your leg from running off on its own. You couldn't hear what was being said onstage because the tide of your loud hatred was rising. And you watched as Abigail turned her cruel eyes to the third row, where you sat in the center seat, her face rippling with awareness of your presence. Beside you, Rebecca, staring ahead, was frozen until she put her hand on your arm to console you. And who crossed the stage next but Glen Meekamp, whom you actually kicked last February while he was on crutches? You will never get over your shame. His wife entered from stage left, carrying a flower vase and wearing a maid's uniform, and you remembered how after you refused to be the surrogate mother of her child she said your womb was not good enough for any living thing.

You told yourself to close your eyes for the remainder of the performance. But you couldn't close your eyes at all. You watched the play. Ninety more minutes. No intermission.

You and Rebecca didn't join the relatives holding bouquets in the lobby and waiting for the actors to appear in street clothes. No, you two walked into the last of the afternoon sunshine. Rebecca's truck was parked blocks away—evidence of her aversion to parallel parking.

"Can you forgive me?" she asked. "Although Paul Bunyan was incredible. I know him." Already you could tell that Rebecca wasn't going to bring up anything personal, and you were grateful.

"You know everyone."

"No. Not that mermaid woman. How can I write about the travesty we just witnessed?"

You couldn't answer. You had watched people who despised you and who couldn't escape from your gaze. You saw people you knew too well wear funny clothes and forget their lines. You heard them strain to make their voices carry. Basically, you witnessed them pleading to be believed. Pretending to be who they weren't. Like who they were in actual life was never enough. You wondered if you drove them to it.

It was still daylight, although a neon light stuttered in the dry cleaner's sign. Through the windows of the bridal boutique two wedding gowns floated like crisp ghosts. If you hadn't been in a dark theater for so long, tucked away from the normal contours of reality, would you at that moment have breathed the air so deeply, would you have been so fully aware of your lungs? And would the stipples of green-yellow on the tips of the maple leaves have looked quite so raised, like actual bumps? You couldn't answer that yet.

Before reaching her truck you told your friend you needed to keep on walking. Alone. As you walked you asked yourself: What if what you experienced in that audience was transformative somehow? You got to see under bright lights the people you hurt and the people you were hurt by. Whatever sins you committed or whatever sins were committed against you could hardly trouble you now.

Your steps became lighter and lighter. Maybe theater worked on the soul more than on the mind? Because, really, your spirit just got a good washing. The past was full of petty cares, and only now could you see how petty those cares had been. Those people who hurt you and whom you hurt—they filled the stage with their humanness, their big vulnerable humanness out there for everybody to see and applaud. They were applauded loudly and long for their bravery, which is a kind of vulnerability.

Soon you were just a block from your apartment, right by the Wells Fargo bank where in late spring one tree filled with buttery platters of blossoms. That tree held its own bouquets, as if every day, no matter what, that tree rewarded itself for a performance. Enormous, those blossoms. Enormous. Almost the size of a human head, those blossoms. Enormous. Well, big deal. Show-offs.

The Wrath of the Norsemen

When I consulted Audrey about my decision we were in a restaurant that smelled vaguely of parmesan cheese and old carpeting—a partly sweet, almost burning smell. Audrey was concentrating on the bowl of olive oil dipping sauce. A fly floated amidst the rosemary, its little arms crossed.

"I'm not going," I announced. I had the sensation of sidestepping a calamity—like in an old movie where a piano falls forty floors but a man walks on, unscathed, dust shooting up behind him.

Audrey reached across the table and squeezed my hand. For all her talk of being sensible, she is a woman of supernatural empathy, the bringer of gift baskets to sick friends and the purchaser of sympathy cards on the occasion of the death of cats.

"You know what?" she said. "You'll go. You've already registered. It will be good for you. Besides, they'll never give you your money back—or not all of it."

The camp was devoted to men like me, men who suffered from anxiety. Normal everyday anxiety for everyday normal people.

Sunlight poured into the car, flecked with sparkles. I imagined that outside the car it was so hot that the pines that dominated the landscape were boiling in their resin. I calmed myself by reading billboards: Home of the Croissant, the Waffle Parlor, Dumpling Dan's. Shadowy blobs in the distance: beef cattle. Another patch of billboards: Advanced Heart Care at Pocono Hospital and then, in devilish irony, The Cheesecake Factory, followed by, fast approaching, a graveyard.

I was feeling guilty on the drive because I hadn't been entirely honest with Audrey. I wasn't only going to the camp because of anxiety. I was going because I had learned the camp was run by someone I knew in high school: Julian Pusser. Now that's a name that can ruin a kid's life, and maybe that's why Julian developed certain capacities. He believed he could channel voices. Old de Groot, principally.

Julian Pusser used to say that Old de Groot strangled him from the inside, like thick hands clutched ladder rungs inside his throat so that Julian would mouth whatever the spirit of Old de Groot demanded. Julian would channel that voice while some of us guys stared at him. Because it was pretty convincing. Julian said that when Old de Groot was alive he wore a frilled collar over a raw neck as reddish-pink as a vulture's. Old de Groot. Julian could gargle and vomit but couldn't get him out of his throat once Old de Groot wanted in. Old de Groot, a mean dirty-minded freak who never had a good word to say to anyone when he was living. He wasn't going to change his habits now that he was dead.

Julian said he didn't even understand what Old de Groot was saying— except it sounded like Dutch. When he stopped gabbling, Julian shook his shoulders, shivered, and became himself again. I remember one time I asked what it was like to be Old de Groot's "host." Julian said it was like a meatball fell on gravel and kept rolling, picking up pebbles, and that meatball flew up into your mouth and started talking.

That was the Julian Pusser I knew. I also knew about some of Julian Pusser's other tricks. I confess that years ago I fell for one—and it's a miracle I'm not dead.

I arrived at the camp in late afternoon. Standing at a picnic table registering, by all appearances, was a guy who looked like a Viking. Gold hair twisted into a thick braid hung down his back. In the heat his T-shirt was stippling like pushpins on a military map. Leaning against his leg was a backpack with a sleeping bag roll and a water canteen. "Is it okay that I brought along a machete?" the Viking asked. I couldn't hear an answer from the staffer. When it was my turn the staffer considered me with what looked like relief.

"Where is everyone?" I asked.

"It's FOB time—flat-on-back time. We ask that you gather yourself in preparation for the commitment dinner. You have a half hour."

"Gather myself?"

"Turn inward. Contemplate your purpose. In silence."

"Oh, shit." It was the Viking. He had stopped in his tracks several feet away but apparently was listening.

Flat-on-back time. I had a cabinmate: George, a market analyst. I'll let you make up your own mind about George. That night I left the dinner early, before anybody spoke or made a commitment. I waited back in the cabin and counted on hearing from George about what happened later. I knew Julian Pusser would show up and give one of his talks about ways to defeat anxiety. I was just too nervous to attend. When George returned he wasn't alone. He brought back the Viking and a gnarly guy named Kevin with the widest cheeks I'd ever seen on a man. George liked to keep at least one other person around him the way some people like to have companion animals.

I wasn't paying much attention to the conversation until Kevin began describing Julian Pusser. "He doesn't move. He hardly blinks when he talks."

George asked, "What are you talking about?"

"I'm talking about our leader," Kevin said. "Julian Pusser. He has enormous self-control. Not to blink."

George sat down next to me on my cot, punching the mattress with both fists, and said, "This isn't as thin as my mattress." He turned his attention back to Kevin. "How does he get anyone to listen to him? That's the mystery. With a name like Julian Pusser." Hearing George, I momentarily felt transported back to high school.

"That's nothing," Kevin said. "I know a guy named Barton Peuker."

"You got the first session, right?" George asked. "Out of everybody, you got the first private session. What did Pusser tell you?"

"He told me to stop hiding."

"You seem to be in plain sight to me."

"Julian, my man Julian Pusser, advised me: Get visible. Be seen." Kevin smiled, flinging his arms out. "Plus, he told me to make a gnome hut. With sticks. A little homemade stick hut for sheltering my fears. It's a spiritual task, he said. He's a man of the spirit and for the spirit."

Kevin called over to the Viking: "What about you? Do you have a private appointment too?"

The Viking, sitting by the door and staring at the ceiling, told Kevin that his appointment wasn't until four o'clock on Tuesday.

Already by then, out of anyone in that cabin and anyone in the camp, except for Julian Pusser, the Viking interested me most. I couldn't figure out why such a vigorous-looking guy was at the retreat. Wasn't he too young to feel anxious?

Up close, he looked especially young. A peach scum of new beard filmed his chin. Maybe I got so interested in him because every time I looked at him I thought of the movie *The Vikings*. Tony Curtis and Kirk Douglas. In the movie Kirk Douglas rides a pony so tiny that Douglas's feet nearly touch the ground. Ragnar—Ernest Borgnine—voluntarily jumps to his death into a wolfhound pit, dying with his sword in his hand. I ask you: Why didn't Ragnar just stab all the wolfhounds? Janet Leigh—she was Tony Curtis's wife, and in the movie you felt the sexual tension between them anyhow. There's a scene where the Vikings are going to assail the castle and one of the extras is smiling in this goofy cheerful way. Brilliant. And then there's the witch's warbling call to Odin when Tony Curtis is chained in the crab pool and the tide goes out. And when Kirk Douglas as Einar busts through a chapel window feet first he cries out to a praying monk, "Take your magic elsewhere, holy man!" Julian and I used to watch that movie together a lot. For a class project we even wrote a collaborative series of haikus about the movie and got in trouble for the words *horny* and *bastard*. I still remember those haikus— although maybe not exactly:

> Heads prickle with prongs.
> Eric's horny heart thunders.
> Northumbria, huh?

> Take time to pillage!
> Let every vat boil with foam!
> Dance on oars, Einar!

Big knees drag on ground:
Einar rides baby pony.
Janet can't stand him.

Einar and Eric:
Brothers! Sorry about that
stab. Bastard, you're home!

"I guess there are people who could find value-added because of
Pusser," George was saying. "I'm not all that impressed yet, but I guess
what he's selling sells."

I couldn't resist. "Obfuscation?" My voice came out in a bleat.

"That sells," George said, patting the mattress between us. "Sounds
like a men's cologne. People feel important, hearing a word like that.
Obfuscation. I bet you felt important using that word. Yeah, that word
sounds like one of those unisex colognes. They're not coming back
again ever, by the way. Women don't want to smell like their dad. It's
that simple. I will say Pusser's got intense eyes. They're like eyes that
see by the light that falls on a playground, and you're walking past
and thinking I bet those kids get splinters in their hands, and that old
tire swing has probably been the source of more than one concussion.
Those are his eyes."

Those were his eyes. I hadn't realized those were his eyes when Julian
and I were kids. As George kept talking, what felt like a barbed hook
ripped through my chest. When the squeezing subsided into a crackling
dart I reflected on the fact that the signs of a heart attack are vague.
One website I consulted months earlier listed as a primary symptom
"feelings of impending doom." That couldn't be abnormal. If I hadn't endured these symptoms for years—acute anxiety masquerading as heart
trouble—I would be headed for the ER.

It was the Viking who said to Kevin, "What's with your face?"

Kevin's hand flew to his nose. Then he pulled it away and gawked at
his own fingers.

"Do you need to lie down?" I said.

The Viking was crouching over Kevin like an umpire and saying, "Lean forward. Pinch your nose."

"No big deal," Kevin said, smearing his chin. "No big deal."

"You look like you've got a head wound," George said. "Isn't this supposed to happen to—you know, to non-adults?" Blood sprayed onto Kevin's sandals.

The Viking grabbed some paper towels George kept on his side of the cabin, handed one bunch to Kevin, and spread the others to catch blood. The Viking kept mopping up, patting Kevin's back, then using his own shirt to blot blood from Kevin's chin and repeating the cycle.

"It's not a big deal," Kevin repeated. By then his teeth were red. "It must be the altitude. My body is more sensitive than I am. I've seen a lot of my own blood. It never fails to surprise me." He spread out his hands. Inside each palm: more blood. "I just never stopped getting these nose problems. When I'm anxious, you know? It's not easy being here."

George was laughing. "You'll need to dunk your head in a bucket, guy." He pointed his sandal toward the Viking. "Come on, buddy, it's not like you're bailing out a rowboat. Calm down. Take your time."

"It's like a faucet," Kevin said. "It's turning off. I can feel it drying up in there. Thanks, guys. I mean it, thanks." A bubble of blood peeped out of his nose.

Abruptly the Viking sat on the floor, his face covered by his gold mop of hair.

In the middle of the night the door banged open and cool air was sucked into the cabin. I switched on the light. The Viking was standing inside the doorway. By then George was backed up against the rear wall. I hadn't even seen him run out of bed.

The Viking breathed heavily and informed us, "I got a discount by saying I'd sleep in the woods. Then I got lost. I came here to gain a sense of direction and I got lost."

"You're lucky. You could have stayed lost," George said.

The Viking sat with his back against the door. After he started to snore, an unexpectedly light snore—like someone sucking an ice cube with a coffee straw—George said, "He's cheap. He bargained for the cheapest rate. Now he's afraid of the woods. Meanwhile we pay full rate."

"He's just a kid."

George snorted. "I would hate to think the program isn't getting the financial support it needs."

A tall man in an elevator handed me a sack. The sack was heavy—so heavy that I woke up and translated: He left me holding the bag. In the dream it was Julian Pusser who handed me the bag.

The next morning, stepping over the Viking curled by the door, I walked out onto the grounds. The dawn light was coming through the pines in shafts. Raindrops clung to bushes. I hadn't listened to so many birds in a long time or seen so many pine needles shining or so much thick brush shuddering with living things. The sizzling sound in the air made me think of Tarzan movies and how sounds were recycled movie to movie—a shriek and a swishing of leaves, the camera panning to high branches. In the next scene Tarzan was standing in front of a movie of a charging rhino. In the end Tarzan sequestered Jane. It was a perfect world for a misanthrope. Rope bridges, towers. Tall plants. Like Pier 1 Imports. Maybe I'd ask Audrey to marry me—ask again. We could have an actual family before it was too late. Even mass murderers were known to have wives. And here I was—a nonviolent man, regrettably not an entirely well-toned specimen. Granted, "A fly swatter could put you to death," as Audrey once told me before she apologized. So what was Audrey waiting for? Other than someone else? Wasn't I supposed to be the one to resist commitment? I resisted nothing. I always felt better around Audrey. In fact, without her to talk to, my insomnia was back. I glanced up the slope at the staff quarters and instinctively ducked my head.

When I circled back to my cabin, the Viking was awake and rubbing his eyes. I was happy to see him. He struck me as being like a giant golden rabbit's foot—a token of luck for anyone but the rabbit and maybe the Viking himself. George was awake too, pulling a shirt over his head and then glaring at the Viking with disdain.

The wall of the cabin shook. I recognized Kevin's voice.

"Can't you knock like other people?" George said, opening the door.

"I'm not like other people."

The Viking stood up. He seemed taller than yesterday, like a good night's sleep had stretched him. "What did you hit the wall with?" he asked.

"A squirrel." Kevin added quickly, "It was not what you might call a live squirrel."

"After you bury that squirrel," the Viking said to Kevin, his voice stern, "why don't you come down to the meeting hall and drink some coffee."

"I think it's actually elk droppings," Kevin said. "It's not exactly coffee."

"So why don't you come down and drink some elk droppings. First, take care of that squirrel." The Viking's voice sounded not only stern but strained, like it was an effort for him to engage in a conversation of this length.

"I don't know why you're so sensitive about that dead squirrel," George said. "It's not like all of Kevin's kinfolk ate squirrels."

The gnome hut was easy to help Kevin make and wasn't heavy, just awkward to carry. Gradually, the other men were out far ahead on the trail back to camp, the Viking towering over George, with a new guy called Dylan gesticulating every few feet at something.

Kevin, who tended to be slow anyway, waited for me as I grappled with his gnome hut. When we were side by side on the path he spoke in a low voice. "I want to tell you something."

The gnome hut dug into my wrists. "Okay," I said. "Tell me something."

"It's about Mark."

"Who's Mark?"

Kevin outlined a refrigerator in the air.

"Oh, the Viking," I said. "Mark." I would never get used to calling the Viking by that name.

"I know why he's here," Kevin said. "His in-laws."

To think that the Viking—Mark—was forced to come here at the command of his in-laws. Sad.

Kevin explained that Mark's father-in-law saw the ad for the retreat, even set up the appointment for an individual counseling session for the Viking. Because, Kevin said, of what happened to the Viking's wife and his little boy. "I'll give you the basic version. Mark and his wife had a fight. After too many beers Mark was sleeping away from his wife in a room off the kitchen. He woke only once maybe. Or was more likely half-awake when he heard a ripping sound above him, like carpet being torn up. Nothing. Squirrels in the ceiling. Nothing. He fell back to sleep. The fire had already spread into the walls. They passed away—the wife and the little boy. The kid was four years old."

I set the gnome hut down.

"How do you know all this?"

"I asked Mark why he was here. He treated it like a punishment—telling me. Part of his punishment was telling me."

"And now you're telling me."

"I'm not telling anyone else. Not George. Don't worry about that." Kevin picked up the gnome hut. "Mark should be watched. He brought a machete. That's weird in itself. He wants to be a chef, though, so that's a good thing. A machete could cut up a lot of fruits. That shows advance planning for a possible future. But still, he should be watched."

"How does being a chef—?"

"That's what she was—his wife."

I was lucky. Not once had I run into Julian Pusser. I went to a session on "Dream Shifting." I was sure Julian wouldn't be there. We were supposed to crawl down into a hole in our minds and meet our spirit guides. We were warned that some people could never crawl down into their hole because they kept getting spewed out to the upper world. I was doing pretty well at mentally crawling down into a hole until the dream-shifting leader put on a recording of drums and I was startled back into my own life.

I'd attended two sessions on meditation and gone on a "wildflower walk" and managed to avoid all the night sessions where Julian Pusser gave talks. Sitting by the campfire seemed pretty safe. According to George, Julian Pusser disappeared after his talks.

The firelight shook and flared comfortingly, and after a while I was the only one left, and then the Viking showed up. We were silent for a long time, companionably looking into the campfire, until he said, "I went to the private session."

"Was it okay?"

"I know Kevin told you about me. I told that guy, that Pusser guy, about what happened. I made myself tell him. He looked at me and wouldn't talk at first. All I felt about myself—it was there. Right there in him."

Across the way a figure limped off toward the lower cabins. A pickup door slammed.

"He said I shouldn't let myself get away with it. He said I wanted them to die. He said I knew what I was doing when I fell back to sleep. He said I was slow, that he'd noticed how slow I was right away. You like to be slow, he said. He called it resistance."

"When he was telling you these things—how did he look, you know, what was his expression like?"

The Viking paused. A chunk of log fell into the fire and flames snapped. "He looked—happy."

The night was growing cooler and damp, like my face was being passed over with a wet brush. Dread locked my knees. Julian was visible in a window of the largest cabin on the rise. The cabin—it was a trick of the dark—was breathing like something made of cells from a lung. My heart was doing strange things. I thought I couldn't take another step. And then Julian was crouching to fit his upper body into the window frame. "Hey!" he called out. "I wondered when you were going to admit you knew me."

I managed to stumble up the steps. Once inside, I was struck by the smell of wet ash. A smell as intense as if the cabin was recently set on fire. Mold speckled the floorboards. A vague piney rot had to be distilled in the walls. A box of cereal had fallen on its side on the coffee table. Some nongeneric cheap cereal. Was it a sign that Julian might be the ascetic he convinced others he was, a spiritual man who lived on wilted cornflakes and liked to breathe the fetid air inside this cottage?

The smell in the room got worse: wet towels left to harden and crust. I sat on a rickety kitchen chair. Julian lowered himself into an armchair and smiled in a way I remembered. "Where have you been hiding all these years?" he asked. He lifted his hands, and the chair's armrests gave off a greasy shine.

"I haven't been hiding."

It was harder than I expected to keep my eyes on him.

"Listen," he said. "You have problems. I tried to help you. But you know what, I can employ you."

I managed to say, "I thought I had problems."

"A long time ago I saw you for what you could be. Except for one thing. Where it counts you never pushed the envelope. But I saw—I did see what you could be."

I thought of what he must have meant. The woman who swerved filed a report. The newspaper reported the incident. But no one ever found out about me. I couldn't be sure Julian had even heard that I followed through. The thing was: I didn't feel braver afterwards.

I remembered the reason for my walk up the path to Julian's cabin and asked, "What'd you do to Mark?"

"Who's Mark?"

"The big kid. The unhappy one. You had an appointment."

"If he's not satisfied I'll meet with him again."

"That's not what he needs."

"All right. You know what he needs. That's reassuring. I'm reassured. I'm not refunding anything. I don't think the retreat's been all that bad, do you?" An easy smile, a shrug. "All my life I've wanted to help people. Some people are easier to help than others. You shouldn't drink. That's friendly advice. You and drinking—not good. Remember that."

"It doesn't work," I said. "What you're trying to accomplish with me." I made myself look into Julian's eyes.

"It never did. You were always good at self-hatred. You should see your face right now."

I was such a naïve kid. Julian had been practicing on me. Practicing his "techniques." He was always smarter, always the leader. For a long time I pretty much worshipped him. Lying down on the highway was the test. A mother of three was driving home from night shift at the hospital. She swerved. I could have ruined her life. I was supposed to lie there—a challenge, a test, to see what I was made of—and I was supposed to jump up at the last opportunity. I didn't jump up. Once I was on my back on that pavement it was like I was paralyzed.

I don't remember walking out of Julian's cabin. I do remember heading down the path, my head whirling, before I felt my body falling into space without landing.

The next thing I knew, the Viking—Mark—was holding me up, and somehow my head was hanging out the window of the cabin and I was recalling something I'd forgotten for decades: In middle school I did two book reports on the life of the great baseball pitcher Dizzy Dean. How did I get away with that?

The retreat wasn't over for two days. What were those men going to tell their wives or partners when they got home? Did they believe the retreat had revealed anything, changed them, made them less anxious, less startled, less prone to insomnia and night horrors?

I was leaving early. As a parting gift, Kevin gave me his gnome shelter. It leaned against the cabin railing like a depressed rodent's nightmare. Before he headed out for a meditation session George said that by leaving I was wasting the opportunity of a lifetime. Mark, the Viking, was curled on the floor in a corner while I packed. He had gone back to sleep after breakfast and missed the testimonials.

When the Viking lifted his head, he looked like he'd forgotten where he was. He looked that confused. And that's when I asked him to do a big favor for me.

I pounded the gas pedal, telling myself I could reverse the sensations I had been getting nearly every day by then, the pliers of anxiety squeezing my ribs. There was a soft snap—something falling off the gnome hut in the backseat. It was like driving a tumbleweed.

Mark, the Viking, had agreed to ride along. I'd told him I was worried about driving back home alone. My anxiety, etcetera. The truth was: I wanted to get him away before Julian did more damage. I knew that the Viking, so determined to be useful, to save anybody from anything, couldn't refuse to help me.

The Viking braced his hand against the dashboard every time we took a curve. I asked, "Why'd you bring the machete?"

"I thought it might come in handy. Like now. Like if you plunge off a bridge I can break a window while we're underwater."

On a billboard up ahead, two people were stuck inside a mammoth champagne glass. A honeymoon resort. I tried to imagine myself and Audrey stuffed in one of those champagne glasses, like shrimp cocktail, and couldn't. I pointed out the billboard to the Viking, who was looking over at me. What was I doing? That billboard wasn't the thing to point out to a guy who had lost his wife.

I concentrated on the scenery to quiet my heart. I tried to imagine telling Audrey about what I was seeing, how ponds were set into the hollows, and the cliffs were dark with slate, with ferns growing in fissures and waving in the wind running down from the hills.

The road ahead was clear—no traffic. Just the same, I kept fearing something in my path—a habit of mine, even though I'd never run over anything, always missed, except once when a rabbit hurled itself at my wheels.

In another mile the Viking proved essential. He took the wheel and got us to the emergency room at Stroudsburg. What saved me: a stent for my heart.

I didn't expect to see the Viking soon after that, and I didn't. But the following summer he stopped by my place. Audrey had at last moved in with me. It only took a heart attack.

"Hello, stranger!" the Viking called out. I was on my lawn picking up sticks from a storm. "Making a new gnome hut?"

I could hardly stop laughing—I was that glad to see him. I had told Audrey about the Viking—Mark—so many times that she'd finally asked me to stop talking about him, and now here the kid was, looking jolly, unscathed. Right away, with pride in his voice, the Viking announced he had a job.

"Great," I said. "Absolutely great."

He said he was going to work for the summer up at the strength retreat in the Poconos.

"Are you crazy? You're kidding, right? You're not going to work for that psychopath. Don't tell me that."

"He helped me out."

"What do you mean he helped you out?"

"I saw him again—before we left. It was just a test, what he was saying to me. Like he was extracting the voices from my head—the worst voices—so I could examine them. He has a method."

"He has a method that could kill people. That's his method."

The Viking clearly didn't want to pursue this idea and said, "I've got somebody I want you to meet—in my truck."

Somebody turned out to be a Malamute. A huge animal with black masklike markings on its white and gray face and a long, dripping tongue. The dog's mouth didn't close, like it was perpetually smiling. Its tail curled up and over and onto its back like a big happy plume.

"He's something. That he is," Mark said. "Yeah, well. They don't allow dogs up at the camp. Liability issues and all that. So many anxious people have trouble with dogs. So I was wondering—."

"No. Audrey—she wouldn't like that. We don't do dogs." I regretting saying "do dogs"—it sounded vaguely sexual. "What I mean is we don't have a lot of room, and we're not dog people. We're not even cat people."

"You mean that? That's something I don't understand. Listen, he eats a lot. He's expensive, but he's a good boy." The Viking turned to the dog for corroboration. "Tell him. You're a good boy." He swung back in my direction. "Actually he's a Malamute. He can't tell you much of anything."

"About Julian Pusser—how could he help you? I don't believe he helped you."

"He told me to get a dog, Rumpus here."

"Rumpus? This is Rumpus? And he tells you to get a dog, but then won't let you bring the dog with you when you work for him? That doesn't bother you?"

"I need the work. He helped me. He has a method." And then the Viking was bending over, hands on his knees, like he was sick. When he unbent he was laughing. "Oh man oh man oh man oh man. The look on your face! I can't keep it up! Man. I gotta stop. I'm gonna have to take you back to the ER if I keep on. Oh man. I'm just kidding with you.

Are you crazy? I'd never work for that asshole. I got a job in Saskatch, New Mexico. Working for a hotel there. Dining services. You believed me about Julian Pusser? Wow. You believed me."

"You were so convincing. Like you had seen him again."

"I did see him. Before you and I left. He was helpful. Actually. He did tell me stuff that was helpful. And to get a dog. He had a message for you too."

"You're kidding again."

"No, man. It was a weird message. I thought you kind of didn't need to hear it then."

"Well, tell me. What did he say?"

"It didn't make sense. Except for one part: He said you need a dog even more than I do. But the rest didn't make sense."

"I don't expect it to make sense."

"Okay. He told me to tell you that the last time he talked to you—at the camp—he said that was Old Goobers talking. Not him."

"You mean Old de Groot."

Mark had to hit the road, and all too soon he drove off. The hours seemed longer than usual afterwards. I was alone because Audrey had left directly from work for dinner and a movie with girlfriends.

It was instinct and a sense of uneasiness that led me, later, to look out the kitchen window. That's when I saw the Malamute, Rumpus. Tied to the walnut tree. I might not have noticed the dog except for the glint of its collar. Otherwise the animal faded into the background, like it was made of camouflage. I hurried and untangled the leash from the tree and led the dog inside. The animal followed dutifully, tail wagging.

"You must be hungry and thirsty. You were abandoned, weren't you? Left to your own devices."

Later, when I talked to Audrey about what happened, I was surprised that I didn't sound angry—and so was she.

"You made it absolutely clear that we weren't taking the dog?" she said, suspicion in her voice. "You're sure you made it clear?"

After I once more recounted the whole incident, Audrey said, "How does your friend know that we won't just let the dog wander off or deliver him to the pound? He's not ours, after all. We don't owe the dog anything. It's a nice-looking animal though." She was petting the dog behind the ears, then shaking its paw, which it kept lifting to her like an overeager salesman. "Aren't you nice-looking?" she said. "Aren't you indeed? Indeedy-do. A handsome fellow."

"Yes, I guess I am," I said, hoping she'd laugh. "Have you ever seen a movie—an old movie called *The Vikings?*"

She thought maybe she had but couldn't remember the plot. I took my time telling her about it. She didn't seem to mind. Soon the dog was resting its head on her feet and sleeping. I told her about the two brothers, how one was a bastard. The brothers didn't know they were brothers. They were trying to kill each other. Audrey said she would watch the movie with me if I picked up a copy or found it on Netflix, but only for the fjords.

Night Walkers

The first thing I noticed about my much-married mother-in-law: She wore jewelry the way generals wear medals—as evidence of successful campaigns where her own blood wasn't shed. And she smoked. More than once I got into coughing fits because of the trapped fumes coming off her sweater, whereupon she told me—absurdly, without irony—that my problem was undiagnosed chronic lung disease.

My mother-in-law possessed an enviable certainty, even though the lights in her eyes were often changing in a way that in anyone else would reveal vulnerability. The thing was, I liked her pretty much instantly, and was grateful for the way she came to believe in me. Upon hearing about my projected divorce from her son, her words proved to be a clear indication of our mutual incomprehension: "Be grateful you don't have children."

My husband used to want a child—at least he claimed to. And then he changed his mind. But the woman he left me for was pregnant with his child, and my husband didn't disguise his excitement about that.

I'd seen pictures of the woman my husband was going to marry. Online. In the only full-length photograph I could find she looked elegant and thin and was wearing a dark fashionable sheath that would make any other woman look like a funeral director. It was impossible to imagine her pregnant. At first. Then I began picturing her as one of those women whose baby hardly makes a ripple.

After I found out the truth I lost my ability to read.

How did it happen? How could reading anything that stirred emotions at more than one level become something I avoided? Suddenly I couldn't stomach fiction or poetry.

And who understood?

Not Beverly. She was the daughter of one of my mother-in-law's friends and must have been recruited to help me. Perversely enough, she wanted me to join a book club.

We were the only two customers in a deli known for its shortbread, and I had the impression that she had followed me. "We've gone from novels to short stories," Beverly said. "No one has the time." She drew her jacket tight, the sleeve ends tucked into her fists. "We're trying, you know, classical works." She pressed her shoulders back, all the better to launch into a prepared speech. "Classic short stories. 'Bartleby the Scrivener.' Stuff like that. You're probably thinking: Why should people join book clubs? Can't they read alone? Does everything require a group—a committee, a forced conversion? What is it about these book clubs? They died out, turned unfashionable, blah blah blah—and then you waited a few years and they were back." She exhaled loudly before going on. "What do you have against book clubs? You wouldn't be forced to read anything you don't want to."

"I just—I like the quiet moments I have with a book. I like my own misunderstandings of the book."

"And we're really together just to, you know—I don't know. And sometimes in the deep past we used to work on puzzles."

"Oh God no."

"Then let's not read." Beverly broke her shortbread in half. "Really. Some of us don't actually read the stories anyway. We could drink? The club's really just social."

"You only read short stories lately? And most of you don't even read them? How could people not at least read a story?" I wanted to ask her: Why can't I just be friends with you, Beverly? Why does a group have to be involved? It would be exhausting enough simply to be your friend, Beverly.

"I know," she said, nodding her head violently. "It's disappointing. But we wouldn't entirely ruin reading for you given that some of us only pretend to read the story each month. My stepfather—wait till you meet him. When we used to read novels he pretended to get upset about the death of Madame Bovary. Like he didn't know it was coming. He taught high school French for twenty-five years. And the Champlain twins, they're shameless. Well, actually, my stepfather's shameless. He had them believing that the novel contains a chapter about the slow death of a horse. But like I said, we're down to short stories. We're maybe the world's laziest book club."

"You want me to join a book club whose members hate reading?"

Beverly was smiling with what appeared to be genuine affection. "So that's why you won't join! You're afraid it will make you feel awkward. It won't. You'll feel superior. It gives us a lot of pleasure to pretend we know what we're talking about when we obviously don't. And we walk at night. We're mentally lazy but not physically lazy—not much. It's a mobile book club. We don't just sit around in somebody's living room and chat anymore. We walk. At night. And talk. Walking. At night. In the woods."

This took some explaining. As I understood it, one member, Enid, who was in her seventies, turned the book club into a walking club. After her husband died she began roaming at night, obsessively. When Beverly couldn't convince Enid to stay home, or at least to walk during the day, Beverly recruited escorts.

I said I would have to think about it—and then, without actually thinking, I said, "All right. Okay. I'll join."

I guess I capitulated because of a burst of hope and a memory. When I was in middle school a group of us girls sneaked out of a pajama party in our long nightgowns and wandered at night by a stream across from the golf course. We were like the spirit of Catherine Earnshaw in *Wuthering Heights*—and ready to jump out of our skin, practically peeping with excitement over the romantic sight we thought we made. We never got caught, and that memory has always warmed me. I still like to imagine us girls sometimes and feel the thrill of it, how powerful we thought we were going to become, given time and the right circumstances and, for me, the right books. Then too, I thought of the story about Beverly's friend Enid—how walking at night served some deep need of hers. And how she had found a way, eccentric as it was, to ease her sorrow. My other hope: I'd start reading again. Eventually. After all, I was joining a book club, even if the members were non-readers (which meant I didn't have to be embarrassed about not reading). At least joining the club was a step toward reclaiming reading, which had been, after all, one of my great pleasures. And a sort of magnifying mirror, or maybe even a mirrorball running around the rim of my life.

The truth about my actual situation was simpler than I've been admitting. I couldn't read anything that was remotely like literature because I couldn't read without thinking of the woman my husband was going to marry—and her relationship to books. She was a writer. Of well-respected erotic literature. That is, of erotica considered innovative and revisionist and transgressive by academics. Academics: often the least discerning and most conventional of readers. Yes, her books were taught in English classes. To students. Out of self-disgust I tried reading one of her slim, deckle-edged, beautifully produced books. The foreword was by somebody whose name I recognized; his essays were in an anthology in one of my literary theory classes in college—a guy who looked like a pimply great-nephew of Harold Bloom. Though the book was written in English it sounded translated from some stiff archaic language spoken only by far-flung Greenlanders isolated on an icy spit of volcanic ash. Anyway, I suffered my way into the book until I couldn't read any more of it, or anything else called literature. To top it off, this woman my husband was intent on marrying after the divorce was finalized, this woman was a librarian. Not just any sort. She worked, if you call it that, at a private library that was slowly being opened to the public through the graces of a foundation supposedly dedicated to preservation. Preservation of its own endowment through manipulation of the tax code. So this woman, this author of erotic literature—"literature" which had as much in common with real literature as "flight literature"—spent her days in a warren of beautiful books. She not only had my husband, she had my preferred life. Except I wouldn't be writing erotic literature. Or at any rate, what I wrote wouldn't be both delicate and raw in that bewildering way, with footnotes.

So books repelled me. Which was horrible. Once an English major, always an English major: that is, a person consumed by optimism who holds out hope that a solitary pursuit might someday accrue a public function—and so this person could be left alone to read. And now I couldn't. I wanted to be comforted by books again. Or absorbed by them again. Or challenged by them again. I did not want to feel rage every time I looked at a book. And so the fact that members of Beverly's club didn't actually read filled me with contradictory emotions, including relief. Plus, I could hardly stand being alone anymore.

So began my membership.

There were seven of us: Beverly; her stepfather, Simon; Jorge, recently divorced and wildly good-looking and attractively unaware of how attractive he was; the Champlain twins—brutal little women who seemed angry I was joining them; and Enid, the widow whose grief compelled her to walk at night.

We met behind Enid's house, which was located in the development where I was temporarily living, and on that first night I kept turning back to search for my apartment. I'd left on two overhead lights to make the place seem less bleak when I returned.

The Champlain twins, in yoga pants and thick sneakers, clung to Enid, one on each side. It looked like tall, thin Enid was being kidnapped by a pair of elementary school cheerleaders. Before long the twins were panting as Enid, more energetic than I had expected, dragged them onward. Within minutes, Simon relieved the twins, took Enid's arm, and managed to get her to slow her pace.

Before a half hour was up I decided it was my turn to help Enid. I guided her on a trail lined by birches, our flashlights trained on the ground. I could smell the creek—a brisk scent of unripe grapes mixed with a faint fishiness.

That first night and almost every meeting afterwards no one talked about books except for Beverly's stepfather and the twins. I could see why the twins resented me. Simon was their sole focus, and at first they must have imagined that I might feel the way they did about him. If Enid was walking off her grief, I suppose I was walking off other emotions, and the twins' chatter with Simon was almost comforting but nothing I wanted in on.

"I thought we were doing 'The Lottery,'" Simon was saying in a pedantic tone I knew instantly not to trust. "It seems to be about small town mores and the weight of the individual conscience."

"So they killed a woman."

"It's kind of like a murder mystery, isn't it?" The twins sounded exactly alike. Only the direction of their voices indicated that two people spoke.

"Many cultures engage in ritual sacrifice," Simon said. "I believe that we do it now—to celebrities. We watch them age and destroy them. Elizabeth Taylor was hunted down like a prize boar."

I turned to look back at the twins. In the moonlight their flesh was undershot with a blue-green wash. They couldn't have been older than twenty-six or so, but something about them made me think of bile-filled elderly aunts in a play Tennessee Williams wouldn't have had the heart to impose on an audience.

"We loved her, didn't we?" one twin said to the other.

"God, yes. We watched *Who's Afraid of Virginia Woolf* it must have been twenty times. She looked like hell. Absolute hell. Double-chinned, ratty-haired. Like an old hobo. Why don't we read Virginia Woolf?"

"There's an idea," Simon said. "But I thought we were reading short stories, although maybe we could read *The Turn of the Screw* pretty soon. It's practically a short story. A novella, anyway."

"What about *The Old Man and the Sea*, Simon—wouldn't you enjoy that? The fish dies. The sharks strip the fish. It's all coming back. From ninth grade."

"It's about the courage to face reality," Simon said. "And about performing to the best of your ability."

"Shoot me now. Weren't we talking about *The Turn of the Screw?* It's shorter, maybe?"

Soon, a pattern was established. Although formerly Jorge had spent part of each night walking beside Enid, I volunteered to replace him. My instincts told me that Beverly thought I would be good company for Enid, although Enid didn't talk, and so I couldn't imagine how I could be good company for her. Gradually I figured out why Beverly wanted me to join. She was being kind to me, yes. But she was attracted to Jorge, and Simon was preoccupied with the twins, and if Beverly was going to have more time with Jorge someone else had to help Enid. By the third meeting I was Enid's designated companion—which I liked. I also liked how each night offered pockets of warm air blown apart by cool gusts. I even liked the flare up of smells—skunk, principally, the closest cousin of gasoline fumes. There were always intriguing sounds around us—cracklings and rustlings made by what I assumed to be shy, invisible woodland creatures. And as for Beverly and Jorge—they were the young lovers who lit our way, for they started heading out ahead of us with their flashlights, farther ahead each night. And Simon began to make me laugh with his mock-pedantic tone, no more self-aware of his effect on the twins than if he'd been Bottom the Weaver.

On the fifth night of walking, Simon asked the twins, "Have you two read *Wuthering Heights?* It's the story of a woman in love with a horse."

I had hoped *Wuthering Heights* wouldn't be brought up by Simon or the twins. Given that virtually every other classic novel came up—including *Adam Bede*—I shouldn't have been surprised.

Unfortunately, one twin responded. "That's Emily Brontë, right? *Wuthering Heights?* You know, you could make a fortune from an exercise program for people who are getting flabby, you know? *Withering Heinies.*"

Simon didn't laugh, but I did—and felt kind of cheap for laughing. I first discovered *Wuthering Heights* at twelve, and my fate was set. Reading didn't become an obsession for me until then. The passions, the sinister attachments, the sheer weirdness of that novel made actual life look small and predictable. I feared that nothing much would ever happen to me and that no one would love me with the sort of love that could ever be called wild. A love so fierce that it practically blasted your skin off, a love that was *wuthering*. For a while I actually wanted to call myself Catherine. If I couldn't share Catherine's temperament I could share her name.

The next meeting, even before the walk started, something must have happened between the twins. They were fuming. Simon, however, was oblivious and chattering on about James Joyce's first horse.

Within a half hour one of the twins disappeared. The other twin beamed her flashlight into the trees as if expecting to see her sister perched on the branches. We called and waited. No answering voice, no signaling beam. The twin with us (the twins had names, but I hadn't learned to tell them apart) ran back in the direction we had come. The rest of us followed, sweeping our flashlights through the shrubs. I was cynical and wondered if the disappearance of the twin was a ploy to capture Simon's attention.

When the path split I walked alone toward the creek. The ground sank under my feet and my shoes began filling with water. Ahead of me something glimmered. I stopped, squinting.

Moonlight reflected off the water onto a crouched figure.

I couldn't see anything clearly for long moments, as if I was stupefied, and then I made out what was ahead of me in the creek: a frog.

An immense frog.

The giant black eyes blinked and filmed over. The skin glimmered as if polished.

I might as well have been slapped across the face. The impact was that strong, that physical. The frog was a woman. And also a frog. A frog that was more of a frog than a woman. Or more of a woman than a frog. A frog woman/woman frog. With powerful haunches and immense eyes. Or was it two frogs? I closed my eyes and then looked again and saw one frog body—with long forelegs. I couldn't get away fast enough and ran to find the others.

When I rejoined the group the lost twin was with her sister again, their arms around one another. Everything around me was strangely unreal— calm, normal, and I was speechless.

Everyone needs, at least once in life, a vision, and this was mine.

In trying to describe my reactions I find myself almost speechless again. I was stunned and overwhelmed. I was proud of the vision and terrified at the same time, for I'd broken through some membrane into another world. I was gratified by the vision and undone by it. My fingers tingled as if I'd touched an electric current.

It was Enid who sensed something was wrong. She broke her silence to tell me, "It just takes time." She knew about my situation. Nevertheless, my first thought was that she was talking about her own grief.

We were nearly at Enid's house when I heard the whispers. Behind me. Whispers and half-laughs. More whispers.

The twin who was speaking to her sister and Simon kept saying, "I couldn't look away. It was the worst thing I've ever witnessed. I just couldn't stop staring."

"Was there a horse?"

I began to understand, in bits and pieces. Right there off the trail. In the woods. In the middle of the creek. For an art class probably. Pornography. The private school over the ridge. Kids making a film. I could hardly contain my disappointment.

Was that all I saw? Pornography? A configuration of bodies that my imagination made into a giant wide-eyed frog or one frog dividing into two?

To say I was deflated minimizes how I felt. I had been so anxious to enlarge my life that I turned the sight of a couple of bodies into a monster. With a burst of familiar rage I thought about the so-called erotic literature my husband's girlfriend wrote and how it was watered down, spineless, less nimble pornography. Her novels were an expense of shame and a waste of experience. And then I thought a new thought. I thought about how my rival made pornography out of her life, whereas out of pornography I made frogs. Which seemed like a higher art.

Something happened later that night: I could read. I knew I could read because I wanted to read. In fact, I downloaded *Wuthering Heights* on my neglected Kindle as soon as I got back inside my apartment. Once again I longed to encounter the ghost of Catherine Earnshaw beating at the window, beating her cold frantic hands against the glass.

But when Catherine says "I am Heathcliff!" I didn't respond the way I had whenever I reread the book in the past. No, this time I thought, "No. No, you're not. And never will you be. You are being ridiculous, Cathy." It occurred to me that I had never been remotely like Catherine

Earnshaw. No, it was my husband, my romantic, obsessive soon-to-be former husband, who was Catherine Earnshaw.

The part of the novel that wasn't ruined for me was the ending, when the lovers' spirits are reunited to wander through the dark. I too knew the appeal of night walking and thought—and still think—that of all visions of eternity it's one of the better ones.

Not long afterwards, our night walking ended. It was too cold to continue. Let's not give Enid pneumonia, everyone said.

Simon took on contracting work that kept him busy and pretty much exhausted, especially given that the twins turned up at his place on too many nights. Beverly and Jorge began seeing one another without needing the club as an excuse. And Enid moved in with her oldest niece and turned to shopping obsessively online. The club would start up again, everyone promised, once spring returned and we could walk in the woods without freezing.

In mid-October a greeting card arrived from my mother-in-law: a turkey caught inside a pumpkin, doing double duty for two holidays.

I was tempted to tell my mother-in-law everything, except about my vision of the frog. Nor was I going to tell her about how I had stopped reading literature for a while. She might humor me about the frog, but she would never understand why I'd let the woman her son was going to marry get in the way of anything that gave me pleasure. I imagined, with some satisfaction, that if she read her future daughter-in-law's erotica she'd be tempted to correct it.

When I got around to calling my soon-to-be-ex-mother-in-law I didn't know if I was ready to explain how anything was going for me. Then I didn't have to.

As soon as she heard my voice she said, "You sound elated. Getting divorced, I tell you, especially when all the loose ends are taken care of, is the best thing ever. Those were the happiest times of my life."

After we talked I wondered what it would be like if, when reconvened, the club became more like a genuine book club. Where people agreed to read at least one book. Some of us would read the book. And some of us would pretend to read the book. And some of us would only read our way through the first half of the book. And some of us would skip right to the ending.

The thing is: At least I made friends. Plus, I'd had a vision.

And, after all, as I have to admit, books are wonderful, but probably books aren't what any book club is about.

The Stone Wall

Something there is that doesn't love a wall.

—ROBERT FROST

Even from a distance we could tell something was wrong with the wall. When we went out to the pasture the ground seemed firm enough, although a few stones had been dislodged. Frost heave, we thought, the result of a hard winter and a spring thaw. Gravity is a stone wall's friend. The stones sink into soil, but there's a problem if the ground shifts or swells, and then a stone wall can bow inward if the stones were never stacked right to begin with.

We didn't think too much about the wall after we tended to it, until a few days later when we discovered several stones scattered in the orchard. The stones were easy to spot. They were the roundest stones from the wall. In the orchard they looked like small grazing animals.

Did we have enemies? Was it a matter of revenge? Or an act of vandalism? Of course we suspected our neighbors' children and not our own.

One morning, the dew wet at our ankles, we walked to the pasture with an intuition that something more was wrong. Those stones our forebears had hefted and knocked into place—none were left. The entire wall was gone. Every stone. We couldn't find any of the stones in the orchard this time. Who could carry off so many stones in the night?

"The troll," one of us said, and we tried to laugh. We didn't tell our children fairy tales. We were sensible people. We believed in being honest and direct. We respected the truth.

Of course we had warned our children. God knows how often we warned them. Educational films, brochures, online quizzes warned them. Our embarrassed homegrown lectures warned them. For years our children were forewarned, forearmed.

At first our children disappeared for only a few hours. When they returned they were almost the same as always, except a little more tired, complaining of dizziness—nothing alarming. Maybe some were shaky, sniffling. A stomach virus was going around. That spring we blamed some of their behaviors on the virus.

No one could predict when one of the children was going to leave us. That child would act almost like the others, a little sleepy, a little angry, the way children of that age often are.

The Dormer girl was the first not to return. We could blame her, or her parents, or ourselves, or the malleability of the young, their brains like a fontanel that hadn't yet closed. We could kneel on the floorboards and beat our heads bloody, and too many of us did.

Some of us counseled indifference: Ignore the problem. The situation would then seem less glamorous to the remaining children. Others counseled aggressive education, the way those people always counseled education, futile to the end.

We begged Irenska not to go when she told us her plan, and she seemed to agree with our reasoning, hanging her head all the way back to her van where her collie jumped at the open window, greeting her with barks of delight. She left the next morning. We waited and we called for her but she didn't come back.

I was the least likely of all of us to climb the mountain. I am not sturdy or strong willed. I am a small woman, given to headaches and rashes, a fearful, quivery sort of person with a voice that sounds pinched. I left the week after Irenska. I went because my son was on the mountain. Otherwise I would never have left my home, my little world of tea and books and Netflix.

It took a long to time to reach the foot of the mountain, and I wondered how the children had ever managed. The slope was covered with whorls of lichen and rocks like marbled steaks, fatty with quartz. There were places where rainwater seeped into limestone and made tunnels. Sometimes the plant called lamb's foot peeled off from the soil, a dull furred green. The few sparse bushes that lined the track flashed silver as if coated with frost. Soon the air thinned and I was afraid boulders would be sent down to crush me. That had happened more than once to ignorant tourists who knew nothing about the mountain.

Gnats circled my face, feasting on my breath. I thought of my neighbors in their houses, each with at least one child's bed empty. Then I began imagining a figure with a backpack watching me, and how he must have come down from the mountain and lured each child. And I thought that the one we all feared, that one with his dried flowers and fine powders, would mistake me for a child and let me pass until he discovered who I was.

The trees far below looked like thick-packed feathers. My boots began to stick to the ground as if I were a bee trying to fumble my way into a hive.

I thought of my son—his glimmering eyes, his small perfect teeth, his hair as silky as a woman's, and as I was thinking of him everything around me wavered. My vision was strained through gauze.

I found myself in a garden. A wave passed through the garden, and another wave of something like energy passed through me as if I myself must be a garden. The air smelled like roses, a fragrance like sweetness except lighter, and the wave passed through me again. I felt lifted off my feet. I knew then why the children had left us, why the mountain's garden was what they came for even though the garden would turn to thistles and weeds that crumbled like ashes.

My hood was yanked back and I was facing my son. I cried out and tried to hold him. He had grown hunched, his teeth broken, his hair in patches. He hobbled away from me, his boots barely holding him up.

"It's too late for me," he said. "I won't let you stay."

I told him I loved him, that nothing could separate me from him.

I was hurled backward, and when I was myself again I was in the pasture where the wall had stood.

For years I had warned my son, and now I wonder if, long ago, I should have told him a fairy tale instead. Maybe then he would have understood what waited for him and what both of us would become.

I shouldn't have climbed the mountain. None of us should.

I knew I'd done something that helped no one, and that all my life I'd want to be there again, on the mountain with the terrible troll and the others, many of them, our children who turned us to stone.

The Tell-All Heart

Their balcony looked out onto their neighbors' pool, which was wonderful: the fountain at the south end with its soft slurring and the dappled turquoise of the wind-stirred water and the way a flock of starlings swooped over and occasionally one skimmed lower, dipping its belly (what else should Char call the underside of the bird?) before flitting away. In the mornings Char tried to let contentment well up under her skin. Sometimes she sat on the balcony and looked downward at the pool and drank her coffee.

Sometimes she sat on the balcony and looked downward at the pool and drank her coffee. Kit wondered if she was sending him a message. Did she know about Kelly? That thing he had with Kelly, which was turning into a bigger thing and becoming a headache but which was maybe in the long run good for his marriage with Char. And now morning after morning Char sat on the balcony and looked toward the pool and he wondered if she was trying to catch a glimpse of Kelly. He didn't need to catch a glimpse. He had plans to see Kelly later. Definite plans. He didn't want to think too far ahead, but he had plans.

When Kit left for work, Char thought about going right back to bed. She was so tired lately. Nine hours of sleep and she was still tired. The weight of the world. She'd been watching too much news lately. Plus, she worked part time at the law library, and that was nothing more than a den of horrors. Sometimes she could hardly sleep, knowing the things she knew. Including the things the lawyers laughed about.

Working part time means you get paid next to nothing, your hours can be dropped at any moment, you get no benefits, and you find yourself listless. Char's hours were almost nonexistent this week. She'd probably be let go soon. At least she had time to herself. Except she really didn't feel like doing anything. She and Kit had lived in the house for half a year already and she'd never, for instance, cleaned out the attic. Well, why should she? You can ignore an attic for a long time, possibly forever. No doubt she and Kit should have insisted that the attic be emptied before they moved in.

It was after one o'clock before she got up the energy to climb the stairs. The air in the attic was thick, heavy. She'd call it airless except the air was so definitely there, concentrated and heated. She felt almost ready to faint and had to sit down. Boxes upon boxes, and there in the far corner an old steamer trunk. The first time she'd seen that trunk she'd been too harried by the realtor even to think about opening it. Now she worried about what she might find. A body? Or more likely a litter of mice or absolute crap—broken dishes or old safety razors or decades of newspapers, bad news festering. The previous tenant was an elderly woman, and the first and second floors had been filled to capacity with useless cheap furniture, including a table so scarred it looked like someone took a knife to it.

Gradually the air was thinning, becoming more breathable, or else she was just getting accustomed to the atmosphere. She crouched next to the trunk and pried at the lid. Inside she found paper, almost like butcher paper, very yellow and old, and obviously something was under the paper.

Clothing. Stained and worn in spots. She expected a strange odor to drift up—sweat and a harder smell, maybe of whiskey, or else mothballs or cedar chips or lavender. No, everything was sanitized by time. She took out each item, spread each on the floor. Men's clothing—a vest, an outer jacket with wide lapels, a blouselike shirt and what looked like a neckerchief or a cravat, a pair of pants, the fibers almost lifting off in her hands. She folded and placed everything back in the trunk, settling paper over the fabric. So much paper. For an instant, the man's wardrobe seemed to fill with air. When she patted the fabric down she found more paper in both pockets of the jacket. The writing on the paper was brown, a swirling handwriting she couldn't read. Apparently someone had stuffed paper in the pockets to keep their shape or to inhibit dampness. Once again she ran her hands across each item of clothing. How carefully and tenderly everything had been preserved. Perhaps the suit had belonged to the great-grandfather of the ancient woman who once owned the house. Perhaps these items from a man's wardrobe were from a far earlier generation than the woman's great-grandfather's generation. She lay down on the floor next to the trunk, overcome by feelings she could hardly begin to name.

That afternoon Char did three loads of wash and scrubbed the kitchen sink and vacuumed both floors of the house. She even cleaned out the refrigerator. Amazing how things tend to hide in a refrigerator. It's like mustard migrates or something.

It's like mustard migrates or something, Char told her husband when he came through the door. Nice to see her looking more animated, Kit thought. He hugged her and asked about her day and tried to listen. It was hard to listen. He was going to see Kelly tonight. When he was going to see Kelly he couldn't concentrate on anything but Kelly. She'd sent him a text at 3:30. Dear God. His mind, it was gone. He'd read once that jockeys use Vicks VapoRub on the noses of horses so they won't smell the females and get distracted from the race. Kelly—she was great. She was bacon. He had one life after all, just one.

He had one life after all, just one, Char reminded herself. And Kit wasn't enjoying his life the way he used to. She felt bad about that. At work they were exploiting Kit, and half, more than half, of his colleagues were such dunderheads. He was always getting called away, could hardly finish a meal before his cell went off and he got agitated. In this economy, the way his employer could make unreasonable demands, it was inhuman. Kit could be texted or called or emailed at any hour. And everybody at all levels wanted instant responses. It was like his life wasn't his own. She was going to be extra-attentive tonight when he returned. He'd be so sweet when he got in—he was always sweet when his hours were long—

and he'd probably hold her during the night before they both drifted off to sleep.

She stayed on the couch, waiting for him, watching an old movie. The plot didn't make sense. She kept falling asleep even though it wasn't that late. It was only a quarter after nine when she heard the thumping. Something in the attic. She'd ask Kit to take a look when he got home. Probably, though, she'd have to call an exterminator. Another sound, this time from outside. A sound like something falling into water. She went to the window. The moon reflected off her neighbors' pool, and a breeze unsettled the surface. It always worried her—what if a kid fell. Good thing there was a gate and that Kelly and Beamer were conscientious about keeping it closed. Still, kids were kids. A teen could scale that fence, bring a few friends, drop some drugs, dive into the shallow end. She remembered what she'd been like—sheer hell. It was a wonder her parents didn't die young.

The thumping again, a scraping, followed by an almost rhythmic sound. This time from above her head. Squirrels. They were having a beat-box competition up there. Maybe she stirred things up that afternoon when she opened the trunk. Had she secured it? Awful to think of the squirrels getting into those antique clothes. If the clothes were in better shape she could donate them to the county museum. But no, the fabric was deteriorating, the threads practically dissolving at her touch. She imagined that if she opened the trunk again whatever was inside would turn to smoky dust. Her head was swimming. The tiredness—you could just about collapse.

The tiredness—you could just about collapse. But Char beat you to it. Asleep on the couch. Poor kid. She didn't suspect anything, he was becoming sure of that. Kit watched his wife. That innocent face. Maybe a little stupid too. Kelly had been on him tonight, making demands, and that got on his nerves. Whereas Char—she was sweet and loyal. Not demanding. And a little too much like a bar of soap. The product does what it needs to do, but you don't remember afterwards much about washing your hands. Kelly, for all her faults, well, you remembered. His thoughts stopped. Sounds were coming from above. That bumping. Had Char invited someone over? Jules, her friend. He imagined going up the steps and finding her in the guest bedroom. He'd always liked Jules—the size of her, the dimensionality. She wasn't pretty, and that made her grateful, and she was competitive with Char, and that was useful too.

Before he reached the second floor Kit knew the sounds were coming from the attic. Great. If it was squirrels he had a method. He opened the door. The sounds stopped. Clever little bastards.

It didn't hit him immediately when he stepped into the attic, the sensation of regret, a slow sinking sensation like the kind he sometimes had in dreams. No, the feeling grew, a regret so deep it didn't seem to have a beginning or an end, just an intolerable ongoing worminess. A trunk was pushed out from the wall. He sat on it. He stayed a long time and never saw a squirrel. Kelly—there were things he'd have to tell her to make her ease up. It might take time. She was temperamental. He had to begin slowly and then let her know the basics: We've got a problem.

"We've got a problem. Last night I heard something in the attic. It's probably squirrels. A heavy kind of thumping. They can get in the walls and lay their babies in there. I don't mean *lay* their babies. They're mammals. I'm so groggy this morning. What time did you get in? Honey, did you hear me? Honey, is everything okay?"

"I'm just sort of down, that's all. If it's squirrels I've got a method."

"Oh, honey, you always say you have a method and then nothing gets done. I'm sorry. Did that sound harsh? I didn't mean to . . . I just want things dealt with, you know? The squirrels were so loud last night."

She thought of telling Kit about the trunk of old clothes but reconsidered. Why would he care? What could possibly interest him about some old gentleman's outfit? Although the gentleman who used to wear those clothes might not have been old. In fact, she had the oddest feeling that whoever wore those clothes was relatively young. The sensation that overcame her yesterday, that extreme tenderness. Before she left the attic, she'd lain down full length next to those clothes and sobbed. Oh, but why should she always be so hard on herself? Kit had loved the strangeness in her. When they were first married he'd said something like that: "I love the strangeness in you." Or maybe not those exact words. Were those words from a poem? She never read poetry anymore. She used to love poetry when she was an eighth-grader. Then high school came down like wolves on a flock and she was the flock. She knew Kit wouldn't love the strangeness in her if he knew all about that strangeness, how two years ago she began "seeing" Jordy whenever she could. Breaking things off with Jordy had felt like violence, like she'd bound and gagged her own heart. Kit never knew, thank God for that. The sad thing, the terrible thing: If you did what she and Jordy did, you ruined any intimacy you could ever hope to have with the person you married. There was always a secret between herself and Kit, an invisible barrier. Sometimes she felt she didn't deserve ever to be happy again. It was, thank God, usually a feeling that dissolved after a while.

It was, thank God, usually a feeling that dissolved after a while. And then it wasn't. Kelly. He needed to see her. It wasn't just a playing-around thing anymore. When he was with Char he was practically itching to get out of the house. He could hear the swimming pool fountain even in the kitchen. Calling to him. The pool was saying: Come on over. Get out of your house. Go.

The thumping upstairs. Maybe the exterminator had to be called.

Maybe the exterminator had to be called. Except Char couldn't find a squirrel-friendly one on-line. According to comments sections on their websites every single local exterminator only pretended to be humane and environmentally friendly. Plus, this might be the season when the squirrels gave birth. Char could live with the squirrels thumping until she located a service that wouldn't destroy the poor things. She could also learn not to complain about the squirrels. Who are you to complain about anything anyway, you whore of Babylon? Jordy had wanted to marry her. She had known him since third grade, and even in third grade he'd wanted to marry her. Maybe things had never gone into the sexual range, but emotionally that was something else. Well, things did go into the sexual range, but only five times. If she forgave herself she would be excusing herself. There were no excuses. And Kit worked so hard and for indecently long hours. He was the only one pulling in real money. Her neighbor Kelly often told her how lucky she was—Kelly, who sometimes popped over with honey wheat bread. Kelly liked to make an extra loaf. She always wanted Char to go for a swim in her pool but Char felt too self-conscious in her bathing suit, the way her upper arms looked all flabby. She should lift weights. Kelly obviously did.

The attic: Once you got used to the air quality, the atmosphere was calming. The heat baked something out of you.

Char hesitated and then at last, after intolerable minutes, opened the trunk. Some of the papers covering the suit looked like they'd been peeled back. The squirrels couldn't have gotten in, could they? She lifted the ivory-colored neckpiece, the vest, the suit jacket, the trousers. She lay down beside them. How beautiful they were in their ancient delicacy. She felt like confessing, as if the vest and coat and neckerchief could absolve her, or as if the man who had inhabited this wardrobe would understand her. She was sure that something terrible had happened to him. Something had happened, and these clothes—whoever found them had packed them away. Were they a bridegroom's clothing? No, they were too worn. Too shoddy in their odd living beauty. Oh, it was her mind fantasizing, fabulating, wanting the clothes to mean more, to carry meaning. Yet it was possible that this man might have been sympathetic toward her, even if he had been born in a moralistic, condemnatory century. Actually, for all she knew, he might have hanged witches. No, not this man. He had done something that gave him pain. His suffering was etched there in the softness, in the creases of the shirt he wore. The shirt was as wrinkled as an old person's skin. The man who lived in this clothing had suffered and yet felt other sensations too, stronger sensations. Under her hand, what he must have worn at his neck, the brownish stain there. She could kiss it. No, she couldn't. No more kissing. But still.

The dream was very beautiful even though she was underwater. Deep under the sea and calling out to a man who was calling too. And then she was inside a castle made of seashells and the man with his dark eyes and high forehead could not reach her. Waves, high and green, pushed him back. She reached toward him, and she herself drew him into her castle. Everything about him was easy to touch. When Char woke her forehead felt as if warm oil had been poured over her in a benediction. She told herself that whatever had happened with Jordy didn't matter. How could it? She was a free human being, and any life was short, and all she had was love. The feeling lasted into the night, even hours after dinner.

The feeling lasted into the night, even hours after dinner. Usually he didn't feel angry at Char. No, he felt pity lately and repugnance. Not this anger. They never should have married. What did they have in common? She wasn't a meat-and-potatoes sort of person. Hardly ever served meat. She did yoga—secretly, because she didn't like to be seen contorting herself. Kelly told him about it—how she could see Char on some mornings doing a bad downward-facing dog.

Kit couldn't keep it up. Supporting Char and breathing the same air as she did and not getting anything back. She hadn't even called the exterminator.

She hadn't even called the exterminator. Hadn't for several reasons, but mainly because she didn't want anyone to go into the attic. It was her favorite part of the house, the attic. She'd started putting extra boxes on top of the trunk to protect the clothes. She hadn't yet seen a squirrel, but she certainly could hear them not only at night now but sometimes during the day. Then, as soon as she stood outside the attic door, the sounds stopped. Can a person be in love with an empty suit? That's a joke, she told herself. There are plenty of empty suits, empty dresses, lots of emptiness to go around. The suit in the attic, that ensemble of men's clothing, was more alive for her each day. Her fantasy: The man who wore those clothes loved her. She could be dead and he'd still love her and find her beautiful. That was the kind of man he was. How could she be betraying Kit when she was only spending time alone with some very old clothes? She wasn't hurting anyone, was she? It was her own life, wasn't it, and yet a new sensation was coming upon her, a sense that the suit of clothes was endangered somehow. What if Kit guessed? What if Kit came home while she was working in the law library and decided to clean out the attic? Sometimes—well, maybe twice—he got urges like that to do something around the house.

She opened the trunk and refolded the clothes, running her hands along each seam. She took papers out of the coat pockets and folded them. She bundled everything into a packet and carried the packet downstairs. Kit never went into the basement. The basement was safe. She could hide the packet in the basement.

What if the suit became damp down there, every fiber loosening, corrupted by mold? She found a plastic bag in the pantry. But no, that was wrong. The fabric shouldn't suffocate. No, and the basement was no place for clothing.

In the bedroom she opened the top drawer of her dresser. Never would Kit look there. If he ever did, and he wouldn't, he might think the clothing was some sort of costume or even an old outfit of her own. He would not be curious. He never noticed what she was wearing. He never noticed her. Oh, she hadn't meant to think that. She didn't want to be disloyal.

She didn't want to be disloyal. No, Kelly never wanted to be disloyal to her husband, but things happen. Big things. And you can't let your life run away without you. You have to make choices. Kelly could make the choice for Kit. Kelly wanted to tell Char, let her know the absolute incontrovertible truth in a way that would be less painful to Char. Kelly said she knew the right words. She was Char's friend, knew where the sensitivity points were. Was volunteering.

"You're crazy, right? You think she should hear it from you?"

"I'm not crazy, Kit. I think there's a way to talk about what's happened between us. You'd be surprised. Char totally deserves to be married to someone who loves her."

"You think so?"

"You think so?"

"Char, yes, I think so."

"I don't know. I think this color looks like death on me. Like cat puke. It's like unrefined mustard."

"Well, I think you look great."

"Ah, you're great. I'll wear it with pride."

"Fabulous. Char, there's something I've been meaning to tell you. About what you deserve . . ."

About what you deserve . . . maybe that is what you deserve, Char. Before Kelly left the house Char stood up from the couch and froze. Catalepsy. She'd read about catalepsy years ago. She could not move, could not throw the blouse at Kelly. No, but in her mind Char had seen the blouse fly from her fingers and hit the wall, splat, and turn the entire wall mustard colored. And then Kelly was gone. Like she disappeared in a puff of smoke. Although right before she closed the door Kelly said something: Kit would not be returning tonight. Kelly said the words in a way that let Char know she was doing her a favor. Otherwise Char would have stayed up all night waiting for her husband to return to her.

The thumping sound was coming from the bedroom. Char walked to the dresser. The floor wasn't under her feet anymore. She was walking on marshmallows—or that's what it felt like. She took the suit from the dresser. She couldn't know that when the author died he was wearing another man's clothes. Perhaps, one theory went, he was kidnapped for purposes of cooping, forced to vote again and again, made to wear different clothes so he wouldn't be recognized each time he showed up at the polls. No doubt his mind was unraveling from too much drink and too many fists knocking at his head. Or perhaps alcohol and desperation and poverty and the death of women he loved—all were enough to destroy him. But there was the mystery. He died in another man's clothes. Where were his own? These—were these the clothes he'd been wearing when he'd been knocked out the first time, a bag slipped over his head? Was that what she pulled from her dresser: the wardrobe from his famous photograph?

How could Char even begin to imagine such things? She could only imagine that she got what she deserved, that her own sins had come back in the form of Kit's cruelty. She slept that night with the tattered vest, the cravat with its gill-like pleats, the dingy coat, the snagged pant legs next to her. Throughout the entire night.

She hadn't slept so well in years. As if for once she didn't have to fear her future. Anyway, she didn't know what her future held. Nor could she know how many other women had felt as she had about the man who once wore the suit, or how the previous tenant had spent some nights of her lonely old age. Besides, Char wasn't aware that the first owner of those clothes famously said words on the order of "The death of a beautiful woman is, unquestionably, the most poetical topic in the world." Ultimately he probably didn't mean what he said. After all, sometimes when we make proclamations we are only talking about ourselves in a roundabout way. What remained that had been Edgar Allan Poe's was beautiful to Char, the most beautiful. Even innocent things, even a cravat tied in a bow and spotted with blood aged to the color of weak tea could be stained even more with the remainders of love: love that travels in and through time.

Char forgave Kit so soon that her neighbor Kelly was disturbed. It was Kelly's own heart that thrashed whenever she ran into Kit's wife. She was hurt that Char would never tell anyone about what happened in Char's ruined marriage. If Kelly enjoyed anything, it was a story about recklessness, the proof that she was desired.

Well, what could Char do about that? You can't please everyone. She couldn't help but forgive Kit and Kelly and make excuses for them. She told herself that anyone's heart has its own language. It takes years to learn the language, and then you mistake half the meanings anyway. Or maybe it wasn't even about language and keeping big secrets. All that knocking, and maybe the whole time your own heart was just trying to get out.

A Story's End

Over the years I've thought less about the morning my sister and I learned our parents died than I've thought about the night before their deaths when our mother read to us from a book I never found again.

In the book, two sisters are lost and wandering in a forest. Most often when I think of those lost girls I imagine them holding hands, their backs to us, surrounded by giant snowflakes. I'm sure I'm remembering the book's cover.

I forgot about the book until three days after our mother read it to us. Darla and I were nearly asleep when the shadow of a passing car swept the ceiling. I pushed off the covers and searched under the bed, on the shelves, and in every dresser drawer, only coming back to bed after Darla cried.

The next morning there wasn't time to search for the book. I stood behind my sister next to our parents' caskets. Darla turned her wet eyes up to mine, and I put my arms around her.

Our parents' car struck the oak at the edge of our lawn. They died in what was called "a single-car accident." How was it possible, people kept asking. Their car wasn't even on the road.

Two days after the funeral, Aunt Abby announced that Darla and I were old enough to sleep apart. Other children would have been happy to have a bedroom of their own, wouldn't they? My mother's sewing and crafts room became Darla's room, and my mother's sewing machine and fabric, spools of thread, ribbons, wire, glue—these Aunt Abby put away. She emptied the closet too. In that closet, days before our parents' deaths, I had found clothing stuffed into garbage bags. When I began to pull my blue sweater from one bag electricity shot up my arm, along with the intuition that I should turn away and not disturb anything. After Abby moved in, I found my sweater once again folded in my dresser drawer.

Abby never changed anything in the house, possibly out of an awareness of how Darla and I clung to anything familiar, the way children in the books we read about the *Titanic* clung to the sides of lifeboats. But I never got over the shock of having Aunt Abby thrust into our lives. Abby—so hapless, so alien, so infuriating. I was already a teenager when I overheard her talking to friends during one of their interminable meetings dedicated to local improvement: *Darla's hair is a rat's nest. Darla is a sulker. And Calista—useless. Hardly any help at all, and her clothes—too short and too tight and it's not easy, not easy.*

Those words stung my proud, vain heart. Even the delivery stung: a loud, jokey voice that must have been strained by her wish for sympathy, for acknowledgment. Back then, my dislike of Abby was chemical. Understanding had nothing to do with it. Resentment—a young person's bottomless resentment—was everything. As if by attempting to take the place of our mother, Abby committed an unpardonable sin.

Within a month after Abby's death I moved back into the house—it belonged to Darla and me now—to prepare Abby's belongings for auction and the house for sale. I had lost my job and had nowhere else to live, and so my days were spent working through rooms stuffed with lamps, mattresses, rolled-up carpets. Abby hadn't exactly been a hoarder, but she came close. I wasn't much better and couldn't part with Abby's glass animals, her old perfume bottles, the set of china plates hand-painted with trout. I couldn't throw out a tiny cracked hand mirror, a box of *Good Housekeeping* magazines tied with purple ribbon, a baggie of white feathers, a cookie tin filled with my miniature paper dolls, and a set of tiny bowls from one of Darla's dollhouses that ended up with those paper dolls.

I knew almost nothing about my sister's life after she left home.

For a long time I tried stalking her online. Darla had never been a joiner—we shared that trait—so I couldn't locate her through a trail of organizations. She didn't appear to use social media. Often I wondered what her life was like during all those years when she wasn't in contact with me or Abby. A person so disconnected from her family—what there was of it—couldn't be happy, could she? Now she and I were all that was left of our family, except for distant cousins on our father's side who, like Darla, didn't bother to attend Abby's funeral.

It must have taken energy for my sister to become an enigma: refusing to answer letters, never giving us her phone number, moving so often we couldn't trace her. Years were unaccounted for, so many that the Darla I knew in my imagination was trapped in that era when the two of us were very young and our aunt was full of warnings. We should be ashamed, Abby often let us know. Ashamed to be selfish. Ashamed to be greedy. Even when we were sick she doubted us. An upset stomach is invisible, after all. A flu required hard evidence and drew suspicion. And evidence, of course, could be fabricated. Though younger, Darla was more resourceful than I was. She could make herself look sick even when she wasn't, whereas when I was sick I crumpled with embarrassment, cringed, even laughed, weirdly enough. Anyway, when I vomited—no better evidence than vomit—Abby was likely to say, "You must feel better now." And that was the end of it. How must Abby and my father have been raised, given how unthinkingly our aunt tried to pass on those ways to us?

And then at last I discovered this much: Darla had started teaching in an elementary school and as a consequence became easy to locate online.

I was pulling into the driveway when I saw a blue compact car parked at the side of the house. I was expecting Darla. I had checked her school's online calendar and it was fall break. In an email I told her to retrieve keys at the realtor's in case I wasn't around. Nevertheless, she hadn't made it clear when, or even if, she was coming.

I set my satchel on the dining room table, careful not to hit the low-hanging lamp. Sliding sounds were coming from above the ceiling. I imagined that Darla was in the attic, pulling trunks and boxes into the hall: Abby's things, and our childhood keepsakes, scrapbooks, clothing that once belonged to our parents.

As I climbed the stairs I let myself imagine my sister, preoccupied with boxes and pretending she owed me no apology for disappearing. The attic was airless and cluttered, and it would take days to sort and clear everything out for the auction. The light was bad there too, the only window thick with grime and plastered with the wings of insects, the glass as opaque as waxed paper. And the flooring was dangerous. Abby always warned us to avoid stepping between the planks. We could lose our footing and fall through the insulation.

I pushed open the attic door.

"We're not finished yet!" my realtor's voice rang out. The young couple with her looked through me. Apparently they were being dragged from room to room on a useless quest. Only politeness was keeping them from hurtling down the steps and out the front door.

"I didn't recognize your car," I said.

"It's my husband's," my realtor said, shrugging and twisting to the side. Days ago she had made it clear that my presence created inhibitions. How can a prospective buyer criticize your taste or, in this instance, your aunt's taste, if the homeowner is in the house? How can a prospective buyer peel off a patch of wallpaper or kick at molding or scuff a toe against linoleum with the full steam-head of disdain?

There was plenty to be disdainful about. And not only in the attic. The dining-room walls were a riot of pink, white, and scarlet peonies. Roses, once red, now tea-colored, crawled the living room walls and those of my childhood bedroom. In fact, in nearly every room the wallpaper was aggressively floral: lilacs in two closets, carnations on raised black velvet in what used to be my parents' bedroom. And giant purple irises in the foyer.

That night, lying in bed, I heard a car pull into the driveway. I threw on my housecoat and hurried downstairs.

Darla had dyed her hair—an auburn that looked almost natural and made her eyes bluer and her skin paler. Looking at her, you would never know that somewhere in our past were generations of Greeks. As soon as she was fully inside the dining room, I asked if she'd like anything to eat.

She averted her eyes, thanked me, and said, "Oh no. I'm tired." Her voice was so quiet I almost didn't hear her. Then I was overcome with feeling. Trying to kiss her cheek I missed and kissed her eyelid.

Before she reclaimed her bedroom she said, "I can help with cleaning out the attic tomorrow. You mentioned in your email about the attic?"

"If you come across any children's books can you set them aside?" When she didn't answer, I went on. "I'm looking for one. There's a picture on the cover, two girls walking in the snow?" I hoped she'd remember.

"I'll just put aside any books at all," she said. "You can go through them yourself then."

I explained that I was looking for the last book our mother read to us, and that I'd been thinking about the book often.

"Oh," she said. "Okay."

She didn't have to promise that she would look. It was inconceivable that she wouldn't.

Early the next morning, judging by the noise, Darla was dragging trunks and boxes into the hallway to create more space to arrange things.

My plan for the day was simple. I'd deal with the contents of the utility room and then make us lunch. Over lunch we'd talk. At 11:50 I reheated the chowder I made the day before and stored in a mini-refrigerator of Abby's. Never yet had I used the regular-sized refrigerator after opening it and finding aluminum foil-covered bowls, assorted bottles of relish and chutney, lunch meat in plastic wrap. There was something sad about those leftovers. The mini-refrigerator, nearly empty, was the safer choice.

Darla's steps clattered on the stairs as loudly as when we were girls. She bounced into the kitchen wearing high boots and a corduroy jacket, like a rich child set to ride a pony.

"Lunch?" I said, trying not to sound too eager.

"There's something I need to do in town." Her voice was so breezy that my heart sank. "No need to bother. I'll pick up something there."

I recommended the Two Cousins Café. My sister was already heading toward the door as I spoke. From the window I watched her get into her car. She backed out of the driveway, hardly looking. There's never much traffic, but there could have been.

The next day I made a point of going up into that sweltering closed-off attic to ask if I could help. The way Darla angled her body, refused to meet my eyes—everything about her let me know I was taking up her time, that she didn't want my help. Yet I couldn't stop wanting to be of use, delivering iced tea, even baking a loaf of banana bread, her old favorite.

On the third afternoon of her visit Darla was in the living room looking over the furniture. Remembering? Deciding which pieces to claim? Cooling her body temperature after hours in the attic?

"We don't talk, do we?" I said.

She looked at me, blinking. "Oh," she said. "We talk enough."

"Are you married?" I asked.

"No." Her voice was flat, although not irritated.

"You like teaching?"

"It's fine."

"Darla, is everything all right? Do you need anything? Is there anything I can do for you?"

"I'm fully employed."

The reproach in her words stung, given my own situation.

Did I remind Darla of a period in our lives when we were vulnerable? Did she need time alone with the house itself, the way I had been alone with the house for a week before she arrived? Why wouldn't she talk to me? It was as if I were her enemy. I had been redoubling my efforts to get my own sister to like me until I resented her.

I left a note for Darla informing her that I'd be out of town for the night. No explanation. No hint of my whereabouts. I knew I was being irrational by trying to be self-satisfied about secrecy. Did that make Darla happy, being a mystery? I could see how it would, the weird bitter sweetness of it.

I tried to batten down my guilt. After our parents' deaths, to all outward appearances, nothing was different between Darla and me. We fought, like normal sisters. Darla followed me around. I ignored her. Or I turned and chased her and laughed. When she cried in the night sometimes I crawled into bed next to her. Her tears would stop. Just as often,

I screwed up my fists and put my pillow over my head and let her cry alone in her room. Anyone would excuse me, would say I was too young to know better. But when we were children part of me stopped rescuing my sister. I couldn't save us, I believed, and I was afraid of my own anger. And Aunt Abby—so ineffectual, alternately stern and then apologetic and muddled. It took me years to realize that her heart was broken, for she loved my mother at least as much as she loved her brother.

A holiday: That's what the British would call what I was trying to enjoy. I could feel liberated from that crumbling memory pit of a house, and from my close-mouthed sister. In the lounge just off the hotel lobby a bored bartender, wearing tight combat pants, watched professional wrestling.

After being ignored, I gave up without ordering and returned to my room. Someone must have snuck cigarettes there for decades. The sunflowers on the bedspread looked like an attempt at van Gogh with a jar of mustard and an oil can. I waded through the heavy curtains (a smell like beef was coming off them) and gazed out at the parking lot and across the highway to a brightly lit truck stop and the sadly named Heidi Ho Diner. I will be the unpredictable one, I kept telling myself when I finally climbed into bed.

Maybe people leave behind psychic residue in hotels, and in this particular room occupants had soaked the mattress with regret. Others must have lain awake on their backs questioning if they should wake up in the morning. Being in that hotel was like finding yourself in one of those tricky stories where you learn that the narrator is dead. I got out of bed and made a discovery: Inside the closet was a stocked mini-refrigerator: tiny gold-banded bottles of gin, silver-rimmed vodka, rum with a label as brown and yellow as an overripe banana.

Remember, you're unemployed, I told myself. These will cost too much—mini-refrigerators: They're like bank vaults. All the more reason to drink. But drinks require salted nuts, bottled water, and a canister of spray cheese. All of which were available on the bottom shelf of the mini-refrigerator.

Later, only a little drunk, I fell asleep. Laughter in the hallway woke me. For a few moments I didn't know where I was. Eventually, to try to drift off, I told myself stories: endings for the book our mother read to us on the last night of her life. For years I had made up endings, never comforting ones. I didn't want to lie to myself entirely, even in my imagination.

The sisters wandered as snow fell around them, fell so thickly they could hardly see. The snow clumped on their eyelashes, clung to their mouths. At last a cottage appeared in the distance. As the girls approached, the cottage door opened. The girls crept inside. Next to a fireplace lay an enormous lion, his mane as bright as flames. A heavy chain on the lion's collar hung from an iron post. The lion opened his huge golden eyes, and the girls slipped the chain from his neck and lay beside him, under his giant paws, but the sisters could not grow warm.

The next morning the sisters left the cottage to find their way home. When they grew too tired to walk any longer they built a small fire and warmed their hands. Suddenly they heard a crackling sound and understood they were atop a frozen river. The sisters buried the fire and dug into the snow, dug until they uncovered ice. In a flurry of wings, swans broke through the ice and flew high into the air.

Over the years I must have invented dozens of endings to the book our mother read to us. Part of me was repulsed by what I was doing. I was a grown woman, why should I cling to the past? What good could clinging to the past do anyone?

When I returned home the next morning, Darla's car wasn't in the driveway. Usually her purse was stashed at the foot of the china cabinet. It wasn't there. Her room was empty, the sheets stripped from the bed. At last I found a note, taped to the toaster. In the note she thanked me for letting her visit.

How stupid I'd been. Resentful just because she hadn't wanted to talk. Why should I have expected she was ready to forgive me? I saw us as children again. By the time I was a sixth grader I no longer hugged her the way I used to. I no longer answered to her "Kee—Ah—Kee," our secret call. She used to chase me to get me to play with her. I hid. And then the years whooshed by and she was gone.

Eventually, whenever the realtor brought over a potential buyer I stopped leaving. The house didn't appeal to anyone anyway. The entire place looked gaudy to people who came by. I didn't have the funds for remodeling and didn't want to remodel. I liked the way things looked. If I squinted, the roses or lilies or peonies or dahlias or irises shifted and swarmed. At night the lamps on the two end tables in the living room pooled gold light so diffusely that the wallpaper's climbing roses appeared to be barely visible veins.

When my realtor's frowning and throat-clearing couldn't persuade me to evacuate the premises, the prospective buyers stopped coming altogether. By then I had stopped sorting boxes for the auction.

Darla had labeled all the boxes in the attic, like the well-organized schoolteacher she apparently was. From one of those I lifted our mother's wedding dress. My fingers stuck to the satin folds as if the fabric were damp. I found my father's clothing too—winter scarves, a heavy plaid coat. Someone, most likely Abby, had filled the box with mothballs. I taped the box shut. What moved me most: the boxes of my mother's sewing and craft supplies. I thought Abby would have given those away. But no, here were spools of thread, packets of needles, wires, fabric scraps, ribbons.

When Darla returned, two weeks later, she parked near the old clotheslines as if she didn't want her car to be seen from the road. I hadn't expected her to warn me that she was coming, and she hadn't.

Her hair was dyed again, this time as dark as mine.

She caught my stare at the smiling turkey on her sweater. "I know," she said. "You have to try to create rapport with the kids. I drove straight from work. It was a half day." She'd never strung that many sentences together during her last visit.

"I'm so glad you're back," I said. "Really. I'm really really glad, Darla."

"I'll just need to stay overnight. Is that all right with you? I'm meeting someone—tomorrow, and I hope you don't mind my stopping over."

"It's your house, half of it. Of course you can stay. Wait. I'll help you get your stuff."

"Don't help me."

"Can I at least open the door for you when you bring your stuff in?"

"I have one bag. Why don't you relax?"

I didn't try to restrain my happiness. "Can I help you make the bed—at least that?"

"I could use some tea first. I'll make the tea. But don't worry about the bed. I'm capable."

While Darla was putting the kettle on the stove I found sheets from the linen closet. When she rejoined me, I made my confession: "The house isn't selling. People pretty much hate it. And anyway, I don't want to sell it." I mentioned to Darla that I canceled the auction because I couldn't stand the thought of our family's possessions winding up at an antique store.

We lifted the top sheet together. The fabric swelled, filling with air. Darla shook a pillow, tugged at the case's seams.

"Stop it."

"Stop what?" I asked, startled.

"You shove people with your eyes. Don't you know that?" Her shoulders were relaxed, as if what she said was obvious. "You've always been like that. I could hardly take it when I was a kid."

"I don't have any idea what you mean."

"It took all my willpower to evade you," she said. "You were always the little mother."

"I was?"

"Yes. It was grueling. Bad enough to have Abby hovering. But you—."

"I didn't do enough for you," I said. "I was awful."

"Not really. Anyway, I don't remember ever not wanting to leave. And other than not always letting you know what I was up to—."

"Not ever."

"All right, not ever. At any rate, I see my life as being my own to do with as I please."

Now that Darla was talking there were so many questions I wanted to ask. "Where were you—for most of those years?" I began.

"In the Upper Peninsula. I got married. It was terrible."

"He hit you?"

"That and other things."

"Are you still married to him?"

She shook her head. "Someone fell in love with him. I'm guilty about that still. I didn't discourage it. She's young. Just out of college. It was like seeing a lamb tied to a stake for the lion. They're not married, at least not yet. But she's still with him."

"It was her choice. She broke up the marriage. She can feel guilty."

I wanted to know more about Darla's life, but soon I couldn't stop telling her about mine . . . though I wasn't the one who had disappeared. Even before I finished talking she was rifling through her satchel. "I almost forgot this," she said. "Is this the book you were looking for?"

My heart knocked with hope and then recognition. "Where did you find this?"

"I took it with me the first time I left home. I love this book."

The dustcover was torn. Inside a yellow circle two children stared out from a pencil drawing, their eyes smudged. I opened the book and the spine crackled.

It would be tempting to lie, even if I weren't such an inept liar.

"It's not it, is it?"

"No," I admitted reluctantly. "But I remember this book too. And the thing is—you came to give me this even though I never protected you when we were kids. I've always thought you must be so angry at me, Darla. I didn't do enough for you."

"Angry at you? I never even think about you."

It will sound strange to say this, but hearing those words made me very happy.

The next morning Darla was getting ready to leave, her satchel on her shoulder, when she swung around and said, "I want to show you something. It's one reason I came. I lost my nerve the other time. I don't want to lose my nerve again."

With each step on the stairway I felt a delay, a suspension in time, until we were in my childhood bedroom. Darla pointed to the window. What was there to see? The lawn, with its rings of thistles and crabgrass, and the road, empty this time of morning.

"The tree that used to be there," she said. "You remember? The oak.

He got in the car after her. The car was already running. She was driving. He ran and opened the door on the driver's side and pushed her down."

"You saw this, Darla? How could you see this?"

"I heard him shouting. He was always shouting. You were asleep. But I saw. Or I think I saw. Sometimes I think I dreamed it all."

"You didn't tell anyone?"

"I never looked out this window again. Abby separated us. I kept begging her to let me have another room as soon as she moved in. She gave me my own room so I wouldn't see this window. I was so afraid of this window—for all those years. Like it was the window's fault. I'm not going to talk about this ever again except to tell you who was the one driving. She must have been going slow, like she didn't know what she was doing, or where she could go. Then he got in and the car sped up. It could have been an accident, right? He just meant to stop her, but one of them pushed the accelerator—maybe struggling after he threw himself in the car. And that did it, that's when the car shot across the lawn. "

"Why didn't you ever tell me?"

"I didn't know what it meant and then, later, I didn't trust that I saw what I thought I saw. Maybe I just dreamed it all. Maybe it's not true."

And then I said, "It's true. I knew too."

In early December I began making shadow boxes or what some people call peephole dioramas. I worked with Ivory soap flakes for snow, wrapped wire trees with crepe paper, and cut out leaves the size of sesame seeds. I felt the way I imagine artists feel, following a natural inclination or a compulsion. If there were moments when I believed my private joy was without meaning, those twinges disappeared as I worked.

My favorite, the most demanding box, required a hand mirror. I'd drawn two girls, scissored them out so that their hair was finely delineated, and backed them with cardboard. The girls, propped on their elbows, lay at the edge of the hand mirror. Cracking through the mirror: one white feather. An accidental drop of too much Elmer's glue made the feather look flaked with ice crystals.

Darla and I talked several times about the book our mother read to us. Her idea: We should post a reward on Craigslist. We could also post a request for information on a listserv for elementary- and middle-school teachers and librarians. If anyone knows children's books, it's teachers and librarians. While writing up a description, Darla remembered more details. She said there's another illustration inside the book, and in the drawing the sisters are standing by a fire warming their hands.

For months I didn't stop imagining more near-endings for the book. I thought about describing those failed endings to Darla—except I knew she would be embarrassed for me, embarrassed for us both, although she would understand. Here is part of the last of those stories:

The sisters wander as snow falls around them, falls so thickly they can hardly see. The snow clumps on their eyelashes, clings to their mouths. In the distance a cottage appears. No one answers the older sister's knock, yet the cottage door opens, and the children tumble inside and press close to the fireplace. They take off their shoes and peel away their frozen socks. Suddenly a mammoth treasure chest glows in the center of the room. Together, the girls peer inside. At the very bottom of the chest lies a loaf of bread. The girls stare with amazement until one girl picks up the bread and hands it to her sister. And then, as soon as one sister eats, another loaf of bread appears.

In this account I imagined myself as the selfless sister, the one who first hands the loaf to her sister. I saw myself as the guilty sister too, always trying to be a better sister while always regretting the past. I saw myself as the melancholy sister, the weaker sister, the secretly angry sister.

So I went on with the story:

The next morning, the sisters leave the cottage to find their way home. It is still snowing. After walking for a very long time they come upon a tree bent to the ground from the weight of snow. They brush snow from the branches, and snow falls from the oak in giant mounds and won't stop falling, and the branches rise higher and higher, freed from the weight of snow. When the sisters turn around, wherever they look is spring, and they have grown into women.

Of course that couldn't be the true ending to a children's story. Somehow my endings never worked.

After I finished daydreaming about the story I thought about the last night our mother had been reading to us. It was spring, and the bedside lamp glowed, and the window that faced the oak tree was open. Am I misremembering everything, or was our mother's voice growing slower as she read? What if she read slowly because she didn't want to return downstairs? What if after Darla and I fell asleep our mother continued reading, silently, taking her time, discovering for herself what happened to those two lost girls?

When she finished reading—when she had no excuse for staying longer in our room—she might have carried the book with her as she drifted downstairs to our father.

All the times I have tried to finish the story in my imagination and failed—what was I trying not to imagine?—while knowing it would have been better, on that last night our mother read to us, if stories didn't end.

Ambrosia

In my early childhood, the people I loved most in the world made sure that I saw a silver tree. I remember taking a giant breath and then swallowing the sight of that tree so that it would never leave me. Late-born, with a far older brother and sister, I must have been a small child to be on someone's shoulders, and the wind must have been blowing so hard that the leaves flickered like metal.

For the past five years I have been the only member of my family. My brother and sister, both ill for much of their lives, died at early ages within a year of each other, and my parents died within a three-month span only two years later. I have photographs of everyone, of course, and scrapbooks of memorabilia, but to feel my family's presence I take turns imagining who cared so much that they made sure to hoist me on their shoulders so that I could see the tree that turned silver.

Maybe not all children necessarily understand that they're children. I found out that I was what's called a child—I made that drastic realization—when I was about four years old and couldn't see anything beyond the enormous legs in front of me. Everyone else on the porch was tall enough to watch the fireworks exploding in the distance over the wheat field. An awareness of my own height must have led to my giant realization: I am not like them. I am, of all things, what's called a child. It was hard to take, this knowledge.

That night we slept at my uncle's house. His friends arrived with children, two little girls, who kissed their mother's mouth. I thought it was required. I kissed their mother too. Everyone laughed and laughed, a seal on my epiphany.

I was renting a house—the sort of place that was partly furnished and partly stuffed with things no one wanted: a broken stepladder, dirt-crusted vases, framed paintings of unnaturally big-eyed children, boxes of books on tape, three pink plastic tubs stocked with half-filled shampoo bottles. I shoved those things back in the pantry next to the kitchen, and otherwise felt I could make the place seem like it belonged to me, although I didn't bother to clean out the downstairs coat closet, filled with jackets and hats and old shoes and canes. The house was too large for me, but the rent was more than reasonable, and I wanted to live far away from the man I nearly married. I didn't know anyone in the area, but that seemed like a good thing for the time being, though increasingly I was thinking of my family and what it would mean to have a family, to have people who knew me and loved me no matter what. Then I told myself I was being weak and ought to buck up. And at those moments I opened my laptop and got to work.

At dusk on the first Wednesday in September I sat on the front porch step and trained my eyes on the distance. Everything was starting to turn for the season, colors taking on a last glimmer.

A sound came from the woods. A cry. Short, abrupt, not quite human. I went inside, chilled by that cry.

That night I began reading the first in a series of crime novels by a Norwegian couple new to the genre. The detective was elderly, tenacious, tracing crimes in the snow. The plot was thrilling, but it was the landscape that held my interest most. The detective was continually commenting on the light through the pines, silver with sudden spikes of gold, and then paragraphs were spent on the fog rolling in from the rock-ringed sea. The detective had a habit of shivering, and when he shivered so would I. Which contributed to my general jumpiness.

After setting the book down I must have closed my eyes. The next thing I knew I was sitting up in bed.

The sounds were coming from the other side of the house, from where the lawn ended and the woods began. I hurtled down the stairs, bumping against a chair in the passage between the dining room and the kitchen, and rushed out to the porch. I looked for movement in the darkness, watching the tree line until my eyes ached.

Had I dreamed the cry? I returned upstairs and was almost asleep.

This time the sounds were more humanlike. Was I hearing a child—a lost child? I threw on an old pair of slippers from the coat closet and grabbed a flashlight. I went stumbling along the lawn where the woods began, grass whipping my ankles. Other than the wind and the oceanic whooshing of cars from the highway over the hill there was nothing to hear.

When I reported the cry to the police the dispatcher sounded irritated. It was most likely an animal, she said. And if not, it's not a crime to cry in the woods.

I slept lightly, waking often before falling again into dreams.

When I think about what happened on the next night it seems odd how calm I was.

I heard crying and eased out of bed, without hurrying, without even taking my cellphone with me. I suppose I was half asleep. My other fruitless attempts at discovering the source of the cries must have conditioned me to believe I'd find nothing. At any rate, I wasn't afraid.

The woman was on the porch, her back to me. When she turned she looked as surprised as I was. A sweater hung unbuttoned from her thin shoulders.

I guessed her to be at least in her seventies. When she wouldn't answer my questions I reached out and took her weightless hand and led her into the dining room where I drew out a chair for her. She ignored the chair and instead circled the table while I asked again and again, "How can I help you?"

She passed into the kitchen, came back into the dining room, circled the table. The lamp over the table swayed. Her pacing went on for at least two minutes, possibly longer, while I stood there, watching.

"Where do you need to go?" I asked.

"I can leave now," she said, in a tight voice. "Please. I live close. I'll head home."

"You can't walk alone," I said. "You could fall. It's dark. You could injure yourself. Wait. Just wait." I opened the closet. A cedar block fell from an upper shelf as I rummaged among discards from the previous tenant. I found a raincoat and slippers.

I drew a white scarf around the woman's neck to make sure she could be seen in the dark if she broke away from me. The jacket I pulled from the closet was huge and heavy. I buttoned the woman into it while she fumed. Then she exhaled, defeated.

The night was moonless, starless. I should have put a sweater on under the raincoat. I was wearing old flannel pajamas imprinted with penguins and shot glasses. My feet were sockless in someone else's slippers.

I didn't question what I was doing, why I was walking in the dark with a stranger who was clearly unbalanced. As it turned out, she was a near neighbor—though she took me on a circuitous route to her condominium. Her place was like an afterthought, set off from the other buildings at the end of a long driveway and close enough to my house that, unaware, sometimes I'd glimpsed her lights while I sat on my porch.

"You won't be wandering around at night again?" I asked, dreading her answer.

"I'll be fine. I'm so sorry." Contrition edged into her voice.

"You shouldn't be walking in the dark. You could fall. Anything could happen."

"I'll be fine."

"You think you'll be fine."

"I will be fine."

Only after she closed her front door and I began the walk back did I wonder what had happened. I didn't doubt that the cries I'd heard on those other nights were hers.

The next morning was chilly. The sky was a wild deep blue, yet the wind was shredding the clouds like egg drop soup. The place I was staying needed a lot of work. Even the yard needed work. The grass had stopped growing, not the thistles. I couldn't find gardening gloves in the house, so I put on leather ones—more leftovers—from the downstairs closet. For hauling away thistles, I found an old red wagon in the garage.

My weed-pulling lasted less than a half hour before an aqua-colored Chevy drove past and did a U-turn, parking on the road's shoulder. A woman with a face as rumpled as an old apple stepped out, wearing yellow sweatpants and sneakers designed for a mall walk. Sunglasses were tucked in the neckline of her sweatshirt.

Her first words to me: "What did you say?"

I had said nothing.

She introduced herself as Sylvia, leaned in close to my face, her eyes a cloudy brown. I felt sure she shouldn't be driving. "I'm sorry I didn't give you my name last night," she said.

I hadn't even recognized her. She seemed entirely sane—like a different woman. We gaped at each other in silence until she went on. "So my question to you is: What's going to happen to this magnificent structure?"

I didn't know what she was talking about. She hobbled closer, her hand reaching out as if to grasp a banister. Instinctively I stepped forward to catch her if she lost her balance.

"Are you eventually going to buy this place?" she asked. Without waiting for an answer she said, "We called her The Kid. The person who lived here." Wind gusted at Sylvia's back, and I caught her by the elbow. I was hot from pulling weeds, but seeing Sylvia shudder reminded me how cold the day actually was.

When I asked if she'd like to come inside she shook my arm off, though her face softened. I tried again. "Can I get you anything? You should come in. Tea? I could make coffee?"

"No. Don't bother. I just wanted to get a good look at you in the daylight. It was almost like seeing The Kid. I suppose you'll think that's not comforting, considering she was in her eighties. Still, there's a resemblance."

After Sylvia drove off, a flimsy red tissue began fluttering and spiraling over the grass like an impish little thing. I chased and caught it. A scarf.

The next morning I was barely out of bed when Sylvia showed up again. She came, she said, for her scarf but would like to have the coffee I'd offered yesterday. Once again she listed to the side, and I reached out in case she toppled.

She sat heavily in a dining room chair, and I felt instant irritation. But relief too. Relief that she wasn't about to fall. I was feeling responsible for her and, at the same time, anxious for her to leave. I brought the scarf out, and she thanked me, shoving it into her clasp purse. I couldn't think of much to say, but she didn't appear bothered; she talked as if coming uncorked. Her topic: her development's board of directors. The directors made a fetish of ensuring that every condominium remained free of decorative flags—grinning pumpkin flags, for instance. Immense effort was currently being spent by three association members against a family who flew a banner of Our Lady of Guadalupe. Other infractions, according to the board of directors: bird baths and bird houses not painted the regulation gray or brown or black. Sylvia said she initially joined the association in an attempt to be civic-minded, but stayed on for the entertainment value.

She clapped her hands and laughed, then rose and swayed dizzily, heading for the door.

It was almost noon by the time she left. After I walked her to her car and returned to the house I found her wristwatch on the coffee table. She must have taken it off while I went into the kitchen to get sugar for her coffee.

Sylvia and I never arrived at an explicit arrangement about her visits. Whenever she called she was already on my porch, her cellphone at her ear, looking like she just popped over on a whim. She limped inside and landed on the couch. Always, she left something behind. A sweater, a coupon wallet, a biography of Teddy Roosevelt, a Waterford pen. She outwitted me, mainly by making requests that sent me out of the room so she could stash something undetected. Of course the item left behind would necessitate my calling her. Next, she'd insist on coming over to pick up whatever she left so that I wasn't "troubled." The minute she stepped inside the house her complaints began. The wretched waste facility and the condominium association were her primary targets. Occasionally she found the condominium association useful.

"Bless their hearts," she said one morning while she made herself comfortable on the couch. "The association officers got rid of the wasp nest near my kitchen window. Did you know that during the winter the female wasps carry around sperm in a ball? Internally. It's called 'dormant sperm.' Imagine that. Their nests are made of wood fibers and their own spit. Funny to think of them spitting. They sting too. They're not like honey bees who sting once and die. They can sting and sting and sting again. You know what to use if you're stung? Meat tenderizer. Animals know how to survive. We could learn something from them."

I couldn't help myself. "Is that why so many animals are going extinct?" I asked.

How could I help liking her? After all, having her stop over helped me to procrastinate. I was working online writing catalog copy about stress-reducing devices and security systems, and so on, for nervous people. I was a nervous person. Consequently I was good at my job. Anyway, who wasn't nervous lately? Lovely good things that were once thought of as precious no longer seemed lovely or good. Who could predict what preposterous affronts to nature were next? The side effects from the sleeping capsule you took could puncture your spleen and make you drive to South Carolina and vote. You didn't even have the chance to worry purposefully. Something you'd never dreamed of was always about to occur. Not just terrorists or uncontrollable viruses. Weird unprecedented events in nature might erupt. Like, say, butterflies that could bite. Or soap bubbles that could suck oxygen out of the sky. "Free us from all anxiety now and at the hour of our death"—that prayer from my childhood still filled me with longing. And how could people defend themselves? The only defense was to defend others. I was volunteering at the tutoring center in town on weekends and turned over a percentage of my salary to charitable organizations. I had already accumulated, because of my donations to various organizations, more address labels than I could use if I sent fifty letters a day for the rest of my life, assuming I'd live a very long life and didn't mind affixing envelopes with shrieking ostriches from the Nature Conservancy or a globe crusted in a crown of thorns from Peaceforall.org. But whatever I did wasn't enough. And so I was grateful for Sylvia after a while. Her visits became oddly calming. Usually I waited to eat lunch until she was with me. I've never enjoyed eating alone.

On a Thursday morning the sky turned golden and brilliant, but by noon gray clouds poured in. Wind stripped loose the bark from the maples and sent branches skittering on the driveway. By four o'clock lightning hooked through the darkened sky. Severe thunderstorms were forecast across three counties. At six o'clock I drew up a chair to the west window and watched Sylvia's driveway, scanning for movement. When the wind died down my heart relaxed—until rain splattered in huge droplets, shaking the window frames in full out war.

Why did my instincts tell me Sylvia was out in the storm? Doing what? Pretending to be a lightning rod? Sylvia was not stupid. But Sylvia was Sylvia—stubborn, driven, compulsive. I had never forgotten how she'd shown up at my place in the middle of the night—and she had never explained why she had appeared. She wasn't an entirely rational person, I was sure. I moved to a south window in case she slipped out another door of her condominium. By eight o'clock my anxiety was overwhelming.

I pulled on a jacket and walked toward Sylvia's place through stinging ice rain. Of course it was likely that Sylvia was actually sleeping. No lights were on in her place. She could be in bed. I was stamping around on her porch and knocking. She didn't answer. Thunder crashed and jolted me to the bones.

As I was about to leave I caught sight of a figure coming up the driveway. Sylvia was wearing the jacket I had given her from the closet and a hat I hadn't seen before—broad brimmed, plastic.

When she reached me, I said, as if it was my right, "Don't ever do this again."

I was heading back to my house, halfway down Sylvia's driveway, when Sylvia rushed up behind me.

"I'm sorry!" she shouted. "I'm sorry. I can't begin to tell you how sorry I am. Do you want to come back to my place?" The brim of her hat kept rain from her eyes while my own eyes were streaming. Unlike me, Sylvia had the good sense to dress for the weather. She leaned against me, trickles of rainwater from her coat pouring under my collar. While I shivered she drew back. She looked more composed than before, even proud. It was the look of a line crewman who, after a hurricane, has restored electricity to an entire neighborhood.

She shouted into my ear, "I'll take better care of myself from now on—but I need you to make a promise."

I couldn't think of a thing to say other than to agree.

"I want you to see my son," she said. "I want you to rescue him."

"What's wrong with your son?"

Lightning flashed, and I could see her lips draw back with annoyance. "Nothing is wrong with my son."

"Please get inside now," I said. "I'll walk you back, okay?"

"No," she said. "I can manage."

We headed to our respective homes. I bent my head and more rain slithered down the back of my neck. It was taking longer to reach my house than it should have. Beneath my feet the gravel was breaking up into pockets blasted with rivulets. When I turned to look for her, Sylvia was safely inside.

The path ahead of me was flooding wildly, scabs of soil floating. I told myself it was a mistake to think Sylvia needed to be taken care of. Thunder cracked so hard the earth seemed to shift under my feet.

The next morning I had a fever. "Please. No visits," I told Sylvia when I called to preempt her. "I could get you sick. It's too dangerous." By the next afternoon I was breathless from coughing and my ribs ached.

I dreamed that I was walking in a field and a high wild cry filled the air, as if my footsteps killed some small, timid, squeaky animal. It was a relief to wake up after that. Then I'd sink again into dreams that were erased upon waking but left an unsettling trace, as if I'd done something horrible but forgotten.

When I finally got my strength back I opened the front door to pick up the mail and discovered a bag of apples leaning against one of the porch pillars.

I was glad when Sylvia stopped by with a Tupperware container of macaroni and cheese, even though it scared me to think of her catching, at her age, whatever it was I had.

"Silly," she said. "You can't be infectious anymore. Plus I'm immune to anything. Or feel like it."

She put her hands on the sides of her head like someone yanking off a rubber mask. It took me a while to realize she was only excited. "Something's happened," I said. "What?"

She ignored my question.

After she closed the door I looked for whatever Sylvia might have left behind and found nothing. Gradually I realized that I hadn't heard Sylvia's car leave the driveway. When I peered through the dining room window she was slumped outside her car against the windshield.

I caught her around her waist before she fell. "Can you come inside?" I asked. "You can move?"

Slowly we sank to the ground.

Her personality was so big that I hadn't fully realized what a small person she was. Her red silk scarf—to protect the delicate skin of her neck from her scratchy coat collar—had come undone and floated across the lawn.

Luckily, her cellphone was in her purse. I followed the ambulance in my car.

The waiting room held only a young couple with two children who stared at me with that look children give when good parents are near and they're thick-coated with protection. Eventually the smaller one, a girl with meticulous cornrows, patted my knee as she cruised past. I felt such gratitude for her tiny comforting pats that I fought back tears. More people arrived. Two little boys played with plastic blocks gray with dirt in a corner bin. A woman on crutches entered with three older women with tight faces, one of whom kept coughing into her hands.

Within the hour I was allowed to see Sylvia. She was propped on a bed behind curtains and wearing a plastic identification bracelet that made her wrist resemble a child's. The overhead light was bright. Her scalp shone through her thin hair.

"I didn't fall, did I?" she said. Her eyes were luminous, not cloudy as usual.

"No," I said. "You—slumped."

"They're just messing with me here," she said. "It's nothing more than dehydration. I heard them talking. A waste of a good ambulance."

Within minutes the doctor, a soft-faced woman with freckles exactly matching the pale brown of her hair, attested to Sylvia's claim about dehydration. The contradictory element: The doctor wore elaborate imitation bondage shoes with straps that ran up to her knees. When she turned away, Sylvia muttered drily, "You can see I'm in good hands." Her eyes sent out a beam of light toward mine. "I do love you," she said. "You know that. I'm going to be saying that to virtually everyone I see in the next eight hours. Don't get nervous. I already told the same thing to an intern."

More tests were ordered. Sylvia had a bad ear infection. Then: a course of antibiotics, hydration.

While I waited for her to be discharged she said, "Will you promise me—you'll see my son? For a dinner at least?"

When I didn't answer she said, "The apples were from him."

With some people we're more alone than when we're alone—that was my resigned assessment. Sylvia's son, Justin, drove us out to a place on the highway called The Three Kings. The menu was Italian. Every place near town was Italian-themed, even though the area was the home of mostly fourth-generation Poles.

"Are you cold?" Justin asked, bending his massive head toward mine. "You look cold."

When did this question strike me as irritating? When the question was asked three times within ten minutes?

I hadn't cared what I wore for dinner with Sylvia's son. Which was the right decision. I didn't think he noticed what I wore because he wouldn't take his eyes off my face. It's a truth not often acknowledged that if a certain sort of man is interested in you, what you look like or how you act doesn't matter much. Not that I've met many such men, but I recognized the rarity when it occurred. Somehow just the sight of me reassured him. His interest in me should have fed my vanity. Instead I felt stifled.

He wasn't a good-looking man and he acted like he knew it. His eyebrows were wild, thick, with a red tinge like you see on a caterpillar. His ears, large, drooped. His mouth was small and bow-shaped, almost like a silent movie actress's. He was one of the ugliest men I'd ever sat across from, frankly.

We both were working over our butterfly shrimp for what felt like hours. Half my beer was left, and I was alternating with coffee. It was a way to stay calm and alert at the same time. It was also a way to stave off a headache, for a headache was coming in twinges, in tiny vibrations, like a train a half mile away you can feel because you put your head on the tracks. We were taking the last stabs at our plates when Justin said, "You don't want to be here, do you?"

I looked up into his honest eyes.

"A mistake," he said. "You were trying to be nice, and look where it got you."

After I shook my head he said, "No. It's okay. Don't apologize. I knew how you felt right away. I felt like a realtor trying to sell a Victorian to a couple who like stainless steel and solar. Let's have dessert. It can't kill us, can it? You write copy—you're a copywriter, right?"

I put down my fork. "Yes, right now I'm working on a catalog. It's kind of like a SkyMall for nervous people."

I explained about my job: finding language to sell things like alarms and carbon monoxide detectors. Deluxe models. It was easy to imagine what a cynic would say, how I was making an income from *cultural hysteria*, but I felt fortunate to have the position. My editor, Therone Binacas, liked nearly every piece of copy I sent. That response differed dramatically from what I was used to. At my previous job, people felt that if they didn't find fault with any copy I wrote they would get fired. As a consequence, everyone was forced to wade through language that wasn't about the products but about the person who was speaking and his or her need to look indispensable.

"I guess a lot of people can't help but be nervous," Justin said. "You won't go broke if that's your target. People are panicked. Fanatics all over the place, on the one hand, and deflation on the other hand."

"What do you mean by deflation—economic deflation? "

He had a way of looking directly at me and then sliding his eyes away, as if he was aware of not having permission, as if he knew how powerful eyes could be, and I did like that. He was aware of himself. Maybe being a large man made such awareness inevitable. He had to watch out to avoid harming other people, stepping into them, accidentally knocking them against door frames.

"The value going out of things," he said. "Not just houses or other properties but the sense that lives lose value. Creeping despair. Is this an awful dinner? I ask you out and just add to the general misery."

"I always feel better when I've had time to think about the general misery."

"Let's stop contributing to it. So you're working for a SkyMall for nervous people. Tell me more. A lot more."

"Weirdly gentle survivalist brochures for people for whom a Swedish knife would be too scary. Meditation gongs. Alarms that aren't alarming. Flower elixirs for the nerves."

"And you like this? I would—if I had the talent to write copy."

"I'll get a discount."

"I guess if anyone thinks we're not capable of living with fear they forgot what our ancestors dealt with. But then again, they didn't live long." He looked down at his hands and swallowed. He was about to say something, I could tell, that he might regret. "I have a product for you," he said. "I just thought of it. I know it sounds stupid. And maybe it has nothing to do with safety, but it would be a curiosity item."

He handed me the breadbasket even though it was empty.

"What is it? Tell me. I promise to laugh."

"You know—cats hate citrus scents? My cousin's cat went crazy on her. It was her perfume. The citrus smell disgusted her cat. So somebody could make a perfume that appealed to both women and their cats. And to other people."

It struck me as one of the most vulnerable things I'd ever heard a man say on a date. "I knew it would sound stupid," he said.

"That's a brilliant idea—the perfume."

"It's never been done, I don't think." He looked at his hands again— his giant hands. What must it be like to stoop under doorways, to have to bend to look people in the eye, to shake hands and worry about crushing them? "Here's another," he said. "A weather radio that's also an inflatable raft with LED capability."

"That would sell."

The waitress, her eyebrow and lip piercings glittering, was standing over us, dessert menus in hand. She handed both menus to Justin in a way that could only be described, nauseatingly, as *sassy*.

"Do you know her?" I asked after she clattered off.

"No." He held out a dessert menu. "Do you want anything?"

The pudding smelled and tasted wonderful—not like the cinnamon roll aroma that clouds airports. There was nutmeg, lots of it, and actual butter.

Our waitress came back with more coffee, splashing some on my saucer. "You know what?" I said. "I was getting a headache, but now it's gone. I attribute that fact entirely to your idea about cat perfume."

He grinned, and I could tell he was holding back from giving the table a happy thump with his palm. There was no one to compare him to, I realized at that moment. He could not harm me, although I knew I could easily harm him. How liberating that was. So often I've heard that love comes when we're not waiting for it. Which sounds like accidental death. Love couldn't be forced. Not the kind that I despaired of finding. And I was relieved that there was no possibility of love between us, although I was beginning to like him, with none of the nervy moodiness that so often afflicts friendships between women and men.

"No one in this entire tri-county area needs anything I'm selling," I said. "They lead bucolic lives in some ways, I think—whereas everything we sell is for, you know, terrified people."

"Oh, they're terrified here too, all right," he said. "They're just terrified in slow motion."

Sylvia came over later than usual the next day. I made us grilled cheese sandwiches and hot chocolate for lunch. We kept a companionable silence throughout the meal until she said, "It didn't go well. Your date with my son."

"I wouldn't exactly say that," I said. Then I corrected myself. "It was awful and then it was really okay."

She pointed away from me. "Have you tried any of his apples? He brought them for you when he heard you were sick. All the way from Vermont. From his orchard. Did he tell you about the orchard?"

He didn't, I had to confess. I had been so busy talking about myself at dinner that I hadn't been polite enough to ask him the obvious questions. And days ago I had set the bag of apples on the counter and forgotten them.

"I would have stayed in Vermont," she said. "Except for the fact that I followed Gloria. My friend. The one I used to call The Kid. Her son and his wife and their little girls were living near here, in town. Gloria came to help them. Eventually they moved and she didn't. Did you know that I used to live here with her? Did you know that?"

"In this house? You mean here, in this house?"

"Yes, this house. Gloria and I. My son wants me in Vermont with the orchard. He worries too much. You could live with him and make him happy. We all could. I knew it when I saw you, the first time. His apples, he brought you apples. That tells you everything. Did you try any?"

It was like something from a fairy tale gone wrong. A promise that must be kept but that disappoints. And now I was supposed to eat an apple. I could have choked with sympathy for Sylvia, but not only with sympathy, with the beginnings of revulsion.

That night I opened the sack on the counter and drew out an apple. I took a bite and almost gasped—the skin gave way to flesh, perfect and crisp. It was like tasting the essence of snow. As if the roots of the tree that grew the apple must have drunk the purest spring water and the leaves flickered with the sort of clear sunlight you only see in early mornings, and each apple grew very slowly, never forgetting it had once been no more than a blossom. I hadn't had such an apple, probably, since childhood.

At around eight the next morning Sylvia called. She was, of course, already on the porch. As soon as she lowered herself onto the couch she announced, "I want to explain something to you. It's about my friend Gloria—and maybe you'll excuse me for the way I've been acting."

"You haven't done anything you need to be excused for," I said.

"That's kind of you for lying."

I didn't disagree with her.

"It can seem like a joke to a younger person," Sylvia went on, "but falling takes on new significance at a certain point—if you're lucky enough to live long enough for the issue to emerge. One fall can spell the end of you, or a long languishing that too often ends with the inevitable.

"So you must take precautions, and a wheelchair is the most efficient precaution for some people. You might think everyone would be kind to a person in a wheelchair. Would open doors and smile. And many do. Others do a good job of frowning and turning away to show they really can't see you. But there are a few who become angry. You shouldn't be in their way, you're taking up their time. I guess I had to chalk up that knowledge to my continuing education."

Sylvia said it was easier to wheel her friend from the parking lot into the specialist's office rather than risk Gloria falling as they made their way to the office.

"We arrived a little late because I got lost. This was a different specialist, and I didn't know the way. After I parked the car I asked Gloria not to move until I could get the wheelchair ready. The wheelchair was the collapsible type, not anywhere near as heavy as it looked." She paused, unclasped her hands, picked up her purse, and nestled it on her lap. "I opened the trunk of my car and drew out the wheelchair, unfolded it, and set the brake. Then I opened the passenger door and Gloria took my arm. Together we squeezed toward the wheelchair. We didn't have much room because I couldn't put the wheelchair next to the passenger door the way I usually did. Another car had just pulled into the parking place next to ours, and that's why things were tight.

"But then it shouldn't have been a problem. We'd done this maneuver in so many parking lots. She would lean against me till she could settle into the wheelchair—I only let her go for just a second while I brought the wheelchair closer. The driver coming up the incline into the lot must never have seen either of us. And Gloria, you know, she was blind. I don't think I told you that. She was entirely blind by that year. The driver, he didn't clip us, only the wheelchair, but it didn't matter. I wasn't able to catch Gloria when she fell."

Sylvia pushed her purse off her lap and put it under a couch cushion. "We lost her within a month after that. Just thought I'd let you know that if I seem strange—it's been hard missing Gloria."

She picked up the couch cushion, patted it, and retrieved her purse. "I don't mean to make you a substitute for Gloria," she said.

"I don't think anyone could substitute for her," I said.

"It would be so good for you if you could rescue my son."

Suddenly my irritation couldn't be held back even though what Sylvia told me about Gloria should have stopped me. "Your son seems perfectly all right," I said. "Why do you think he needs rescuing? What's wrong with him?"

"I mean that it would be the right thing for you. It's you I'm thinking about. The best thing in the world—to have the chance to rescue someone."

"From what?"

"Didn't you get a good look at him? Don't you think a man like that deserves every kindness? And you? What about you?"

"Neither of us needs to be rescued."

"My son would love you beyond reason," she said. "When he heard you were sick he drove all the way down from Vermont to deliver those apples. And he hadn't even laid eyes on you yet. Do you think people like that grow on trees? You're just like him. Who else would put up with me stopping by every day? Who?"

"Plenty of people would," I said. "Frankly, it's easy. I work online. I can fit you into my life. And it's not as if I don't get irritated by you sometimes. You know I do. I'm not an easy person. Although neither are you. But I can't love your son."

"Oh dear, honey, you are so naïve to pass up a blessing. You are such a child."

I have admitted already that it took me a long time to know that I was a child when I was a child. I suppose I won't know that I'm old when I'm old either. But if anyone was a child it was poor desperate Sylvia.

She spoke carefully, as if I needed to remember her exact words: "Gloria said she would send me a sign. You're the sign. I couldn't live here anymore without her, and no one would rent this place. For a year. Then you did. You're the sign."

I told her she wasn't feeling well, that she should get some rest, that she shouldn't talk like that to me again.

Sylvia stopped showing up at the house. I called to make sure she was all right, and she made excuses. I imagined she'd found some other woman to pester about her son. By then, everything felt different. Even the house I was renting felt different. I saw what I'd missed that now seemed obvious: A blind woman had lived there. Thus, the audio books, the railings on the dining room wall, the steel hand grips over the bathtub. On the last Friday of October I learned from a woman at the post office that Sylvia had moved. Her son had taken her back to Vermont with him. Two weeks later the woman at the post office—an older woman with enormous staring eyes—told me Sylvia had died.

I sent Justin a sympathy card at the forwarding address. Sylvia hadn't wanted a funeral, the woman at the post office said.

After I found all this out I felt, inexplicably, as if something of Sylvia's had been left behind in the house. Or—and this makes no sense and seems wildly wrong—as if I had been left behind. I couldn't stop feeling guilty.

In early December during a warm spell I finished the last book in that Scandinavian crime series. I wasn't going to be reading any more about fjords and glaciers and the ring-rocked sea. The translation was done by multiple authors, and whoever finished up the series must have hardly known English, so nothing made sense.

The unseasonable warmth soon made things feel out of kilter too. I felt suddenly very old, very withered. I wasn't old, I kept reminding myself. I wasn't even forty yet—not for another month. I couldn't be old. Then the warm spell broke.

On a Tuesday in the second week of December snow began falling. At first the snow fell lazily, almost like flakes drifting in oil. I had been longing for a full deep snowfall, as if a change in the weather would initiate a turn I needed in my life, and now at last outside the window near the desk where I worked snow was feathering the air.

In the next half hour the snow sharpened into fine crystals. I turned on the radio and learned that more than a foot was expected. Before long the roads would be empty and silent. I was tired of staring into my computer screen and didn't want to miss the sight of so much snow relentlessly falling. And walking in such snow—it was a feeling of being taken out of myself, like a feeling someone in love enjoys when her love is returned—a profound self-forgetfulness. Snow tracing and then covering the branches and the trunks of the trees, how could I have let such a sight go unseen? And the silence. No other silence is like snow silence. It would be ungrateful to stay inside during a snowstorm.

As I walked on the road that runs past the development I was breathing snow, as if the air were only snow, when in the distance two lights, softened and diffused by snow, drifted sideways. I was thinking that the ice would be worse on the bridge at the exact moment when the headlights disappeared.

I ran toward the spot where I had last seen the car. A shadow crawled from the ditch and struggled up the embankment.

At first I couldn't decipher the shout. Then I understood.

"I came to see if you were all right! Are you all right?"

The absurd question was shouted twice more. Of course I was all right. Justin was the one who had just crawled out of the ditch, epaulets of snow shedding from his shoulders.

His mammoth hands, ungloved, must have been stinging from the cold, and his big earnest face was blurred by snow, and I thought about being loved beyond reason and yet within reason and I thought—I don't know what that means. Do I have to know what that means?

"I'm so sorry," I said when I reached him. "I loved your mother."

"I know," he said.

I lost my footing. As I slipped backward he grasped my hand and pulled me up. Together we began walking to my place. Ahead of us everything solid was invisible. Only snow was visible, and where it wasn't silver it was gray and slate blue. Justin kept slipping too. The silence was everywhere for a long time until finally, knowing the consequences, accepting the consequences, and maybe needing the consequences, I spoke.

"Thank you for the apples," I said.

ACKNOWLEDGMENTS

I'm grateful to the editors of the following publications in which some of these stories appeared, sometimes in other versions and under other titles: *Bennington Review; Cimarron Review; Cincinnati Review; Ecotone; Fairy Tale Review; Idaho Review; New Ohio Review; Notre Dame Review; Per Contra: An International Journal of the Arts, Literature, and Ideas; The Roanoke Review;* and *World Literature Today.* "Ambrosia" was published in the Working Titles series from *The Massachusetts Review.*

I could not have a more wonderful and discerning editor than Michael Griffith. Infinite thanks for his insightful suggestions and abiding care—and for his brilliant fiction. Everyone at Louisiana University Press has been marvelous, and I extend special thanks to James Long, Lee Campbell Sioles, and Mandy McDonald Scallan.

I owe a unique debt to Elizabeth Allacco, whose account of an art project in which she smoked cigarettes filled with hair inspired the best man's art project in "Hello! I Am Saying Hello! Because That Is What I Do When I Say Hello!"

I'm grateful for the support of my colleagues and students at Lafayette College.

Enduring and special thanks to Patricia Donahue, first friend at Lafayette and lasting friend. Many thanks to Alix Ohlin, who kindly suggested that I submit the manuscript of this short story collection to the Yellow Shoe Fiction Series.

My gratitude extends to others who have been supportive as I wrote these stories: Jody Bates, Anthony Caleshu, Chelsea Cefalu, Paul Cefalu, Anna Duhl, Alexis Fisher, Evan Fisher, Marilyn Kann, Ana Ramirez Luhrs, Neil McElroy, Kirk O'Riordan, W. P. Osborn, Carrie Rohman, Emily Schneider, Randy Schneider, Beth Seetch, Diane Shaw, Jim Toia, Sylvia Watanabe, James Woolley, and Susan Woolley.

Thank you to my incredibly inspiring in-laws, Yetta and Theodore Ziolkowski.

Thank you to my sister Alice Faye, dear and loyal and steady.

I write always with the sustaining memory of my mother Rose, my father Charles, my brother Joe, my sister Lana, and my niece Carla.

Thanks to Dan Bishop—for the happiness he has brought our family.

Unending gratitude to my daughters, Theodora and CeCe. To Theodora, the first reader of my fiction, for her valuable suggestions, and for her ambitious and beautiful fiction and poetry. To CeCe: iconoclast, gifted and provocative visual artist—many thanks for your brave example.

This collection is dedicated to my husband, Eric Ziolkowski—always, with love, through words and beyond words.